TALE FOR THE BLUEBIRD

TALE FOR
THE BLUEBIRD

BY GERALD WEALES

HARCOURT, BRACE AND COMPANY 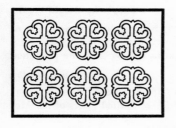 NEW YORK

I want to thank Yaddo, where most of the first draft of this book was written.

first edition

Library of Congress Catalog Card Number: 60-10933
Printed in the United States of America

For Nora

Do I resent the wind when it chills me, or the night when it makes me stumble in the darkness?

BERNARD SHAW

CONTENTS

TALE FOR THE BLUEBIRD

ACCIDENT ON COLLEGE HILL

 IT BEGAN in Providence. The city in Rhode Island.

The *why* of my being there is of no importance, and, yet, all information is finally relevant. The curiosity that drove me out of the warm kitchen in Bridgeport to the cold streets of Providence, doubled and redoubled, was to lead me from city to city and from name to name as relentlessly as a bored young man leads a tired pony and a smiling child around any pony ring in the country. You can accept —with difficulty, perhaps—that I had come to Providence. Busses, trains, and highways bring people to that city every day and there is no reason why I should not have been one of them. That I had come, possible; that I had come in search of a restaurant, incredible. That would be my feeling, too; so perhaps I should explain.

I had been visiting The King, my brother, in Bridgeport (he lives in one of those dark streets round behind the gasworks). I had kept Christmas there and seen the new year in. Time had already nibbled two weeks out of the ripe new January that evening, when The King and I sat, in sock feet and undershirts, at his kitchen table, drinking cans of beer.

"Do you two know what you look like?" screamed Queenie from the other room. My sister-in-law worried about such things. "Do you two know what you look like?

Slobs, that's what. Suppose somebody came in now. What would they say?"

"If someone came in now," my brother answered calmly (a man of infinite patience, my brother), "we would ask them to join us in a can of beer."

"And to take off their shoes," I added.

Queenie appeared in the doorway. "Your jokes I don't need, Connie, your jokes I certainly do not need. I have to live with The King, but I do not have to live with you and your jokes, Mr. Constance Firth."

There it is. I knew I would have to say something about my name before I got very far into this story. Constance. I have no idea what my parents were thinking of when they hung that on me. Constantine, perhaps. Or Conrad. Or Cornelius. Something surely that boils down to Connie. Not that I care much any longer, but even an old cross— one that you no longer have to carry—is a burden.

Queenie stood there wrapping her tongue around my first name, tasting its incongruity and spitting it at me, as though it were a peach seed. Although I had been C. M. Firth for fifteen years—since I was twenty, in fact—I still bridled a little at the name. Once when I was in Switzerland on some doubtful business or other, a chance meeting—a girl of great beauty and an unbelievable appetite— led to an invitation to spend a few weeks at a villa on Lake Constance. I could not bring myself to accept. Reluctantly, I said farewell, crossed over into Germany, and spent a lonely two weeks in a tiny hotel on the Bodensee. Years later—it was the time when I had begun to read atlases for pleasure—I discovered that it was one damned body of water. Nomenclature had done me out of a good thing. Since then, I have learned to control my natural sensitivity

(I cry like a baby at the movies), but still I take a little umbrage at open displays like that of Queenie's.

"Out," said my brother, who understood how I felt (The King, after all, was not his given name). "Out." He pointed past Queenie, into the other room. "We have things to discuss."

Queenie snorted, but she also departed, and left us to taste our beer, to wiggle our toes in our sock feet, and to talk.

"I heard an interesting piece of news today," said The King. "I was filling the machines over at the bus station." That's the way my brother makes his living, gets the cash to buy his beer and to give Queenie so that she can buy white curtains to pull shut so the neighbors, sitting in their kitchens drinking their beer, cannot see The King sitting in his. . . . He is a soft drinks distributor, which means he drives the truck and carries the bottles. A wearing job, physically and spiritually, but The King likes it. Although I am the wanderer, my brother, too, is a listener and a looker, within his appointed rounds, and the cases of bottles are prop and excuse and wherewithal.

"I got to talking to this bus driver about food. Don't ask me why. Because you're in town, I suppose. Anyway, he tells me the best food he ever ate came from a little restaurant in Providence."

"Providence!"

"Honest to God, that's what he said. I got the address written down here." He walked over and began to fumble in the pockets of his shirt, which was hanging on the handle of the refrigerator.

"Don't bother looking," I said. "I don't believe it. There is nothing edible in Providence. I know, I've been there."

"You're too hasty," said The King. He pushed a fresh beer toward me and with it a slip of paper, a barely legible address penciled on it. "You like to check on things. Go have a look and let me know."

So it was time for me to go. My visit in Bridgeport was over. A man of infinite tact, my brother.

"Perhaps you're right," I said. "This may be worth looking into." The King smiled his thanks and we lifted our beer cans in a silent toast.

"Queenie," he called, "come here a minute, will you?"

Her face, wearing its scowl, looked in at us. "What is it now?" she asked. "You want to take off something else?"

"Be nice," said The King. "Connie tells me he has to be leaving."

"I have to run up to Providence on business," I said.

Queenie's face fell. By rights there should have been a smile, but that is not the way Queenie's mind works. She smiles only for arrivals; for departures, she is sad. The scowl grows in between. "You're not going because of what I said, are you, Connie?" she asked. "You know me, I didn't mean anything."

"I know you didn't, Queenie," I said. "That's your little joke."

"Well, I wish you'd told me earlier. I would have fixed something you like for supper instead of those lousy wienies."

"Plenty of suppers in the future, Queenie. I'm not going forever."

"He'll be back to see us some one of these days," said The King.

"And you make it soon, Connie," Queenie put in, meaning it, what's more. "Don't you stay away no year like you did last time."

☐   ☐

So I left Bridgeport. I had no place in particular to go and, since there was an outside chance that the bus driver really knew something, I went to Providence. I was right, of course. There was no good restaurant at the address my brother had given me. There was no restaurant at all—just an empty store with a For Rent sign stuck on the inside of the window and dirty words printed, misspellings and all, in the dirt on the outside.

To the settled man, my trip to Providence might seem a little odd. To the family man and the employed man and the social man, my having no place in particular to go might seem a little strange. But that's the way I am. I travel. I do things for a living. Even when I have no particular business, I go places. I look around. I have been going and looking since I got out of the army more than a dozen years ago. I am not at all sure just what it is I am looking for, but I do know that I have not come across it yet. So it makes as much sense—to me, at least—to look for a restaurant in Providence as to look for uranium in New Mexico (which I have done) or to look for missing persons in Kansas City (which I have done) or to look for a Northwest Passage to the Pacific Ocean (which was done before my time). The important thing is the looking.

My wanderings are my own. I belong to no group and no generation. I have no theory and no philosophy. I do not GO; I simply go.

Although I have seen a great deal of the world and have met an unlikely collection of people in my time, I cannot think of myself as an adventurer. They are a special breed. They wear trench coats and speak only in wisecracks. They are fast with their fists and with a gun and they are, reputedly, irresistible to women. My information is based largely on the movies and paperback novels, for, strangely, despite the amount of territory that I have covered, I seem never to have run into a real adventurer.

Life, it seems to me, is more careless about casting problems than even the poorest independent moviemaker. I would never have chosen myself for the lead in an adventure story and, in its way, this is an adventure story. I am too amiable for one thing. Although I have hit men—and even women—on occasion, I cannot remember taking any real pleasure in it. I am as physically wrong as I am spiritually. I am too short of breath (the hills in Providence proved that) and I certainly have not got the looks for the job. At best, in my early twenties, I was an innocuous young man with a face that even my best friends could forget. I went into the thirties, fifty pounds heavier, and now, at the top of Dante's arch, I am a plump, bland man who would look perfectly at home behind the prescription counter of a chain drugstore. My only qualification for the part that I am going to play in the pages that follow is that I have that itch that will not let me stay behind a prescription counter, or any kind of counter or desk.

The snow had been falling when I got off the bus in Providence early in the afternoon. It continued to fall while I avoided the double-name, high-tariff hotels (other times, other resources, I would have checked in immediately) in search of a reasonably clean bed in a reasonably quiet house. Checked in, rested, washed, I went out into the now heavily falling snow to find the address that my brother had given me. Downtown, the streets were full of people, on foot and in cars, fighting the snow, their own tempers, each other. Wheels spun, policemen shouted, nervous female drivers broke into tears, tense male drivers swore.

To a man with no destination, the spectacle had its comforting side. Checking into a cheap hotel is always a sobering experience and I needed the snowstorm so that home and family would balance fairly in the scales with the transient's loneliness. I stood on the curb and watched. In the car in front of me, a thin-faced man in rimless glasses clenched the steering wheel as though it were the handrail in the front seat of a roller coaster. Suddenly, his face an apoplectic red, he screamed, "Chains! I forgot my goddam chains."

I lifted an imaginary hat to him. "Not at all, sir," I said. "Not at all." I left him staring and made my way through the milling people in the general direction of my brother's mythical restaurant. Exhilarated, I decided to walk all the way. I puffed up one of the city's seven hills (those hills and the Italian population are all that Providence has in common with Rome), skirted the edge of the university, and walked along one of the city's eighteenth-century streets. Except for an occasional slithering car, here there was quiet. The snow was still white on the ground, and the houses, worn and wracked by daylight, were Christmas card illustrations in the dusk and the still-falling flakes. Benignity settled on me as the snow settled on bushes and trees so that by the time I reached the address, in the heart of what had once been the Portuguese section of the city, I merely shrugged at my barely visible image in the dirty window, an obscenity scrawled on my chest.

The details of what followed my shrug are unnecessary. The luncheonette on the corner—its size, its shape, its smell, its dust and dirty dishes—who cares? It is enough to know that I came plodding along Benefit Street, now disenchanted with the snow and the city, a ball of regret and luncheonette food in the pit of my stomach, in time to hear the happy shouts of the pan-skiers who were taking advantage of College Hill before the municipal dustmen came with their authority and their ashes to make the steep incline safe for wary motorists.

Pan-skiing is a collegiate variation on an old and honored sport that I knew in my childhood. After a snowfall, the kids without sleds headed for the nearest hill with whatever substitute they could devise—flattened cardboard boxes and trash-can lids were favorites—and, as like as not, the sled owners became so impressed by the devil-may-care unmaneuverability of the makeshifts that they abandoned their store-bought certainty for the excitement of surprise.

The pattern on College Hill was well set by a short but rigid tradition. (This I learned from a drunken ex-pan-skier who carried his arm in a sling: old athletes often go that way.) At the first sign that a snow will be a heavy one, the hard knot of pan-skiing enthusiasts (a rigid center to the flaccid circle of the student body) desert classrooms and laboratories, bridge games and afternoon naps, and head for the college kitchens. They assault with determination—the kind that it takes to get through an institutional meal—and come away carrying their prizes: cookie sheets and tea trays, roasting pans and pie sheets—any utensil that is big enough to hold a scrunched-up human body. They assemble at the top of College Hill as soon as night falls and spend happy hours sliding, spilling, and rolling down it until their enthusiasm brings the authorities and sends them scattering to their dormitory shelters. The next day the pans, showing the marks of the night's revelry, appear at the refectory door. There is a touching scrupulosity about returning them which does not quite compensate, in the eyes of the administration, for the condition in which the pans come back.

The pan-skiers are mostly men although there are a few enthusiasts from the adjoining woman's college. For the most part, the girls who do appear at the top of College Hill are those who have been brought there under duress —by threats or promises or bribery. We shall be momentarily concerned here with one such girl, a flaxen-haired beauty called Ellen, whose full name the police now know, but which delicacy forbids that I should make public.

The politics of social life in Eastern colleges is so complicated a subject that only a sociologist could do it justice —and then only after a battery of interviews. The one rule that holds firm, however, is that no inmate of a man's college (Harvard, say) will willingly date his opposite number from the local woman's college (Radcliffe, say) for an important occasion if he can possibly find an import from one of the other girls' schools scattered along the coast.

Which explains why Ellen was pan-skiing. A young man, named Aubrey, had been coffee-dating her off and on for months—an occasional movie at the Avon, an occasional egg roll at a Chinese restaurant, a quick kiss and clutch in the shadows outside her dormitory. With the approach of the major dance of the winter, Ellen, whose grandmother had been a leading feminist (she had known the best jails in New England), had asked point-blank if Aubrey was going to take her. The young man, with feelers already out toward Northampton and Poughkeepsie, pulled in his horns (and his feelers), calculated quickly, and demanded a fair trade. He would take her to the dance if she would do something that he wanted. Ellen gulped, swallowed hard, tightened the edges of her mouth with decision, and agreed. Aubrey, an enthusiast, asked that—come the first snowfall —Ellen join him in pan-skiing. It could have been worse.

When the snowfall came, however, Aubrey was lying on his bed, deep in a paperback novel about a mythical people who wear blue jeans and ride motorcycles and have uncanny luck in their choice of riding companions. He never saw the falling snow, nor heard the scuffle of pan-skiing boots in the corridor. He might lave lain until the three-cycle crash conclusion if Ellen—the soul of honor—had not appeared at the door of the fraternity house, looking apprehensively through the opening between her bright orange stocking cap and the long, school-color scarf that was wound around her throat and up over the edge of her chin. A brother . . .

If this were a philosophical work and not a fast-moving, taut, tight adventure story, I would interrupt to make a few generalizations about that unlikely usage.

. . . roused Aubrey from his literary lucubrations and sent him downstairs to his waiting lovely.

While the would-be pan-skier had been sidetracked by long-haired young men on Harley-Davidsons, developments of importance to this narrative had been going on in the refectory kitchen. The assistant dietician, a wiry young woman and one with determination, had decided to make a fight for her equipment. She had lost the first few skirmishes, but, by the time Aubrey put in his appearance, she had alerted her bridge club. When he made his belated entrance, he was met by the dietician and her companions —a phys ed instructor from one of the local high schools, a girl with a mean right hook; a tall typist with the reach on Aubrey; and a deceptively gentle librarian with a reputation for dirty infighting. Armed with soup ladles, serving forks, and carving knives, they were ranged across the kitchen intent on protecting the pots and pans as they would their honor, and with more reason. Aubrey retreated.

In Ellen's breast—which is not really our concern here— there came alive a sudden though faint hope that her obligation to Aubrey might be written off. The flicker of hope died quickly, stamped under foot by Aubrey's American ingenuity—an until-now latent inheritance from an insurance-executive father. He remembered an old dishpan kept to ice beer for picnics and informal Friday evenings at the house that was hidden away in some corner at the fraternity. Unearthed and held up in triumph, the dishpan proved to be an ordinary deep-dish dishpan, circular with a pair of handles, the kind in which a generation of small boys were washed because no self-respecting mother wanted their alley dirt tracked into her still unfamiliar bathroom. Arm in arm, hand in glove, heart in mouth, Ellen and Aubrey proceeded to the top of College Hill.

I should not have kept the camera so long on Aubrey and Ellen. They are, after all, not characters of any importance in this story. They are instruments, devices. We shall never know how things went with them the night of the winter dance or what the future, as sentimental fiction has it, held for them. We are lucky to know as much as we do about them. Only the infinite research resources of fiction could have uncovered as many details as sprinkle the pages above.

It would be wiser to get back to me, to my concern with my heavily laden stomach and my walk through the Providence snow. My momentary preoccupation with myself (preoccupations with self are hardly momentary: they are central to existence—but that is another matter altogether) was arrested—as I indicated above—by the joyful shouts of the skiers. I stopped at the corner of Benefit and College and watched with amazement and a little envy the skill and the exhilaration of the young men and women as they raced down College Hill on their tea trays and cookie sheets and persuaded their precarious vehicles to make a sharp left turn at the corner where the Athenaeum stands (a building no one of them had ever entered) into the comparative safety of Benefit Street. A jog to the right would have carried the improvised sleds down a second and more precipitous section of College Street and would have brought them, finally, dangerously into Main Street, busy —for all the snow—with the familiar traffic of the city.

I made my own jog to the right. Spectator sports—American myth notwithstanding—are possible only in small doses. Almost tenderly, I watched one foot cross and come down ahead of the other as, gingerly, I descended the hill. Although my eyes were on my feet, my mind had hurried on ahead and was back in my hotel room busy about my impending (and unregretted) departure from Providence. Not until a medley of delighted and horrified cries . . .

Somewhere recently I read about a group of students at one of our leading Eastern colleges who gathered on a balcony and cheered while a house burned down. Well, it takes all kinds . . .

. . . rushed down the hill behind me and plucked insistently at my shoulder, did I know that something—Ellen, of course—out of the ordinary had happened among the skiers.

Aubrey and Ellen had at last arrived. A gentleman, whatever his other qualifications for existence, the young man stepped aside and gallantly offered the dishpan to his lady. Ellen, doubtful but determined, settled herself as comfortably as possible in the space where dirty dishes or cooling beer would have been more at home, and nodded fiercely—a gesture that she had learned (and Aubrey had learned to interpret) by sitting through an unreckoned number of movies about the early days of the airplane. A well-placed foot, a sudden straightening of the leg, and the dishpan was hurtling down College Hill, the rider hunched over in fear and astonishment, her hands clinging pathetically to the tiny handles.

The cry went up when the dishpan began to spin. Ellen, with no practice in dishpan handling (in any way) and no inclination for it, could only hold on as tightly as possible and send up whispered prayers to whatever socially acceptable God the Eastern schoolgirls relied on at that time. A few of the men scattered along the hill, plodding back to the top with their own kitchen utensils, stepped out into the street as though they would try to save her. One made a genuine effort, got his hands on the rim of the pan, and had time to cry out, "I've got it," before the force of the descent ripped the pan out of his hands and left him standing with scarred knuckles and an inescapable sense of being ridiculous.

Drawn by the shouts, my mind flew back from the hotel to find its occasional home in my body just as I turned to see what all the commotion was about. Ellen and her dishpan, having failed the turn at the Athenaeum, came careening down College Street, spinning like a souped-up Catherine wheel. The dishpan, like the malevolent machines of science fiction, raced madly to some obscure destination of its own; the rider, all hope abandoned, screamed incoherently into the snow-filled night.

I had almost reached the foot of the hill before my attention was drawn to the run-away dishpan. It held me so completely that I was only vaguely aware that a figure was passing behind me, walking along Main, stepping out across College. I turned, following the path of Ellen's incredible rush down the hill, and in the instant before the dishpan struck I got a glimpse of the victim. He was a small man, dressed in a black overcoat and a black stocking cap, an incongruous figure set like a moving target against the white snow. Some kind of box was stuck beneath his right arm, pressed all the more tightly against his body because, in his right hand, he held a small notebook which he seemed to be studying in the occasional and insufficient light that came from windows and street lamps along his path.

When the dishpan hit him, his right arm flew up, showering the box and the notebook at my feet. Without thinking, I stopped and picked them up, putting the notebook in my pocket, holding the box in my hand. The force of the blow sent the little man reeling onto Main Street, in the path of a city bus, which gently finished the work so violently begun by the dishpan. Ellen was knocked out of her vehicle by the collision and lay unconscious at the juncture of College and Main, while the dishpan, still possessed by some demon of its own, clattered angrily under the wheels of the bus before it finally subsided.

The street was immediately full of solicitous and intruding people. The college kids had raced down the hill in the wake of Ellen's mad ride. The passengers poured in a seemingly endless stream from the bus doors, like respectable clowns in the old circus joke about the midget car. Onlookers sprouted suddenly on every corner as though they were winter flowers that had just been waiting for an occasion to break through the snow. The inquisitive, who live always within a block of disaster, hurried eagerly to the scene.

The accident became the occasion for revelation. Those in the crowd who were essentially spectators told of other, more horrible accidents they had witnessed; those who were basically participants described, in detail, their own collisions or, in even greater detail, their near misses. One woman, small and bespectacled, with a bathrobe clutched around her and a voice like shattered glass, rode her hobby-horse into the center of the group and began to make a set speech. "Those college ruffians are at the bottom of this. No one is safe from their . . . total disrespect . . . completely selfish . . . unbelievably immature . . . bordering on the criminal. . . ." A wave of protest swelled up through the gathered pan-skiers, who had been momentarily humbled by the stunning of one of their own kind, breaking finally in a direct and carelessly phrased attack on the bath-robe-clad Cassandra and her ancestors. Goaded by the situation and a hypersensitivity of his own, one boy—without the mental capacity to be an intellectual or the physical capacity to be one of the boys, and so forced to be a clown—began to recite Karl Shapiro's "The Wreck" in a high, hysterical whine. His performance variously amused or angered everyone in the crowd, except a poker-faced, preoccupied gentleman, dressed neatly in spats and a Homburg, who passed among the gathered gawkers, picking pocket after pocket, before he went on down the hill, obviously to a formal celebration of some kind—perhaps the annual dinner of his trade association.

While the crowd busied itself, trying to domesticate the accident, to make it sit up and beg, to make it heel at the correct (read, magic) word, the police and the ambulance arrived to replace the functionless passion of the spectators with their own passionless functioning. The little man was scooped up—not ungently—and placed in the back of the ambulance. Ellen, once again conscious, sat shakily in the street where she had fallen and tried, lamely, to answer the few questions that the policemen asked her; then, she, too, was taken to the hospital. Aubrey and several other students left in the police car to tell their own imagined versions of the accident to the officials in an official setting. Even the dishpan was taken away.

The skiers disappeared, their pots and pans put away for that night. Traffic resumed. Normality came back to Main and College. Only a tiny knot of people lingered on the corner, determined to hold on to the unusual as long as possible. At first animated, the group slowly ran down like a coasting bicycle, and then it flaked off into individuals who disappeared in various directions, each one's head busy with details of the evening, sorting and polishing them for proper display the next morning in office or shop or classroom.

The last of the stragglers was a woman who crossed the street and came to where I still stood. She was tall and slim, with wisps of gray hair pulled loose from the bun in back, hanging stringily over the earpieces of her glasses. She bit her lower lip repeatedly, as though to make sure that it was still where it should be.

"Wasn't that terrible?" she said longingly. "That poor man. Wasn't that a terrible accident?"

"Yes," I answered, "it *was* terrible."

"Have you ever seen anything more horrible in your life?"

I looked into the woman's hungry, empty eyes. "Yes, I have," I answered. "Often." One more nibble at the lip and she had turned and disappeared. I was alone, except for the passing cars and the falling snow.

ENCOUNTER ON FEDERAL HILL

THE PROCESS of separation is, I suppose, the most important activity that a man can indulge in. There is identification, of course. But that leads to compassion or contamination. I stood in the falling snow and separated furiously. By an act of will, I managed to disassociate myself from the woman with the nibbled lip, the neurasthenic poetry reciter, the Saint Joan in the wrapper. I was in that crowd, not of it.

Wisdom is an occasional thing. It is also, like landscape, a matter of perspective. If I had not needed to feast on the prostrate body of the little man in black (take, eat, this is my body broken for you . . .), it may simply have been the luck of my comparative freedom. But even the floating kidney does not float very far. If someone had been able to stand so that he could have seen me against the background of the accident, as I had seen the crowd. . . .

Such thoughts are dangerous. It is all right to talk about culpability because spoken words are magic spells. Communication is instinctive self-protection that turns nibbling guilt and fear into hard, round, audible objects that bounce meaninglessly against another consciousness. Ears are not instruments; they are receptacles. If I had been on a train, I would have gone into the club car, cornered a traveling salesman, and invented for him a series of sexual exploits that would have served him as raw material for weeks of traveling. To keep my mind away from the big generalizations, traps for the soul, I worried it with the box in my hand, the notebook in my pocket. I sent it on a hundred small errands, imagining me through the lobby of my hotel, stretched out on the bed, my shoes off (for comfort and to placate the nagging ghost of childhood that still whispered that I must not put my shoes on the bedspread), safe from the snow, the night, the hint of self-identification in the winter air.

In not many minutes, my body, like a dog with a newspaper in its teeth, its tail wagging, had followed my mind to my hotel room. Stretched out, unshod (the child *is* father to the man), I began to examine the refuse from the wreck on College Street.

The box was not much larger than the standard cigar-bearing variety—a little deeper perhaps, not so wide. It was wonderfully ornate. Tiny birds played in explicit foliage, fluttering their carven wings as they darted in and out of clusters of leaves, as real as autumn, with color borrowed from the cherry red of the wood. All six sides were so crowded with sylvan busy work that I could not have told which end was up if there had not been four rosebuds, one about to burst open, in each corner of the apparent top. A carved ribbon ran across one edge of the box, tying two of the rosebuds together.

I could not get it open. The lid—if the beribboned, be-rosebudded side was the lid—was so tightly pressed against the rest of the box that only the faintest line testified that the work had not been carved from a single piece of wood. I tried to get my fingernails into the almost invisible split, but I keep them bitten down and so had nothing to work with.

◻   ◻

The box, I decided, must have a secret, like those lacquered jewel cases which, along with wooden tea sets and kimonos, form the bulk of the Japanese trade with American soldiers, and other innocents, abroad. I poked and pushed and prodded at all four rosebuds, at the ribbon, at the birds and the leaves, but nothing moved, nothing gave. No sliding panels, no first step in the Japanese puzzle that leads finally to the interior of a disappointingly empty box.

Except this box, I could have sworn, was not empty. I cannot quite say why I was certain that there was something inside, but I was so convinced that, for a moment, I was tempted to break it open, to rape it of its secret. It was the box that stopped me. Not its beauty, for I am as indifferent to beauty as most human beings, except, of course, when it is plainly labeled Art or Nature, or bathed becomingly in sentiment (They're playing our song). As I held the box in my hands, looking down at it, toying with the possibility of its destruction, it seemed to move, the softest kind of flutter that passed through my palms, up my arms, into my body and settled, caressingly, around my heart. I am a gentle man; I cannot kill, not even a box.

I am as inquisitive as the next man . . .

I am the next man. We all are.

. . . but I do not take kindly to the idea of an ornamental box—particularly one that I hardly know—which chooses to breathe on me. Especially when its slightest flutter seems to make an immediate demand on me. Affection for The King, yes, and a little for Queenie, but a man cannot get involved with every animate and inanimate soul that crosses his path.

I put the box aside and took up the notebook, which turned out not to be a notebook at all. It was a diary, bound in black leather. Inside on the flyleaf was an inscription, dated June 7, 1923, "To my darling son Solvent on his eleventh birthday. With LOVE from Mother." Solvent, I wondered as I looked at the lady's handwriting (thin-nibbed pen, bold strokes), what kind of a name is Solvent? Like Increase Mather, I guessed, only edited for an age in which marketing has stolen the march on production.

Opposite the flyleaf, on the inside of the front cover, a small boy's scrawl, penciled lines that had withstood more than a quarter of a century, protested the mother's dedicatory message: "Solly Derritch, 1164 Grahame Str." What city? Where had eleven-year-old Solly Derritch had to take his stand against Solvent, the darling son?

In every city in the world. *They* hang labels on you right from the beginning. Dig out! Dig out!

"Solly," I said out loud. "Solly, boy, Connie salutes you." I hoped that he had won that fight before the coed-carrying dishpan and the anonymous city bus had freed him from Solly and Solvent forever.

Reading another man's diary is one of those caressing secret pleasures, touched in degree only by opening someone else's mail or peeking into parked cars in a lovers' lane. There was little enough in Solly Derritch's diary, heaven knows; still the inquisitive hairs may be rising on the inside of some reader's thigh, so I will repeat, as nearly as I can remember, the complete contents of the little man's private journal. The first entries were in the boy's hand that had appeared on the inside cover.

July 7, 1923. Today was my brithday. Eleven years old.
                I am tall for my age. Daddy took me to the

Circus. It was a good one. There was no
rodeo. I like rodeos. Mother gave me this
Diary.

July   8, 1923. Today was the day after my brithday. Nothing happened.

July   9, 1923. Today I played cowboy with Charly Hessly.
He is a big fool.

July 10, 1923. Today it rained.

At this point Solly apparently lost interest in a record of
his life and times. The next entry was in a small, neat hand.
Black ink. As though it mattered, the writer had followed
the form that the child had set down for him. Following
the date—July 11 of the old year that I had just seen out in
Bridgeport—were these words: *Picked up the box. Oh, God,
I hope I'm finally going to find it.*

That's it. That is about all that diaries ever add up to.
Or letters, for that matter. Or parked cars. Today it rained.
But, Solly, old son, let us never forget that the farmers need
it.

I skimmed through the empty pages just to be sure.
Finally, on the last page, I discovered a list. There were
nine names with addresses scattered all across the country.
They were written carefully, the margin straight, the letters colorless—the hand of July 11, apparently that of the
mature Solly Derritch. At the bottom of the page, in pencil,
these words: "Hotel Chevron, Providence." On an impulse,
I tore the sheet out of the diary and tossed it on the bedside
table.

At this point, my small voyage of discovery over, I realized that I should have turned the box and the diary over

to the police an hour ago out on College Street when, note-
books in hand, the automatons in blue had been jotting
down the details, highly conjectural, of disaster.

I am not one of those people who hate policemen or
fear them. I will ask a direction, or report a burglary, or
even—the sun and my singing soul in conjunction—stop at
a busy intersection to pass the time of day with the man on
duty. Though I doubt the direction and expect the burglars
to go free, there was nothing personal in my dereliction. It
did not cross my mind to turn in the little man's scattered
belongings. They had fallen, like manna, at my feet. For
that moment, they were mine.

Now it was too late. I could see myself, standing before
the desk sergeant, saying, "I picked up these things up there
where the bus ran over the man. I somehow . . . some way
. . . somehow . . . forgot to give them to the poli . . . officers
while they were there."

"Forgot, is it?" the desk sergeant answered (in dreams all
cops are Irish). "Now, me bhoy, don't be handin' me such
a gallous tale."

At which point, since I hate stage Irish, I shut off my in-
vention and lay back on the bed, staring at the ceiling (one
water stain shaped like a bird, and me with no salt), wondering what to do next. My eye wandered, caught at the
edge of the page that I had torn from little Solly's diary. I
picked it up and read the list again: New York, some town
in Virginia, Atlanta, Los Angeles. . . . Like an insurance
man's list of prospects, but what a territory! The Hotel
Chevron notation sent me to the phone book and there it
was on one of the Federal Hill streets. I asked the switch-
board operator to get me the number and after a long few
minutes, an exasperated voice (the desk man: no switch-

board at the Chevron) complained, "This is the Hotel Chevron. What d'ya want?"

"I want to speak to Mr. Derritch."

"Who's he?"

"He's staying there, isn't he? This *is* the Hotel Chevron?" That last in an intimidating voice, with *you idiot* as the implied noun of address.

"What's that name again?" Querulous, but a little cowed.

"Derritch. D-E-R-R-I-T-C-H." The intonation hinted that under other circumstances I would have been prepared with *cat,* C-A-T. "Mr. S. Derritch." For Solvent or for Solly. The race is not always to the swift.

"Oh," said the voice, making a discovery. "Derritch. 32. But we got no phones in the rooms here. You think this is the Kah-reeb-hilton or somethin'?" The reasserting self.

"I'm sorry I bothered you." I could afford to be gracious; I had what I wanted.

"That's O.K., buddy." By now, just tired. "I don't think he's in anyway."

If any man can tell me why he puts on his left sock first of a morning, why he ritualistically crosses a particular street catty-corner in the middle of the block, why he salts his food before he tastes it, I will explain why I got up from my hotel bed, put on my overcoat, slipped the diary into my pocket and the ornamental box under my arm, and headed for the Hotel Chevron. The habitual is as irrational as a single chance decision. I went.

Perhaps I was nagged to the Hotel Chevron by an incompletely remembered pattern of the social dues of death. The call on the bereaved. Did I imagine that S. Derritch had taken a wife, that a rumpled, wilted little woman, puffs of white around the eyes, would meet me at the door of his room, would accept the useless comfort of my hand holding hers, of my voice assuring her that he looks just lovely?

Perhaps I saw myself, younger, shy, dressed in the creased and crumpled khaki of heroism, bringing Solly Derritch's *memento mori* back from the battlefield, back to his mother, she of the bold stroke and the darling son. An elegant woman, Mrs. Derritch, tall and slim, proud head held high, the neck of a swan bound loosely with a string of pearls no whiter than her skin. In green silk, she sat, her long tapering hands as still as marble in her lap.

I held out the ornamental box and the diary, which had become an identification bracelet ("To my darling son Solvent on his eighteenth birthday. With LOVE from Mother.") and a pack of tattered letters tied with a GI shoe-string. "I thought you would want these, ma'am."

"Thank you, Mr. Firth." A silence. Then, "Were you there?

"I was there, ma'am, and I want you to know that Solly. . . ."

"Solly?"

"Solvent, ma'am. We called him Solly in the outfit. Your son died a hero's death."

From under the quiet plaster hands came a handkerchief, touched—just barely—to the corner of the right eye. She put her hand on my arm. "Thank you, Mr. Firth. Thank you for telling me how it happened." A silence. The hand still on my arm. "You were Solvent's best friend, Mr. Firth. May I call you Constance?"

NO, NO, NO, NO, NO.

Perhaps I headed for the Hotel Chevron simply because I had grown impatient. I was opening without jacks or better and hoping that I could draw a winning hand and never be found out. I went.

☐   ☐

The streets on Federal Hill might have been a place to walk when the markets were open in the summer and the fruits and vegetables spilled out onto the sidewalk. In the winter, the shops pulled into themselves, steamed their windows as if in self-defense, built a wall against the stranger. My taxi slushed past the faceless stores, pulled up finally to the curb.

"This is it," said the driver, the pronoun hanging like a bridge to the unspoken, "and you can have it."

The Hotel Chevron is legion. There are such chevrons on the arms of every city and town in America. It was no flophouse. It was simply, undeniably a cheap hotel, too casual about changing linen and choosing its guests ever to get onto even the lowest rung of the guidebook ladder that leads up to five stars and prosperity. It was four stories high, with a façade on which a few furbelows of onetime elegance, acorns and trailing vines in masonry, were blurred and lost in the grime of years. A stunted marquee stuck out over the sidewalk, like a reluctant public service, a rain-catcher for loiterers, delinquents, bums, and housewives caught between the market and home. A barely legible sign whispered: TRANSIENT, PERMANENT, Rooms $1.50 and up.

I pushed open the outside door and stepped into the sour-sweet lobby. A smog hung over everything. Years of cigarette smoke, mingled with the food fumes that had come creeping down the stairway, past the faded sign, NO COOKING IN THE ROOMS, almost hid the desk clerk in a mist without magic. I followed the path that a million steps had marked through the nap of the carpet, past the three leather chairs, hollowed out by a thousand behinds. Where two roads diverged on the yellowed carpet, I took the one most traveled by—headed toward the stairway on the left, not toward the desk directly in front of me.

Just before I turned, the desk clerk, who had eyes, ears, nose, mouth, a face—who remembers?—said, not pretending that he could, or that anyone can, "Can I help you?"

"No," I said.

"Where you going?" Not a question, but a demand.

"Up." Not an answer, but a fragment of defiance.

Up two flights of a narrow stairway, along the dim and dirty hall, I found room 32. I lifted my hand to knock but stopped myself, my doubled fist still hanging, ready, in the air. I remembered that Solly Derritch was not at home.

Perhaps he had never been. *Oh, God, I hope I'm finally going to find it.*

I turned the knob. The door was not locked. I pushed it open, stared into the darkness, groped successfully for a switch to the right of the entrance and then, glancing up, I found myself, as they say in private-eye novels, looking into the muzzle of a snub-nosed automatic.

"Solvent Derritch, I presume," said the man holding the pistol.

Oh Solly, Solly, so you did not win that battle. *Requiescat in pace,* Solvent, my darling son.

The speaker sat in an armchair facing the door. Not so much sat as was poured. Immense, he spread out, like an amoeba, or marshmallow on a sundae, filling every corner of the chair, dropping over the edges so precariously that, if he had been a sundae and not a man with a gun, I would have picked nervously at him with a spoon, trying to tidy his edges before I began the serious business of eating. His chins were like a ruff around his neck. One plump little hand, self-contained in the midst of such flow, like an exotic ripe fruit with the sick skin of a white peony, lay along the arm of the chair; the other, of course, held the automatic. He wore an overcoat of blanket cloth (perhaps, actually a blanket designed to cover the expanse of him), thrown open now against the stuffiness of the room, and, incredibly, a straw skimmer on his head. His Stanley line spoken, he lapsed into a low cheerless hum, which worked its way up from deep inside him, shaking his wattles as it came. I barely recognized "Bye, Bye, Blackbird." The words of the song trickled up and out, following the hum, and fell on the rug between us:

> Make my bed and light the light
> I'll arrive late tonight

The words became hum again. I waited for them to come around once more, half imagining that I would come in on "No one here can love and understand me," but the heavy man broke in on his own music with, "Well, Mr. Derritch?"

"I'm not Solly Derritch," I found myself saying, against a background of "Bye, Bye, Blackbird." The hum only stopped when the hummer was forced to speak. "I'm an old friend of his. Name's Eddie Anodyne."

It was an old routine. *What's the trouble, ladies, what's the problem, men? Don't go all to pieces, stop and count to ten. Is your husband cheating? Are you short of tin? Let me tell a story, try to make you grin. Let me sing a ballad, prove the world is fine. I've the news to cure the blues, name's Eddie Anodyne.* A night-club comedian I once knew in Kansas City used that as an opener. Unhappy fellow, never quite made the big time, killed himself, they say, over a girl in Wichita Falls. Men have died and worms have eaten them. . . .

My pistol-packing pachyderm had apparently never been in Kansas City, at least not when I had. All he said was, "If you're not Derritch, where's Derritch?"

"I thought he'd be here," I said.

"He isn't." Then, almost to himself, "He didn't say there would be two."

"Two what?"

"Two of you. What do you think I mean? Two guys in on this."

"In on what? You crazy or something?" I decided to play for outraged innocence, which was not very difficult, considering that I did not have even a hint of what the dead Solvent and his overweight, anonymous friend were involved in. "I come by here to see an old army buddy and I find some nut with a gun talking all around the barn. I'm going to get a cop. Jesus, you must be just out of the funny farm or somewhere, wearing a straw hat in the dead of winter and swinging that gun around at total strangers you've never even met."

"You shut up about my hat," said the fat man, running his free hand around the brim, the fingers barely touching the straw, straightening and caressing. "*I* wear this hat," he said firmly, as though he had to convince me. "I call it the last straw." And he giggled.

"We all have to clutch one," I said. He glanced into my eyes and, for the barest moment, I thought that he might recognize the brother in me. But his eyes were pale, weak, watery, could not see beyond his straw hat and his immediate job. They came to rest on the box under my arm and, this time, there was recognition.

Before he could speak, I went on. "I run into this old army buddy of mine, good old Solly Derritch I haven't seen since Italy, and we have a few and tell a few lies. So he comes up to my place and first thing you know he's screaming drunk. Old Solly didn't used to drink like that. Best drinker in the outfit. The stuff never fazed him. Civilian life must have knocked the guts out of him. He goes yelling out of my place, and the last I see of him he's slopping down the street in the snow singing at the top of his voice about roll me over in the clover, roll me over and lay me down and do it again. And he left this goddamned music box"—I waved the ornamental box in the fat man's face —"or whatever the hell it is. So I bring it over here to his hotel, like the buddy I am, and no Solly, just you and that gun."

At this point the hum again turned to words: "Oh, what hard luck stories they all hand me."

There was no artist in the man. Having accidentally stumbled across a moment of poetic irony, he hurried, unheeding, into prose, demanding—and getting—the ornamental box. He turned it uncertainly in his hands, stared at it as though he intended memorizing the pattern of birds and branches, finally nodded acceptingly, setting up a wave of fleshy shuddering at his neck.

"Would you know anything about a diary?" he asked, waving the hand with the gun in it. I watched the movement—not a threat, an explanation—and saw that the sweep of his arm took in the room. The closet door was open; a single suit coat hung there, precariously askew on its hanger, the suit pants in a heap on the floor below. A suitcase, pulled half out of the closet, lay open in the doorway, its meager contents rumpled. The drawers of the dresser were open; one of them, a small drawer that should have sheltered handkerchiefs and socks, had been pulled out and tossed on the bed. "You see," he said, "it's not here."

"What's not here?" I asked, involuntarily touching my right pocket where Solvent Derritch's diary lay.

"The diary, Mr. Anodyne, the diary," the heavy man repeated. His voice had grown peevish. "I was told to get the box and the diary. And not to hurt anyone if I could keep from it."

I was nagged by memory. Somewhere I had heard that voice before. As the fretful repetitions of *diary* slipped up and out of his pouting mouth, I realized that it was not this particular voice, but a similar one that was playing cat-and-mouse with consciousness at the back of my mind. Years ago, when we were cruelly kids, we used to tease a big, stupid boy—almost feeble-minded, I suppose he was— who placidly took all that we offered until he could take no more. Then, his voice mixed decision with a whine, as the fat man's had just now, and he slowly, painfully warned us, "You better . . . you better not . . . better not do that . . . once more, or I'll . . . I'll . . ." and he would, too, and we would finally go home crying.

One of the difficulties of living, or so it seems to me, is separating the tormentors from the tormented. Finally, I mean.

The fat man hooked me with one of his casts—"You may not know anything at all about the diary, Mr. Anodyne, but I can't tell"—and reeled me in from memory. Brought up, gasping, on the dry land of dirty rug in this cheap hotel room, I suddenly saw the value of not being Eddie Anodyne, wartime buddy of Solly Derritch. I had gone into this maze without a borrowed thread from Ariadne that would lead me back out . . .

Technically, I had not gone in at all; I had built the maze around me as I talked. That's the way of men with mazes.

. . . and my only hope was to push one of the walls down and escape in the confusion.

"Could this be it?" I asked, pulling the diary from my pocket. "I found this under a chair at my place. It must have fallen out of Solly's coat. I don't really think you ought to take it. It may be private. Of course, I didn't look. . . ."

He was up and out of the chair so quickly that he caught me in midsentence. Before I could say "inside," he had flicked the diary from my hand and moved across the room, his gun still on me, where he began to riffle the pages as though in search of something. For all his bulk, he had moved swiftly, lightly. He only seemed ponderous. Perhaps that was the way with his mind, too. I decided to go easy, and if possible, just to go.

"I don't see any list," he said. My mouth went dry; I felt a chill wind playing around the small of my back, trying to work its way up my spine. The true adventurer (the fictional one, that is) would have been unmoved, but then the true adventurer would have torn the list from the diary on principle, not on impulse. He would have known, instinctively or intuitively or logically, that it was of importance, that it would lead finally to the crown jewels, the stolen plans, the head of the syndicate. I wished the missing page back into the diary, wished so insistently that if there were any magic on this earth—other than the incredible magic of just being on this earth—the page would have slipped across Providence, the wound of the tearing would have healed, and the fat man in his riffling would have found what he wanted.

"I don't see any list," he repeated. A silence. "But then I may not know where to look." He put the diary into his pocket; he picked up the ornamental box, which had fallen to the floor when he made his diary-snatching dash across the room, and slipped it into some voluminous inside pocket of the blanket coat. "I've got the box and the diary and that's all I'm supposed to worry about. Mine not to reason why," he dredged up from his schoolroom past.

"Yours but to do and die," I added, involuntarily.

"What kind of crack is that?" he said. Then he grinned. "Oh, I get it." He looked suddenly like a man who knew too many limericks and I hoped that we would not settle down to a poetry-quoting session at this time of night in this unfamiliar room with the spirit of Solvent Derritch hovering over us.

"I had better be going," I said.

"Turn around," he commanded. I turned.

"And not to hurt anyone," my lips were soundlessly saying, praying, picking up his earlier phrase. I heard just a snatch of "Bye, Bye, Blackbird," and then felt a sharp pain and a heavy weight on the back of my head. Then nothing.

CHAPTER THREE

THE GLADDEST HAND OF ALL

WHEN I came to, I began to cry. I sat, cross-legged, on the floor of the late Solly Derritch's hotel room and cried because Dopey Frankie—that was our name for the big kid on the block—had hit me again—never mind who started it—and I no longer had a home to run to for comfort. Growing up is learning to cry by yourself.

Dopey Frankie began to recede. Through my tears, I focused on the hanger where the coat of Solvent Derritch's other (best?) suit hung crazily, as though it had not yet decided to join the pants on the floor of the closet. I wrapped the tangibility of the room around me and climbed slowly back into the moment, using the open suitcase, the now-empty armchair, the small drawer lying on the bed as handholds to pull myself back into complete consciousness. All that I found when I got there was a patch of blood-matted hair where the fat man's pistol had hit the back of my head and a long, dull ache that clung to my skull the way that heat, on a summer's day, masses at the ceiling.

The sickly first light of the winter morning poked its way through the accumulation of dirt on the window as I struggled to my feet, wavered on their new uncertainty and, with more bravado than assurance, closed the door of Room 32 behind me and headed for the stairway. The desk clerk dozed, a sleepy Cerberus, at his post. Outside, no taxis in sight, I began the long descent to my own hotel and, having reached it, bathed my bloody head and stretched out to sleep my way toward the tag end of the morning.

There are moments when I am quite rational, when, as easy as shredding wheat, I decide to act in my own best interests. I awoke to such a moment. Thus far, I cried, and no farther. If I still felt, or thought I felt, the tremor that the ornamental box had sent through my body, if the hint of promise still played, shyly, around my heart, I was wise enough (*pace, pace*) to banish all such considerations from my brain. The fat man in the blanket and our last night's charade at the Chevron were as dead as Solvent Derritch; the ornamental box and the diary were forgotten, like vows of constancy (what's in a name?). I packed my few belongings.

It was a fluke, or ingrained tidiness, or a personal demon that made me fold the list of names that lay on the telephone table, and stick it into the centerfold pocket of my suitcase.

The first train out of Providence was headed for New York. I got on it. There are more painful ways of deciding on destinations.

New York in April is as beautiful as birth. I got there in January. Soot dripped out of the gray sky. Dirty snow was piled along the edges of the sidewalks, like improvised altars on which beer cans, brown paper bags, and copies of the *Daily News* had been sacrificed. The inhabitants, encased in coats and scarves, like peripatetic cocoons months before butterfly time, scurried along the streets on private

errands, too self-preoccupied to be suitably indifferent to
their neighbors.

I was conscious of no particular pattern to my days. I
wandered a great deal, bad weather and all, reminding myself of the way the city felt. I found busy work for my
mind and my eyes and my feet, partly, I suspect, to keep
from feeling too settled down. Only later, after the inter-
lude at Pacific Hall, did particular scenes leap out of the
generality of those first weeks in New York and form what
the movie boys call a montage.

Memory is, after all, the process of turning almost facts
into nearly symbols.

Image 1. I had hardly settled into my new home, one
room in the decayed splendor of an upper West Side hotel,
when a knock at the door brought me a stocky lady clutching a portable phonograph. "May I come in?" she said.
"May I play a record for you?"

"No, thank you," said I, gentling the door toward her,
hoping that she would step back and let it close easily. I
knew the routine. Some message or other about God's love
and the new elect, wrapped in a pitchman's gimmick. The
unwary, so goes the hope, caught off guard by the sight of
the record player, throws open his door to the benign May-
I, perhaps with the prospect of a fast fox trot (the wife
being out) and finds, instead, that he is waltzing (I am
speaking metaphorically) through the halls of Heaven while
the rest of the world rots below.

Her right Enna Jettick, a sizable doorstop, came forward
and stopped my gentling in midpassage. "The word of
God . . ." she began.

". . . on 78 r.p.m.," I countered. "Or is it LP?"

"At Armageddon, you will no longer smile," she said firmly.

At Armageddon, in the name of God, your God, my God, everyman's God, who is going to smile?

"This message is for your salvation, young man," she insisted.

"Lady," I said, "I've got scarlet fever." I pushed the door determinedly and at last her short-stopping foot began to give, but not until she had thrust her free hand around the corner of the door and forced a cluster of pamphlets into my fist. I dropped them into the waste basket as I walked back across the room.

Image 2. In the subway, the Eighty-sixth Street stop, I think, I killed the waiting time by looking at the posters. On one, a prettily scrubbed family, dressed in pastels, leaned into hymnals while the light of God played through a stained-glass window behind them. GO TO THE CHURCH OF YOUR CHOICE, the poster demanded. Written in black crayon across the oatmeal face of the father was this message: Maxie fucks LaVerne.

Image 3. I stood with one foot on the bottom step of a narrow stairway that led to the second-floor blare of a Puerto Rican Pentecostal church. Down the stairs drifted the sound of the celebration of God—in the antique and honorable sense of celebration—an evangelical tango, so to speak. I did not go up. I yearned upward, but I did not go up. Nor did I mount a stairway a block later which led to a clubroom or dance hall where the same strains and the same celebration poured out of windows, opened onto the late January night, past which whirled dark girls in bright orange dresses and black lace shawls, in the arms of miniature, coffee-gray dandies.

Image 4. An old gentleman with a broad-brimmed hat and a straggling gray beard stood in front of a West Side synagogue. He muttered to himself in a language that I do not know, but I stood beside him, stared with him at the notice board, and understood without understanding his words. Next week's sermon: The Mythos of Diaspora: A Critique of Leopold Meyer's Best-Selling Novel, *Next Year in Highland Park.*

"Old man," I said in English, "you are my father." And, then, just like a father, he turned and walked away and left me to find my way home alone.

Image 5. On a cold Sunday morning—early February—I stepped into one of those dressy churches down on Fifth Avenue, or Madison—one of the clean streets—as much to warm my body as to save my soul. A neatly dressed male mannequin, playing hooky from Altman's window, pretended to be an usher and offered to take me to a seat. I shook my head and stood quietly in the back. The sermon was in progress. I listened to the minister develop a long metaphor in which God was likened unto an insurance policy (30-pay-life, I suppose, and all in pieces of silver, although he did not put it just that way). As his unction, relative, not extreme, poured across the hungry souls in his congregation, I watched a very elegant woman try without opening her mouth to tongue out a piece of breakfast that had lodged in her teeth: a bit of ham between the molar and the incisor is a cross of sorts. I stuck it as long as I could, but I knew that as soon as the minister saw and understood the facial contortions of the suffering lady, he would come down from the pulpit with a propitiary offering of dental floss. I went back out into the whipping wind, in which bits of snow now followed each other around in circles . . .

God, too, is a symbolist.

. . . and found that, at least, it was warmer outside than in.

Image 6. An old man, unshaven and unwashed, sat in the reading room at the New York Public Library eating a hard-boiled egg and reading the collected letters of Evelyn Underhill. He had a strange, soft light in his eyes and a bit of yolk stuck to his lower lip.

Now, after the fact, I can see that these shards of broken days, pieced together, were forming an arrow, a hand with the index finger outstretched, pointing me the way to Pacific Hall, sending me back to Solvent Derritch's list of names, in search of the ornamental box.

What is it that never having had a man knows that he has lost?

In point of fact, it was a missing cuff link that brought me back to the list of names. I had decided to take a girl named Maureen Gretz dining. Here, under ordinary circumstances, you might expect a long, lyric, and lurid description: a night on the town, the tinkle of piano music ricocheting from an April sky (it was still February), an early morning walk through deserted streets (how's come those young lovers in movies never get mugged?), a shy game of advance-and-retreat beginning badly in the foyer and ending triumphantly as we lay, body-proud, cut by strips of new-morning sun coming through the Venetian blinds, our fingertips—now, oh, now—barely touching in thank you and good night.

Actually, Miss Gretz, whatever cause I may have to be grateful to her, has very little to do with the story that I am trying to tell. The one relevant fact about her is that she has a genteel fondness for what she calls "nice places." I sensed when I made the date that, in the vernacular of my youth, there might be something doing, so I decided to risk some ready in the hope that she was. Candlelight, real silver, a peripatetic violinist—all these mean, among other things, a clean shirt and, the occasion demanding, French cuffs. Ordinarily, my jewel box, which once housed paper clips, contains a single pair of cuff links, a Brazilian coin of doubtful value, and a thin chip of colored rock that I picked up once in Montana and have been carrying ever since. On the evening in question, showered and shaved, immaculate in clean shorts, my one French-cuff shirt hanging, like a half slip with peek-a-boo sides, down around the mail packets (no pun intended) that sailed relentlessly around my underwear, I went, my cuffs flapping like crippled wings, to the dresser drawer, opened my paper-clip box, and found the coin, the chip of rock, and a single cuff link.

At which point, flapping cuffs or not, immaculate or not, I had to go to the closet and drag out my suitcase. A paper-clip box, as everyone knows, crushes easily, collapses in panic, and opens at the end, spilling paper clips—or cuff links, as the case may be—as freely as water from a street sprinkler on a hot day. My box had come from Providence to New York, as it always travels, in one of the large pockets on the centerpiece that divides the suitcase into two compartments. In the first of the two pockets, there was only lint. In the second, I found the cuff link—a small silver bird, sitting quietly, not singing—fashioned, I think, by a Danish craftsman if anyone cares for details. I found, too, a crumpled piece of paper, jammed into one corner.

Daintily, forefinger and thumb, I pulled it out of its hideaway, rolled it more tightly into a ball and lifted my hand above my head, ready to toss, ready to see if I could possibly hit my wastebasket with so small a missile and from a sitting position on the floor halfway across the room. I tossed. I missed. I pulled myself to my feet and walked across the room, coaxing the silver bird to a perch at my wrist as I went, and then, for what reason I cannot tell since I am not compulsive about such things, I stooped and picked up the crumple of paper that had fallen short of its mark. I held it over the wastebasket, ready to drop, when it came to me to wonder what piece of paper had found its way into my suitcase.

So the list of names that I had torn from Solvent Derritch's diary came out of the shadows in which it had been crouching into the bright light of my *now*. I smoothed the rumpled paper and placed it, weighted by an ash tray, on my dresser and, my toilet finished, went out to Miss Gretz and romance.

It was the next evening before I was quite myself again.

Of all the clichés in common use, that phrase is the dirtiest. Oh, says the young mother, having marked the soul of her son by screaming abuse into his child's ears, I'm not myself today. Oh, menstrual mother, let me introduce you to the migraine professor and to the gentle, gray-haired grandmother who carries kleptomania in her knitting bag.

In the post-Gretz haze of late afternoon, I at last made myself aware of another day. After dinner in a cafeteria (balancing the Gretzian expenses with common-sense, post-coital frugality . . .

□

It would be interesting to know how many savings accounts are opened in the wake of successful seduction (I'm giving the girls the benefit of the doubt, like in that Pinero play), but it is a matter that lies, as we say when there is some job we just do not want to do, outside my professional competence.

. . .) I retired to my room with a book. I had just begun to sort out the young men, to realize which one was supposed to flutter the pulses of which Miss Dashwood, when my mind wandered away from Sussex and settled on the rug a few feet in front of my chair. I watched it lie there, chugging nervously, trying to harness its power for some practical purpose. It failed. Finally, tired of humming pointlessly, it leaped to the top of the dresser, danced once around the glass ashtray and settled on the list of names. I joined my mind at the dresser and, picking up the list, returned to my armchair and contemplation.

If the first name on the list had not had a New York City address, it might all have ended there. I had not yet been sucked into the active orbit of the ornamental box . . .

We are all born with that gravitational pull on us, but there are degrees of resistance.

. . . and if I had had to go farther than East Eighty-second Street, my curiosity might not (but who really can tell) have been strong enough to send me out to take a look at Rodney Salvay.

As it was, I did not go until the next morning. I walked across Central Park, at its best, deserted, on a winter morning when a new snow has touched the landscape clean, and wondered, as I went, how and in what guise I should meet Mr. Salvay. It turned out to be easier than I expected.

The street number was fixed to the heavy door of a four-story gray stone house, more elegant than the omnipresent brownstones. Not a town house any longer, but not an apartment building either. A polished name plate proclaimed, quietly, as the street seemed to demand, PACIFIC HALL and underneath, even more softly, Rodney Salvay, D.D.

I stared at the building, trying to guess from its correct front, its pulled drapes, its whispered promise of peace, just who and what Rodney Salvay was and what he had to do with a fat man with a snub-nosed pistol and a dead Derritch under a bus's wheels in Rhode Island. I became aware that someone was looking at me looking at the building. The man who was eyeing me leaned, contemplatively, contemptuously, against an urn, full of dirty snow and candy wrappers, that graced the front steps of a house across the street from Pacific Hall. I crossed over to speak to him. He was a small man, wearing a leather jacket against the February cold, and with the wispiest fringe of graying hair to protect his bald head from the weather. He chewed nervously at a matchstick and his words slithered out around the stick and dropped nastily off the edge of his resident sneer, venomous words that sounded as though they had been strained through bad teeth on the way out and had picked up a little decay in passage.

"Pardon me," I asked. "Do you know just what that building is used for?"

"You mean Redemption Rodney's salvation parlor?" A charlatan-collector, I could tell. You always know them. They try to beat the Holy Ghost to death with wisecracks, but tears keep coming through.

In, around, under the strained patter, information. Pacific Hall was a church of sorts. Its structure, nonhierarchical; its theology, nondenominational; its dogma, non-existent. Its function, consolatory. The faithful (my informant said that word as though it were an obscenity) gathered every evening, not for services in any formal sense, but for a meeting at which Dr. Salvay spoke rather than preached. During the day, there were private consultations. A steady stream of cars, some chauffeur-driven, flowed to the door of Pacific Hall every afternoon. That, I thought to myself, explains how Pacific Hall can afford to be and can afford to be in such a neighborhood.

In the middle of the improvised lecture, the small man broke off in midsentence, slithered into a hiss. "There he is." The door of Pacific Hall opened and through it stepped the mildest, blandest-looking prophet that I can remember having seen. The face might have been called handsome by certain ladies in late middle age who like the suggestion of babyhood in their men. To me, Rodney Salvay, D.D., looked like a blanc mange. The Homburg and the dark blue overcoat made more pale and puffy a face that was already far gone in that direction. Secret vices, I always think when I see one of those walking roast porks, skinned of its crackling, but nothing could have been more correct than the founder of Pacific Hall as, clutching a rolled umbrella in his gray-gloved hand, he stepped out of his home, his church, and, turning toward Third Avenue, walked briskly along the sidewalk, off probably on some mundane errand.

"That son-of-a-bitch," snarled my new acquaintance. "That son-of-a-bitch really believes the shit he sells." Viciously he yanked at his already-closed zipper, pulling it tight at the neck. (I hear you knocking, but you can't come in.) He turned and stomped away.

"Well, there he goes," I said to myself, out loud. "There

he goes in both directions." For a minute longer, I stood and looked at the house across the street and then I, too, moved off, ready to make a day of making a day.

At eight o'clock that night, I was back in front of Pacific Hall. Light filtered through the drapes, seeped into the street. The impression was one of restrained activity inside —the feeling you sometimes get as you pass a house in the evening and know for a certainty that the people who live there have asked a few friends in for dinner. The double nature of Pacific Hall momentarily paralyzed me. I did not know whether I should treat it as a church and simply walk in or treat it as a home and make use of the ornate knocker that decorated the door. I decided on the former, imagining that, if I made an error, a touching apology might ingratiate me with those inside.

I turned the handle and pushed at the door, which, oiled and easy, opened with no strain. I found myself standing in a hallway bare of all furniture but a single chair, on which, I supposed, the congregation sat, individually, to remove its overshoes. The evidence stood in neat pairs along the wall. From a room on the left came a block of light and a tinkle of soft voices.

As I stepped into the doorway, four faces were turned toward me. One of them, as sweet as a child's, was attached to a delicate little woman, gray washing into the gold of her hair. Her hand, veins visible in the fragile translucence, went to a brooch, a bird's head that held her orange silk dress together at the neck. She jumped from her seat, spilling some kind of magazine to the floor, and hurried toward me, still fingering the clasp at her neck.

"You are a new friend," she said, extending her hand. I

took it and held it for a second. When I released it, it flew back to its nest, the brooch.

"I came in without knocking," I said. "Have I done wrong?"

"Dr. Salvay always says that doors are to open," said the little lady.

And to close?

"My name," she continued, "is Marie Destine. Miss Destine. Let me introduce you to the others."

"I am Charles Seeker," I said, out of nowhere. "I am a stranger in the city." On *Seeker,* she put her hand gently on my arm; on *stranger,* she gave it a reassuring pat.

I followed Miss Destine around the room, shaking hands with a stout lady with a bun, who sat alone reading a Grace Livingston Hill novel, and with two men, both intense, both in slightly dirty shirts, who interrupted a complicated discussion of brotherhood as an abstraction to make my acquaintance. Miss Destine shepherded me back to where she had been sitting, insisted that I take the seat next to hers. "And how did you happen to come to us?" she asked.

"Your name," I answered. "I happened along this street this morning, and saw the sign that said Pacific Hall. If there is anything that this world needs—don't you agree, Miss Destine"—she nodded—"it's peace. I asked a neighbor what the nature of your group was—an amiable man who is, I believe, not a member, although he seems interested in your work. I determined to come back this evening, and the reception you have given me makes me think that I was right to come."

She patted my arm. "Dear Mr. Seeker, how charming."

A pause in which Miss Destine prepared herself to clear up any misunderstandings that I might have about Pacific Hall. "You are quite right about peace. The world needs it badly. However, do not misunderstand what we are trying to do here. We are not political." I shook my head, meaning that Charles Seeker had never thought for a moment that Marie Destine and her crowd were political. "Oh, no," she went on, "not political in the least. It is personal peace that we want."

If wishes were horses . . . and strangely enough a beggar occasionally gallops a mile or so before he finds himself rolling in the dust. Marie Destine, wherever you are, may you have a long and gentle ride.

While we talked the room filled up, if a dozen or so persons can be said to provide a filling. We sat on chairs, facing one end of the room where there was a raised platform, a kind of stage. Two large vases, stuffed with enormous white flowers, sat one on each side of the platform; a heavy white curtain hung on the wall. At precisely eight thirty, Rodney Salvay, dressed completely in white, even to his shoes, parted the curtain and stepped through it onto the stage. Only then did I realize that there was a small spot fixed to the right wall, up near the ceiling, which sent a blue-silver light over flowers, curtain, platform, Salvay, draining away any color that might inadvertently have crept in to spoil the carefully calculated effect of peace and purity. Did he know that he looked like a barely animated corpse? Was death part of the effect?

When the voice began, "Well, friends," I was startled. It was too cheerful for its pure-white, soap-white setting. Salvay was like a restrained YMCA director, no bounce, but with the suggestion that, given the right conjunction of time and a volley ball, he might clap his hands and start things humming. He suggested a small-town minister, conscientiously relaxed for a secular occasion. Within the first few sentences, I knew that Rodney Salvay was right. The setting was mesmerizing; the voice was release. It was as though the fly, having accepted the hypnotic invitation into the spider's parlor, were forced into the most comfortable chair, given a nice cup of tea, and convinced that the magic word *brotherhood* would erase all the differences in the insect world. Looking around me, I saw that everyone in this fish bowl of a room had risen to the surface and was feeding on the speaker's words. Had, I wondered, the spider-fly metaphor come appropriately?

Better to be burned in a candle flame, said a moth I know, who is also a poet, than to mope away your life in a dark closet, munching synthetics.

The speech was completely innocuous. *Well, friends. What kind of day has it been? Did you smile? Did you smile when you wanted to frown or to cry? Was there that one person against whom you felt anger? And did you put down the anger? Did you smother the anger in love? My friends and my brothers, if there is one thing that is stronger than anger, it is love. If there is one road to peace—the peace that rises in the heart—it is the roadway of love. Every small triumph of love, every smile is a step toward personal peace and the peace of the world lies just beyond the edge of our own gardens. Let us work on our own small patch of ground. Let us weed our gardens. Let us make flowers grow. Bloom, bloom you marigolds of the heart. Smile, my friends, and your smile will brighten the whole world. Love, my brothers, and your love will brighten the whole world. Make room for the love and you will make room for the peace. Peace, my brothers. Peace, my friends. Peace. Peace.*

There must have been much more than that. Still, one paragraph will give you an idea, although to tell you the truth, I am rather sorry that I cannot issue the message on records, like those that the stocky lady brought to my hotel room, for only then would you be able to wrap yourself completely in the words of Rodney Salvay. Wrapped, rapt. That is what his hearers were. When the double *peace*, the second one almost a whisper, although something of an embrace too, fell over the audience, they sat hushed, receptive. Their faces had that vacant look of contentment that is seldom seen outside a Turkish bath. Their spiritual muscles which had needed were kneaded and they were given a few minutes of relaxation to pleasure them before they stepped back into the world and felt the soul-muscles begin to knot and twist again. Was there that one person against whom you felt anger?

Mine is a limited show-business experience, but I supposed that, the last *peace* having gentled over the congregation, Rodney Salvay would step back through the white curtain and leave only his spirit and the echo of his voice to see the room emptied. I was wrong. This man knew how to play variations. His speech finished, the lights went up, and Rodney Salvay, now simply a pale and puffy young man in a white suit, stepped down from the platform and took the hand of a lady in the first row of chairs. The comforting touch of his hand, the look in his eyes, the softer, more intimate voice, and the peace of the platform became indeed a personal peace. He was son and lover, prophet and God's vicar behind the tea cozy, and the lady, a hatchet-faced woman who looked vaguely dangerous, melted like cheese in a rarebit and oozed toward him. As he passed

from person to person, the same scene was played again
and again. With men as well as with women. *The son-of-a-
bitch,* I heard again the voice of the morning, and wondered if, once upon a time, the man in the leather jacket
had come here and had barely escaped the presence of
Salvay, only just got out and home where he could pick at
his wound in private.

When Salvay was at last in front of me, being introduced
by Miss Destine, my adopted aunt Marie, I could see that
he was not quite a young man although he might pass for
thirty in the dusk with the light behind him. His eyes, pale
blue, washed-out, were disconcerting because, when he
turned them on me, they were expressionless, for all the
hint of sincerity. They were like blanks which I was supposed to fill in according to my need. He took my hand
and held it noncommittally, uncertain whether he should
squeeze it in comfort or shake it in fellowship.

"What is your difficulty, Mr. Seeker?" he said quietly, as
Miss Destine moved away, leaving me room in which to
unburden.

"Mortality mainly—like everyone in this room." I read
the line simply as though it were a fact—which indeed it is.

There was a flicker of interest in the pale wash of his
eyes. "Just looking," he said. "You're not sure that I can
help you in any way."

"No one," I answered, feeling as though I were playing
some kind of game with him, "is quite sure of his motives."
I was glad that Miss Destine had stepped away because I
would not have liked her to hear me invent a profession.

How the innocent do make us feel guilty.

"I'm a writer," I went on. "I had heard of your work
here at Pacific Hall and I came to look for myself. Partly

out of curiosity, I will admit, but partly because I am interested in what you are trying to do. Personal salvation as a microcosmic infecting cellular unit." He nodded, understanding, but his face assured me that he would never have put it that way. "I would like to have a private talk with you some time; perhaps I might even do an article about you and your work."

I had him. Whether he was a charlatan or a bona fide prophet, I had him. When the roll of the publicity drums is heard, we will all be there.

"I believe that I have a free hour tomorrow afternoon," he said, pulling an appointment book, a prop, from his pocket. "Would that suit?"

"Fine for me," I agreed.

"About three?" A nod, a handshake, and Rodney Salvay moved on, passing among his followers who had not yet been greeted. Charles Seeker, a top-level journalist with maybe a youthful novel to his credit, smiled a good-by to Miss Destine and left Pacific Hall. He went to my hotel room and I put him to sleep by counting sheep that looked like Rodney Salvay.

At three o'clock the next afternoon, I banged the antique knocker against the door of Pacific Hall. It was apparently the right thing to do, for in a few seconds the door was opened by Rodney Salvay himself and I was shown in and up the stairs.

"On this floor," he said, as we paused on the second landing, "are offices. Here I hold my regular interviews. You're a special case, though," and he smiled, "so we might as well go on up to my apartment. It's more comfortable."

There is no causal connection between unctuousness and

home furnishings, but still, with his business and his ear for the exact colorless word, I expected chintz and anti-macassars. The other possibility would have been chinoi-serie with the essence of poppy heavy in the air. There was pleasure in my surprise. The sitting room into which he led me was simple, unpretentious. The chairs were com-fortable, chosen for sitting; the colors were subdued with-out being dull; the one painting was an original by one of the more conservative American abstractionists and the woodcuts were vaguely German.

"Will you have some sherry?" he asked, seeing me first into one of the chairs. He gestured toward a bottle and glasses sitting on a heavy desk in the corner of the room.

I took the sherry and sipped it. I am no enthusiast, but I do know what the stuff is supposed to taste like and this had not come from the A & P. "Good," I said.

"Yes," he said. "It is good." For which I liked him.

The amenities out of the way, we got down to the busi-ness at hand. I cleared up his doubts first, tidying the path along which I would have to walk to get inside his head and heart, to the land where I hoped the secret of the ornamental box lay. I assured him that I was a free-lance writer and implied, with becoming humility, that I was a figure to deal with in contemporary publishing. I was un-sure for whom I would write the article, but—he need have no alarm on this score—the magazine would both be re-spectable and have a large circulation. The ease with which he accepted my statements indicated that he had not spent the morning doing research; a quick trip to the library, a glance at the *Reader's Guide,* and Charles Seeker would have been exploded. But men talk to interviewers the way they fall in love.

We spoke first of the nature of Pacific Hall; it remained as yearningly vague as it had seemed during Salvay's talk the night before. "Dogma?" I asked.

"There is none," he said. "No one who comes to me wants concepts. They all want comfort and that I can give." I was about to open my mouth when he stopped me. "And next you will ask about God. I could say, there is none, but I would never say that on the platform downstairs. There is certainly no God in Pacific Hall, no official God that is, but most of the people who come here bring some idea of God with them and mix Him in with my generalization."

"Generalization?" I caught onto the word. "Isn't the word deprecatory?"

"I don't think so," he said. "Brotherhood, love, peace— what could be more general? The words soothe, like a hand on the forehead. Like all that white I use downstairs."

"And what do you get from all this?"

"The sense of having done a little kindness. I really like the people who come to me and I like the idea that I make life easier for them."

"By fooling them?"

"But I'm not fooling them," he said. "Some things, like my D.D., may not be genuine, but about essential things, I'm not fooling them."

"And all this?" I asked, making a gesture that took in the desk, the painting, the woodcuts, the sherry.

"I like nice things," he said. I made no comment. After the suggestion of a silence, he went on. "Yes, Pacific Hall pays for all this"—he made my gesture—"as you call it. Some of my followers are rich. I comfort their souls and they comfort my body. Is that wrong?"

"I don't know. Is that wrong?"

"You are a journalist, Mr. Seeker. You write on call, for

money. Is it impossible that you should take pleasure in your work and still get paid? That you should think an article well done and still accept money?" He had me there, except that I was no journalist. I was plain Connie Firth, a seeker, not Mr. Seeker.

One of me answered, "Your point is a good one, Mr. Salvay. A doctor doesn't have to cut out a cancer for free to stop the spread of decay."

Salvay smiled. He nodded toward my now-empty glass and, when I did not protest, he picked it up and walked to the desk. He stood, his back to me, pouring the sherry. "But if you have both physical and spiritual well-being," I began slowly, watching his back carefully, "why are you involved with the ornamental box?"

He gave a sudden, violent tip to the sherry bottle. The wine spilled over the glass, over his hand and dripped, dropped to the desk beneath. He set down the bottle and the glass. He turned, leaning against the desk, looking toward me. He began to cry.

There he stood, Rodney Salvay, D.D., whose spiritual strength was as the strength of ten, with great tears rolling down his yeast-dough face. He lifted his right hand, still wet with sherry, and reached toward me. "I need it . . . I need it, too."

"Need what?" I snapped.

"I need it," he repeated through his tears. "Whatever it is, I need it."

"Jesus Christ," I said, aloud, to no one, and left Salvay leaning against the desk, still crying helplessly.

CHAPTER FOUR

THE CRY IN THE IVORY TOWER

NOTHING unnerves me like the sight of a man crying. I plunged my stumbling way—dabbing occasionally at my eyes with the rough sleeve of my coat—down the two flights of stairs and out the door of Pacific Hall. Eighty-second Street seemed placid in the brightly useless late afternoon sun of February. "Rodney, Rodney," I whispered back over my shoulder as I hurried toward Lexington. "Pull yourself together, Rodney. You owe it to your audience." Then, incontinently, I began to laugh.

We are doomed finally to speak only in advertising slogans and when that time comes the few survivors of the age of incongruity will die laughing and be buried without honors.

I ran, laughing, past Park, past Madison, across Fifth and into Central Park. There were tears in it by this time, cold on my face. *Was there that one person against whom you felt laughter?* Rodney Salvay, said my mind, if you were my son I would buy you a two-wheeler with an artificial foxtail to tie to the rear fender. I collapsed on a park bench and laughed helplessly. There is no one road to compassion.

"Whatsamatter, mister?" said a voice. I looked up at a little girl, bundled in a snowsuit, peering out of round, rimmed glasses, all that was visible between cap and scarf— an owl in Baby Bunting's rig. "What're you cryin' for?"

My hand against my cheek told me that she was right. "I lost my balloon, little girl," I said. "I lost my birthday balloon."

"Gee," she said. "That's too bad."

That was her last word of comfort. "LA VERNE!" screamed a siren dressed in Persian lamb. "You come here this minute." LaVerne went. Where had I heard that name, I wondered, as I watched the sweet bundle of brotherhood stumble back into the orbit of distrust. And then I remembered. "LaVerne, LaVerne," I whispered, "beware of a kid named Maxie."

The mother did a basilisk, but I kept on breathing just the same. There may have been justice on her side because all that her stare could pick up was my strangely swollen face (exertions of the soul) and my mumbling lips sending a soundless message to the snowsuitclad back of the retreating LaVerne. The mother snatched the child's hand, a gloved snake pouncing on a mittened mouse. "Dirty old man," I heard her mutter, but I did not much care. I could take five of her years and still call her big sister, and I did wash regularly with a brand-name soap.

I did not have time to focus my eyes and mind on the leafless branches of the nearest tree, had that been my pleasure, before LaVerne's place was taken by a dirty old man. A real one, this time, or are all such designations relative?

"Buddy, can you spare a dime?" All trades have their jargon.

I was off again. Somewhere under the laughter, I heard him. "I'm hungry." Not even hunger can take the edge off hysteria. I found a handful of change and forced it into his willing old hands. "Go, you, and do likewise," I screamed.

"God bless you," I heard him say, and that topped everything that the afternoon had offered. I jumped from the bench and embraced him fondly (he smelled) and then I turned, still laughing, still crying, toward Central Park West and, beyond that, my hotel. The old boy thinks I am drunk, I remember saying to myself, on pale Rodney's one glass of sherry. And why not? Home at last, I crawled into a pint of Irish and slept like a baby.

I did not wake up until the next morning, fourteen hours later, and, strangely, I found myself at one with the world. My body felt as though it had been lately in front of a high-pressure fire hose, up close to the nozzle; it lay limply on the bed, all strength drained away, and little fantasies of warmth and friendliness danced up to its helplessness. I smiled and went back to sleep.

Finally, at noon I got up and out. Over a cream cheese and chive on roll, I thought, calmly, of Rodney Salvay and his reaction to my mentioning the box. "Oh, God," Solly Derritch had written, "I hope I'm finally going to find it." Squeezing my tea bag with my fingers to get the best of it, I decided to disassociate myself from all that need. No more ornamental box for me, said I to me, wiping my tea-wet fingers, like Pilate, on a paper napkin.

Like the village alcoholic at the revival meeting, I had signed the pledge. All that remained to be done was to break it.

Those people who do not like to see the hero of a book gainfully employed may skip over the next few paragraphs. They are not integral. Still, they do have some relevance. I took a job as night counterman at one of the Bickford cafeterias. If you are a Bickford devotee, you know that the work is not, as the placement boys say, challenging. One just stands behind a counter passing cup after cup of coffee,

English muffin after English muffin, into the hands that reach out from the other side. I took the job so that I could fill the Solly-Rodney corner of my mind with a new family. Every Bickford's, every Horn and Hardart, every all-night cafeteria in America has its regulars, a band of the old and the poor, the rootless and the tieless, who find in one another home, family, and lover. The counterman, as dispenser, is an important tangent to the circle; he is not in it. The pattern of demand is set by the conventions of trade: said Simple Simon to the pieman let me taste your ware; said the pieman to Simple Simon show me first your penny. Any smile, any joke, a not quite disguised catch in the throat is a purely gratuitous gift of the gods, which means from one man to another.

I would not have stayed long at Bickford's in any case— I was too out of condition for the long hours on my feet— but my resignation came sooner than I expected. On Wednesday night, my second week at the job, I was leaning over the fruit salad, spooning grapefruit and peach and a little pineapple into a dish, when a voice said, "I hope you're sober tonight."

I looked up into a familiar face which I plainly did not know. The speaker was an old man in a tattered overcoat —his unwashed face half hidden in a grizzle of beard. I thought first—don't ask why—of the egg-eating mystic that I had seen in the public library, but when he said, "Or do you only drink in the daytime?" I knew him for laughing boy's pal from the park.

I made some kind of silly joke about being on the wagon because the old man made me feel guilty—and grateful, too. Like when I go out with my fly unzipped and discover it all by myself hours later, no one having said anything, no one apparently having noticed. I always feel a fool or worse, but I am glad that no one has publicly declared my fool-dom. I had been bare-ass soul-naked in the park that February afternoon, but now it was March and the one dangerous witness chose to see me as a drunk. A mask, even if it is unbecoming, *is* a mask. "My doctor won't let me drink after six," I said with a television smile, handing the old man his porridge. I was rewarded with a cracked titter.

Old John—for that was his name—returned the next night and the next and the next. He became a regular, transferring his letter, so to speak, from some cafeteria farther downtown. Something—the handful of change or the embrace—had served as adoption papers; I was his. Having staked his claim, he came to work it nightly—for smiles, for jokes, for teasing banter: "You're late tonight, Old John. I bet you've got an Old Jill staked out somewhere in this neighborhood." The titter. Oh, that titter!

Of all the ridiculous discussions that go on in college dormitories and army barracks, the silliest of all is the one about whether or not you would marry a girl for her money. There is always one man to insist that he would, whatever the circumstances, and a few who think they might be willing if the woman in question were good-looking as well as rich. But *no,* say the mass of men. The money would be lovely, runs the argument, but the man would become simply a piece of property. Considering the way some rich women take care of their property, that might not be such a bad deal, but that is not the problem here. All of you priggish, world-weary, discussion-happy boys out there in the dormitories and the barracks, listen to a man of experience. If you really want to know how it feels to be owned, don't marry for money—let someone marry you for money.

☐   ☐

A week of Old John and I had had it. I left not only Bickford's, but the city. At this distance, I can see that I should have gone back and said good-by, for how rough it must have been on the old boy to come in—his titter ready —and find no one to press the release mechanism. Good-by, Old John, and God bless you. Now laugh, goddamit.

I caught a Greyhound for Ravenna, Virginia. My reason? The list, of course. The second name was Edward Pick; the only identification, an address in Ravenna. It would have been easier for me to compose my face if the late Solvent Derritch had taken the trouble to identify his friends (colleagues? conspirators? competitors?) by trade, age, and hobbies, but things, as Jean Arp has shown, can be arranged according to the law of chance. Which is how I got involved with an academic on the make, and give me an insurance salesman every time.

I was preoccupied with myself when I got on the bus, busy swearing off of swearing off, deciding to follow the names on the list until I came to the one who really could tell me what was in that box. As if I cared. Of course, I cared.

We were through the Lincoln Tunnel and almost to the Turnpike before I bothered to look at the person sitting next to me. It was the smile that caught my attention. The young man—it was a young man—was grinning like a high school boy who has managed, for the first time, to get his hand inside a girl's blouse. The most corrupt smile of all because it cancels girl and breast, shouts *look at me, look at me*. I looked to see what he had to shout about, whom he was canceling.

In his hand he held a few sheets of printed material, too

few to make a magazine or a pamphlet, at which he stared
with consuming fondness. By which I really mean *consuming*, saying, with that smile, like the high school boy, I will
eat you up and you will make me strong and that should be
enough for you. Poor girl, poor pages. A close look, an
intrusive one considering the nature of the communication
between the man and the print, told me that the pages were
a reprint from some scholarly publication or other, something like *The Journal of Chromatic Philology*. You know,
those spotless quarterlies you see in college libraries lying
close to the dog-eared copies of *Life* and the *New Yorker*.
The title was "An Image in Hegel and Bret Harte: An
Intuitive Borrowing."

"I doubt if Bret Harte ever read Hegel," I heard myself
saying, although if there was one thing that I was not interested in at that moment it was a literary discussion.

"Who cares?" my neighbor said, looking at me, still smiling.

"Whoever wrote that article cares," I said, and the discussion was under way whether I wanted it or not.

"Oh, no, he doesn't," said the young man. "I wrote the
article and I don't care a damn about whether or not Bret
Harte read Hegel. I'm covered. See that word there." He
pointed. *"Intuitive.* You know what that means?"

"I've done a little in my time," I said. So it was Bret
Harte and Hegel that he was canceling. "There are all
kinds of ways to fondle a breast," I said out loud, "but
there are some ways that I just do not like."

He looked at me suspiciously. After waiting in vain for
me to follow my declaration with a dirty story, he asked,
"Is it a riddle?"

"No," I said, "it's a point of honor." Then, "Why didn't
you say *accidental?*"

"*Intuitive* is better," he said warmly. "It suggests that there is some kind of connection."

"What are you, a matchmaker?" I asked. I could see this pushy little bastard getting Hegel and Harte (sounds like a musical comedy team when you say it that way) into the same room and introducing them—Georg meet Bret, Bret meet Georg—and then walking out and leaving them with not one damn word to say to one another.

My remark must have pleased him. At least, he began to fumble busily at a battered brief case sitting at his feet. "Perhaps you'd like a reprint," he said, straining at the catch which kept the mouth of the brief case shut. Would that I could have done the same with myself.

"What would I want with a reprint?" I snapped. Then, when his eyes clouded over, I modified, "I mean why waste one on me? You'll want to send them around to the rest of your bunch."

"Oh, I've got plenty of them," he said. This time he did get the case open and he insisted that I take one of his treasures.

At the foot of the article, in the neatness of italics, was the label: *Peer Gray, Spitzer College.*

"Peer Gray," I said. "Peer. What a coincidence. My name is Rosmer. C. M. Rosmer." It passed right over him. What kind of education are they giving these young teachers? Tired of talking to myself, I said, "What is this Spitzer College?"

"The end of the world," he answered. "A positive hole. But don't you worry"—I was worried?—"don't you worry. I'll be out of there and on my way in no time."

"On your way? Way where?"

"To the top," he said, and expanded like a soufflé. The poor little bandit meant it. "That's why I'm on my way to

Ravenna. I've got to go down there and snow old Professor Pick."

"Edward Pick?"

"Is there another Professor Pick?"

"Not that I know of," I said, speaking the truth. I was glad enough to know that there was one.

"Are you going to the celebration?" he asked. When I admitted that I was not and played him with one question after another, I found out as much about Edward Pick as I needed to know this side of intimacy. An eminent classical scholar, he had chosen to stay at Ravenna College, a small but respectable place in Virginia (even I had heard of the Ravenna Lectures), instead of getting involved in the organization shuffle of one of the big universities. Now, after forty years as a teacher, he was retiring and the college was throwing a large celebration that was supposed to attract Pick's fellow scholars, his old students, and, the public relations man fondly hoped, one or two of the national magazines (*Life* Goes to a Wake?).

"And you were one of Professor Pick's students?" I asked.

"God, no, I never met the old crank."

"Then what are you doing butting in on his celebration?"

"I'm the fair-haired boy," said the young man. "I'm the heir apparent." I must have looked my doubt, for he went on, "You look like you don't believe me. Probably you just don't understand these things. In my business . . ."

". . . racket," I amended, trying to get the man and his mind together. He happily agreed.

"O.K., in my racket you've got to have a gimmick. I haven't had one; that's why I played around with Hegel and all that image crap. A publication for my personnel record. But now I've got one. A gimmick, I mean. I read somewhere about old Pick and about how he was all tied up with some North African poet back in St. Augustine's time and how he'd been working for years on translations of the guy's stuff. He's an old man, Pick, I say to myself, and I begin to read all his other stuff. And don't think that's easy. Greek and Roman and all that. Who cares, I wonder. Anyway, I wrote him a letter saying how interested I am in Avis—that's the poet—and throwing in a few casual hints that I've read this and that and the first thing you know we're pen pals. Now I'm invited to the party. And if I don't end up with all of the old man's notes and translations and a job at Ravenna too, I'm not Maisie Gray's little boy Peer."

After that, conversation languished. I sat there wishing that I had brought along my Buck Rogers disintegration pistol. But the road from New York to Ravenna is a long one and it was impossible, given Peer Gray's galloping fondness for confession, that silence would prevail. I was even forced to uncover a little. I admitted that I was traveling as field representative for a new textbook company (Anodyne and Seeker) and that I was on my way to Ravenna and hoped to see Professor Pick. Gray tried to force a second reprint on me when he heard of my publishing connections, but I escaped it, just as I escaped him as soon as the bus touched in at Ravenna, pausing just long enough to call over my shoulder, "Beware of button-molders."

I avoided the Ravenna College Inn, assuming that it would be rather preciously Old South, a visiting mother's cup of clam broth, and also that it would be full of Pick's friends, his fellow scholars and a few grave robbers, like Peer Gray. I went instead to the Hotel Ravenna, a pleasantly ramshackle place, that was permanent home to the town's professional lady and temporary home to countless drummers, where I might have sat long hours in a rocker on the gallery and listened to stories if I had not felt that I ought to walk over to the college and see if I could get in on Professor Pick's party.

The publicity man was as easy as autumn. It could not have been my newly discovered publishing company that did the trick. My guess is that the grand occasion was being undersubscribed, that ex-students and scholars alike were finding good reasons for not traveling to Ravenna in March.

Dear Ed: Which one of the Romans was it that said, age has its excuses. I would have liked to have been on hand to toast your retirement, not so much for all your scholar's achievements, real albeit they are, but in memory of the summer of 1912 when we followed those two English school-marms all around the Grecian isles.
Resignedly, Clyde.

Dear Professor Pick: Damn all this administrative non-sense! Now that they've made a Dean of me—when all I wanted to do was be a teacher like Edward Pick—I find I'm tied to my desk and can't get back to alma mater and your dinner. Best wishes, all the same.
Frederick Pall, Dean of Men, Gribsey A & M.

Dear Pick: I'm not coming to your deification; promise not to come to mine two years hence. Get on with the Avis translations.
Yrs. Melsen.

Walking across the campus, my invitation in my pocket, I thought for a moment of Professor Pick, gentling into the grave, his honors like scars on his head. But campus-walk-ing is not for thoughts of the aging. March, even in Vir-ginia, is a little too early to litter the grass with couples playing touch-and-promise across open but unheeded sociology texts and volumes of Victorian poetry; still there was the young activity of the campus: youth on the move, as the editorial writers and commencement speakers say, meaning, in this case, from class to library to class to dormitory to class to snack bar. Put a name on an eighteen-year-old and he begins to grow characteristics to go with it, but nameless and impersonal, he looks like everyone else—male or female—although there are beguiling differences in shape. As I walked across the Ravenna campus, scrubbed, healthy, eager faces spread out before me, like mirror image on mirror image, testifying that life, if not love, springs eternal. For that moment they were a single shape under the sun. A bird sang somewhere. On other days, in other moods, I might have wanted to drown the litter.

I stopped to annoy one couple who stood in private communion outside the PolySci building. Annoyance was not my goal, but it was an inevitable by-product of any intrusion on their exchange of bromides. The young man was dressed in everyone's chino trousers and flannel shirt with a light jacket, almost the color of the pants, to complete the impression that he read the better men's magazines, and the girl, in a Morrison plaid skirt and short jacket, had also learned the meaning of *casual*.

That word is probably responsible for more tension, uncertainty, and ulcers than any other word in the American ad-man's lexicon.

"May I ask a question?" I said after I had attracted their eyes out of each other's heads.

"Do your worst," said the young man. He had decided to play it . . . well, *casual* . . . there's no other word to describe his calculated effort to use me, a stranger, to impress the young lady.

"Do you know Professor Pick?"

"Yes," said the girl, coming in so quickly that she caught the young man still trying to think of a cute way of saying yes.

"They're having a dinner for him tonight," said the young man, determined to get something out of the conversation. "A funeral would be more appropriate."

"Oh, Charley," the girl giggled. She pushed at him with her hand, her wrist flabby, a gesture that was a hit and a pat and a wave. "You are *just* awful. Professor Pick is really a sweet man."

"The best fifth-century mind on campus," said Charley.

"Oh-h-h-h, you *are* awful." She folded confidingly toward him.

He turned to me for approbation, too. "Take the advice of an old straight man, Charley," I said. "Get yourself a new writer." That's the trouble with most conversations; they pull you down to their level. I walked away with the uncomfortable feeling that all the well-washed faces swimming past me belonged to killer sharks aching for the smell of blood. Professor Pick was *sweet,* then, like a puppy in a taxidermist's window.

The testimonial dinner was held in the refectory. A baronial hall, all dark wood and dim light filtered through high leaded windows, it seemed to belong as little to the classic exterior as it did to the three-button neatness of the men and women who had gathered to honor the retiring professor. Across one end of the hall stood the head table. There was assembled everyone closely related to Professor Pick (a widower) by blood or inkhorn and there of course sat anyone who had even a single line of praise to read. The rest of us were scattered at four-man tables.

I shared mine with a member of Ravenna's biology de-

partment, the biologist's wife and a minor politician—
clerk or treasurer—from a neighboring county, all of whom
had been students of Professor Pick. The three of them
assured me that the guest of honor had been an excellent
teacher. Then followed anecdotes. There was the time, of
course, that Professor Pick had turned two pages of his
notes at once and gone on reading without noticing the
hiatus. There was the time, absorbed in explaining some
complication in Roman poetics, he fell off the platform and
sat, one leg folded beneath him, and followed his point to
its conclusion. There was the time that a bright student,
playing a joke or caught in a bind, handed in a few pages
of one of the standard translations of Lucan and got it back
marked "C –: Not up to your best work." And so they went.
The stories were contradictory, condescending, plainly un-
true. All of them were designed to prove that Professor
Pick, a man with a birth certificate, a blood type, and a soul
of sorts, was really the most unforgettable character that I,
you, he, *Reader's Digest* ever met, all tweed and pipe smoke,
absent-mindedness and simple wisdom.

When the anthropology boys get tired of comparative
religion and move on to comparative pedagogy, they will
find a Golden Bough cluster of anecdotes around one professor on each American campus—the same stories edited to
fit any discipline. No universal sun god or scapegoat may
grow out of the material, but at least we will see clearly the
outlines of the academic archetype—the father-fool.

"Do you still read Greek and Latin?" I asked, which was
a little like turning over a glass of water in their collective
laps.

"Heavens, no!" From Mrs. Biologist, the frankness of
spontaneity.

"You have no idea how many scientific journals I have to

keep up with" from Mr. Biologist, who, I will wager my job with Anodyne and Seeker, takes *Time* and the *Saturday Evening Post*. He grumbled into his parfait—we were that far along in the dinner—half afraid that he was being accused of selling out Latin for the laboratory (thirty species . . .?).

"Not much call for those languages in my line," said the clerk (or treasurer). "Why would I be reading them?"

"For pleasure," I answered. "I meant, do you read them for pleasure?" The air became stuffy around the table; several of us found it hard to breathe. At a distance I glimpsed Peer Gray, talking earnestly to his tablemates, explaining, probably, how he had spent the afternoon stealing pennies from dead men's eyes, and I suddenly saw myself for the amiable son-of-a-bitch I was being. "Of course, a great many classicists don't read Greek and Latin either— except when they have to," I announced. (Do not ask me where I get my information.) The air cleared. Mrs. Biologist beamed; her husband smiled in a friendly fashion. The politican coughed affectionately and began a story about Professor Pick's outwitting the trustees, which was fortunately interrupted by the dinner knell—the sound of a spoon tapping a half-filled water glass. Attention, attention must be finally paid . . . .

One of Pick's colleagues in the Classics Department, a dumpling of a man with a sense of humor like the early years of radio, acted as toastmaster, making leaden-footed witticisms that crawled painfully away from the head table and died before they reached the nearest potential laugher. Most of them involved multilingual puns. The president of the college, a retired cement manufacturer, spoke his piece prettily—a PR, suitable-for-all-occasions insistence on the honored guest's (fill in correct name) importance to the

college. He smiled from the opening quotation from New-
man's *Idea of the University* to the closing quotation from
Barzun's *Teacher in America:* if it had been a eulogy, he
would have done the same routine with a straight face. An
eminent outsider (all expenses paid), a classicist who had
discovered, much to his and the television audience's de-
light, that he was photogenic, gave the main speech of the
evening, an appraisal of Professor Pick's contribution to
classical learning in America. "If Epictetus could have been
here tonight . . ."—but I do not have to go on; you know
the way it went. An articulate man in middle age (a state
senator, I was told) spoke for all those who had been students of Professor Pick; a nervous young man, who,
strangely in this company, seemed to mean his warm words,
spoke for the present student body. (Charley had said a few
words on their behalf in the afternoon.) Two or three more
people, whom I never quite identified, got into the act and
then the toastmaster remembered a stack of congratula-
tory telegrams which he felt called upon to read, comically
putting in all the *stops.*

Finally, when the audience had retreated to sleep or the
sense of being trapped, Professor Pick stood up to acknowl-
edge the praise that he had received. He was a tall man,
well over six foot, lean, sharp-faced, alert. He wore a black
suit, obviously cut by an English tailor from a rough cloth,
plainy as durable as its wearer. He did not smile, but there
was a glitter in his eye, which—at my distance—I could not
read. He stood quietly just long enough for everyone to pay
him the compliment of nervous attention. Then he spoke.

"The one thing that I have learned in forty years of
teaching is patience. The one consolation for the classroom
is the library. No man need long for more. Many of you
know that I have been working for several years translating

the poet Avis, almost unknown in English, so unlike the other poets of his time. I would like to read one of my translations to you.

> The wise grain of sand
> Knows the desert.
> He does not hear the other grains
> Who will find God
> Uniquely in a single size or shape."

Professor Pick sat down. In time, the applause came.

The dinner ended in a rush of informal words and the shudder of chair legs pushed away from tables. There was a melee of recognition in which friend greeted friend, acquaintance, acquaintance, associate, associate, many of whom had not seen one another for four hours, since the afternoon curriculum meeting. A fast tap of steps—including Peer Gray's—beat its way to the head table. I watched Professor Pick shake hands with everyone who approached him, warmly with a few, perfunctorily with most. Gray got a warm handshake, but that is the way things always are: the wronged wife is the last one to know. Above the changing pairs of clasped hands, Professor Pick's head moved back and forth, a continual shake of *no,* of refusal. At last, when the crowd was thin enough for him to move through it without anyone sticking to him, Pick walked the length of the refectory and left the room and the building, alone.

I followed at a distance. The professor walked deliberately, not hurrying from, not hurrying to, across the campus and then turned up one of the neighboring tree-lined streets where faculty homes stand like ordinary houses, unaware of their semiofficial position. The space between us closed as I outstepped his deliberation, finally catching up with him in midblock.

"I enjoyed your speech, Professor Pick," I said, as I came abreast of him.

"You weren't meant to," he said simply, and then, turning toward me, he realized that I was a stranger. "Do I know you?"

"I think not. My name is C. M. Rosmer."

"Do you want something from me?"

"Probably. Doesn't everyone?"

We walked then in silence for the length of two lawns, past a scattering of flower beds and a single tricycle left out for the night.

"About now," said Professor Pick, "you should tell me how much you admire my work—in very general terms, of course."

"In very specific terms," I said, "I've never read anything you've written."

"That's a refreshing confession. I prefer people who admit ignorance of my work to almost everyone—except those who really do know what I've done."

"That explains the success of the boy vulture," I said, as much to myself as to him.

His only reaction was a startled "What?"

"Oh, never mind. Just something that came into my head."

The next silence was shorter and ended in his laughter, soft and deep. And something else. Was the other note simply intelligence or was there a little bitterness in it? "You mean Peer Gray, I take it."

"Yes, I mean Peer Gray. How can you put up with it?"

"Have you ever been seduced, young man?" Before I could answer—and I had not even thought of a suitable answer—he waved his question away. "Don't bother. I'm speaking rhetorically. Flattery does not cease to be pleasant simply because you know that the flatterer is false. Besides, there is at least as good a chance that Avis will convert Peer Gray as that Peer Gray will corrupt Avis."

"I'll put my money on Gray."

"I put mine on Avis long ago."

"I'd never heard of him until today."

"Don't apologize."

"I'm not. But judging from the poem you read tonight he is worth listening to." The professor nodded that he was. "Still if the grain of sand were all that wise he would know that the other grains have a point, that a desert is not always and only a desert."

"That's true," said the professor. "Avis has a poem that says that, too."

"And does he have one about your patience?"

"My patience is my own. I've acquired it slowly."

"Is it enough?"

"It is enough."

"Then why do you care about the ornamental box?"

"*Who are you?*" The cultivated voice of the professor became the high, shrill scream of an old man. (*Was there that one person against whom you felt anger?*) He stepped away from me, backing himself against an iron fence that bordered the lawn past which we were walking when my question came; his hands reached behind him and clutched the rails. There he stood, almost impaled, like impatience on a monument, facing directly at me and screaming into my face. "*Who are you?* I'm seventy years old and I've as much right to that box as anyone in this country. Don't you come around here telling me I'm off the list. I'm on the list, on it, on it, on it. Do you hear me? Damn you, do you hear me?"

I reached out to put a hand on his shoulder. Still clinging to the fence, he kicked out at me with his kindling-wood legs. "Don't touch me! Don't touch me! Don't try none of that."

"It's all right," I whispered. "It's all right, Professor Pick. I don't want your place on the list. I don't want your place on the list."

Lights had come on in the house behind him. I soothed and coaxed and finally I got the old man's hands free of the iron fence and led him off up the street. The two of us walked slowly toward Professor Pick's house, he making the turns instinctively, I looking for a street and number that I knew from the diary. Like a fragment of some kind, he rattled as we walked, words bubbling up out of him disjointedly. I said nothing except perhaps, *now, now,* or *it's all right, Professor Pick,* vowing as I walked—no more direct questions. *Go round about, Peer,* I said to myself, but the quotation set up unhappy echoes of my bus trip and I went back to the simple, nonliterary—no more direct questions.

He was almost calm by the time we reached his front steps. I started to go up with him, but he stopped and put his hand, like a weight, on my shoulder, indicating that I was to go no farther. "I'm all right now," he said. "I'll be all right now." He climbed the two steps. At the edge of the porch, he turned and said, "You weren't sent, were you? I'm not off the list, am I?" I shook my head and mumbled something like *accident.* He crossed the porch, but at the door he turned and looked at me again. "Rosmer? Did you say, Rosmer?" I nodded. He laughed softly. "O.K., Rosmer, don't take any wooden millraces."

I could have kissed him.

A FAMILY AFFAIR

 THE ONE THING I have learned in thirty-five years of being is patience.

Professor Pick did not appear in class on Monday. This I discovered from Peer Gray, whom I met that afternoon in the bus station where I had gone—following the list—to check schedules for Atlanta. His boy's smile was distorted by disappointment (he had not managed a private talk with Pick) and worry (his small failure might portend a greater one).

"I can't understand it," he said. "I just cannot understand it. The old man was so friendly in the letters he wrote me. And did you see how he shook my hand at the dinner?"

"Like the return of the prodigal," I agreed.

"But he wouldn't talk to me on Saturday or Sunday. I went to his house twice and no one would come to the door. He was home. I know that. I called up and he answered the phone and said he was sick. Sick, my ass. He was healthy enough on Friday night when he made that snotty speech."

"I liked the speech." He ignored me.

"Only maybe he really was sick or something. He didn't come to class this morning because I waited around to catch him then."

"You make him sound like a fish."

"Fish. Fish. I'm not sure who's the fish in all this—if

you mean sucker. I dragged myself all the way down here from New York. And for what? I ask you, for what?"

"To pay honor to Professor Pick," I suggested.

"Balls," said Peer Gray. "You know what I came for and you see what I've got to take home."

As he talked, Peer Gray pushed at his suitcase with his foot, gingerly, as though it were a sleeping Pick that might rise up and swallow him whole. Still, there was force enough in the pushes to carry the bag, in short slides, hobbling stops-and-starts like a crippled animal, from the door of the bus station almost to the ticket window. And with two free hands: one to clutch the brief case, now empty of reprints; the other to assault the air with gestures of futility. With every sentence, each new helping of exasperation, the foot came more sharply against the suitcase until finally on *and you see what I've got to take home* the young man kicked out angrily. He pulled his foot away quickly; a mild moue of pain—too small for an *ouch*—crossed his face. He snatched up the bag and carried it the remaining two steps to the line at the ticket window where he took his place behind an ample woman carrying a wicker basket. As he half-turned to find out whether or not I was to be his traveling companion on the journey back to the North, the suitcase nudged the lady in her fleshy backsides. "Are you . . ." he began. *Splat* went the suitcase. ". . . going back . . ." he went on, straining farther. *Splat* went the suitcase. ". . . to New York . . ." another twist of his head and shoulders. *Splat* went the suitcase.

Fury broke loose in the bus station. The fat woman whirled around and brought her wicker basket (empty, thank god; I had visions of eggs) down on Peer Gray's head. With a scream, the young man dropped the suitcase and brought his hand up to his reddening ear. The offending bag, left to look after itself, fell on the woman's instep and set her off once more. With an oath, she brought the basket down again, this time on Gray's protecting arm. Now, no quarter. She moved in, raining blow after blow on the bewildered young man. Gray threw his brief case to one side and brought the other arm up with the first, a crossed defense against the battering basket. He tried backing out of her way, but with heavy steps she was on him, still pounding.

The two or three would-be ticket buyers who stood in the line behind Gray scattered before him as he scrambled to escape. One of the others, a pale and fragile girl whose lipstick smear insisted she was a woman, forgot to snatch up her suitcase as she ran, and Gray, blind in his backward plunge, fell over it. Shiny and new though it was, it was cheap, and the inexpensive catches gave under the falling man's weight; the suitcase opened and its contents rolled with Gray on the station floor. He struggled, enmeshed in Woolworth laces and silks, one foot caught in a pale pink Suspants, and tried vainly to rise, while the fat lady, now tiring, dropped occasional, weakening blows on him, and the girl danced around him like a demented sparrow, chirping her outrage. Through all this came Peer Gray's plaintive counterpoint, "What'd I do? What'd I do?"

The whole sequence, from provocation to prostration, passed so quickly that no official, nor any officious bystander, had time to step in and disrupt the precision in the flow of events. Calm came quickly after chaos. The announced departure of a bus for Charlottesville sent the fat lady, winded but unrepentant, muttering that she was, after all, a lady, to the ticket window and then, ruefully examining her badly bruised basket, through the doors to the loading

platform. A bus official of some kind—stationmaster perhaps
—put in an appearance—finally and fussily—but by that time
Peer Gray was on his knees beside the pale girl's suitcase,
trying clumsily to repack it while she knelt beside him,
snuffling quietly.

It was a scene that I did not want interrupted. I explained to the official that the girl's suitcase had been spilled
open by a lady who had just got on the Charlottesville bus
(forgive me, you warrior with the wicker basket, but in a
way it was true) and that the young man was helping her
pick up her things. Satisfied, he prissed off to his office and
left the two of them on their knees in the center of the
station. The girl was now between a sob and a sigh, the
catchy breathing of a child who no longer wants to cry but
does not want to lose the warmth of being comforted.
Through her tears she could see that Peer Gray, for all that
he meant well, was making a distressing male mess of her
suitcase. She began to rearrange things as he put them in
and, within a second or two, he began to hand them directly to her, first dusting at them shyly (you, there, with
the knowing grin, have you ever shaken out a half slip in
a public waiting room). There they knelt, he passing each
piece of clothing to her, an acolyte to her priest, a nurse to
her doctor.

The repacking was at last finished; the spell broken. Peer
Gray got to his feet and helped the girl to hers. She took up
her suitcase and went her own way, retaining who knows
what memory of her fellow communicant. By this time, I
was holding the young man's brief case, collected from
under the bench where it had gone when he sent it flying.

"Mr. Gray," I said, holding the case toward him.

"Thank you, Mr. Rosmer." He took it, grudgingly, as

though his tentativeness would make me disappear, would make me not ever have been there. He tried on a laugh, but it did not fit. "That was quite a show, I guess."

"From accidental villain to conscious hero, Mr. Gray. You looked all right."

"Thank you," he said, the strut gone from his voice. There may even have been a blush but it would not have been visible what with the flush of the unaccustomed activity and the still-red marks of the basket. "I started to ask you if you were going back to New York on my bus," he said, and added, "before I was so rudely interrupted."

"I have to go to Atlanta, but not today. I mean to stay here in Ravenna for a while."

He understood what I had not put into words, although he could not have known why I should be concerned. "I hope the old boy's going to be all right." As soon as the line was out of his mouth it rang falsely against the memory of our Friday's conversation and he felt that he could only make me believe it by insisting. "I really mean it. I do hope he's going to be all right."

Before I could say *I know* or *I believe you,* he turned abruptly and went to the ticket window. I stood where I was. The ticket bought, he walked to the door marked TO BUSES and stopped this side of it to put his suitcase down. He turned, not smiling, and lifted his hand in farewell; then, shifting his weight, he picked up the bag again and passed through the door and out of my life. Three days before I could not have predicted the fullness in my throat.

I have no way of knowing how long it took for the brashness of Peer Gray to come back, like armor fresh from the dry cleaners, or if it came back at all. I do not care. I see him still, the golden boy in ashes, the heir apparent of Professor Edward Pick on his knees alongside the tear-stained girl, and I will trade him decades of wheeling and dealing for that single moment.

What I could not do—although God knows I was willing —was go on my knees alongside Professor Pick, to help him repack all that was spilled on Friday night when the two of us ran together.

The while of my stay in town became several weeks. I claimed for myself one of the rockers on the gallery of the Hotel Ravenna and there I sat, weather permitting, one with the loafers and the tellers of tales. I could not bring myself to leave for Atlanta without some assurance that Professor Pick had found his way back to the shelter of Avis, but neither could I think of approaching the man himself.

The hotel proved a good observation post. The shyer boys from the college, too cautious to make the decisive move with one of the coeds, came to visit the Hotel Ravenna's most famous inhabitant. Mae Glin was about my age, somewhere in her thirties, but she was as placid and comfortable an image of the earth-mother as you could find outside of an O'Neill play. A visit to Mae never sent a boy slinking back to campus, riddled with guilt; he went instead swaddled in ease and easement. It was a simple matter for me, in my rocker, to stop the young men as they came down from Mae's room, still full of warmth and well-being, and to ask them about Professor Pick; and for some reason they were as garrulous after a half hour upstairs as Mae was in her off-business hours.

I am giving the wrong impression. There was not a steady tramp, tramp, tramp of loafers and white bucks across the porch and up the stairs to Mae. Her collegiate customers came intermittently, so now-and-then, that if I were a worrier I would wonder how she managed to pay her rent and buy the occasional delicacies which she set out when she had some of us in for a purely social call.

Professor Pick—I discovered—returned to class at the end of the week. At first, he was particularly withdrawn (he had never been one of the academic jolly boys) and a perceptive student reported that his manner was the one that he displayed on those days when the dipped flag on the administration building announced that one of his contemporaries had died. But now he wore his mourning face for more than a week and the flag flew in nonmortal splendor at the top of its mast. (Professor Pick was crying at his own bier, but the kid could not have known that.)

Within two weeks, Professor Pick was apparently himself again and still I stayed in Ravenna. Once in the supermarket where I had gone to shop for late night lunches in my room, I caught sight of a thin, black figure bending into the soap powders. He saw me at the same moment and, snatching up some detergent or other, he tossed it into his basket and pushed off in the other direction, the click-click-click of the inevitable twisted wheel on his cart sounding his retreat. I stayed where I was until I was certain he had left the store. I was glad to have seen the old man, but I no more wanted to talk to him than he wanted to talk to me.

The encounter in the supermarket should have been the signal for my release. But Ravenna was an infectious town. Like an extra in a movie, I sat on the hotel veranda, nodding sagely, making conversation about the nothing that went on around me. I lingered, I told myself, because I felt comfortable, unhurried, wonderfully lazy. If the voice of the ornamental box called somewhere beyond the click of my rocker, I did not want to hear. At least, not for a breath or two.

It was Lester Kenner who finally got me out of my rocking chair. A drug salesman, a massive man, big-boned and muscular, barely under seven feet, he rode into the hotel one late April afternoon on the wave of his own voice. The regulars greeted him by name and he answered in kind, although, in the first shock of hearing him, I wondered how he had ever managed to shut his mouth long enough to find out who they were.

"I've got to see Mae," he boomed. They could have heard him in the mausoleum out east of town. "Is there anyone with Mae? I've got to see her right now." Boom, boom, boom, and he was through the screen door and passing, like a distant cannon, across the quiet lobby and up the stairs.

"There's Lester for you," said the man in the rocker next to mine.

"He's not shy about announcing his needs," I said, not having taken to Lester. "Does he make a fuss like that when he goes to the bathroom?"

Mae Glin, forgive me. We talk that way and sometimes —God help us—we act that way, but there is no plumbing fixture made in Toledo that is your equal in grace and warmth. Mae Glin, forgive me.

"It ain't what you think," said my neighbor. "Lord, you don't think Lester would carry on like that if he was going to see Mae in a business way, do you?" I shrugged that I had no way of knowing. "Him and Mae's from the same town and whenever Lester comes through he gives her all the news about her folks. Course she can't ever go back."

"Of course not," I said. I think I must have meant something else, like *why not,* but the correct words did come out and the speaker, accepting them, lapsed into silence and turned again to watch the inactivity in the street.

One by one, my fellow porch-sitters drifted away. When Lester, emptied of his home-town news, came out to find an eating companion, I was alone. I was elected.

Over dinner, I learned that Lester Kenner's heartiness was not a business affectation (if it was a defense—and why not?—he had long since forgotten when he put it on) and that it was flawed by a surprising primness. He roared no salesman's jokes at me; he spared me the confidential details of sex and drink. He even took exception to one of those casual remarks that drop from me like leaves from an autumn tree and with no more malice than that.

"I suppose I'm the first drug salesman you've ever met," he began by way of introduction.

"I do know a couple of pushers," I said, meaning nothing.

"I don't think that's funny." His mouth pursed reprovingly, an unusual operation on so large a head, and he withdrew behind the menu. I felt properly chastened.

"You're quite right. It isn't funny at all." The menu dropped and he came out smiling. I was forgiven. The stream of his words began to flow again and I floated along on them. He talked about the South. Not the South that we Northerners know today, the bad, bottom half of the argument over integration, but about battles and generals, churches and colleges, towns and cities, buildings and gardens, all that South which any of us could come to love if the Negro shacks and slums were not standing in the shadow of the crinoline.

I cannot quite remember how or when I managed to pass information on to Lester Kenner, but by the end of the meal he knew that I was bound for Atlanta and that I was bound by no schedule. He invited me to join him, for he, too, was headed for Atlanta to make one of his infrequent appearances at the regional headquarters of the company he represented.

"I have to be in Atlanta by the twenty-fifth," he said.

"Big sales meeting?" I asked.

"Gosh, no," said Lester, using his rawest swear word. "Confederate Memorial Day in Georgia. I always try to spend it in Atlanta."

It took us five days to cross the two Carolinas and cut deep enough into Georgia to reach Atlanta. We stopped frequently—sometimes, the drug boys would be happy to know, so that Lester might do a little business. More often we stopped because there was an antebellum mansion or a battle marker that I—as my guide put it—needed to see. Finally, on the eve of the great day, we entered Atlanta. Kenner dumped me at a hotel like my Ravenna sanctuary but puffed with pride, a big, comfortable, massive-veran-daed building out on Peachtree Street. My drug-peddling Virgil also checked in, but he had friends to see, things to do, and so he left me, promising to meet me in the lobby at noon the next day, to see that I got to Oakland Cemetery in time for the memorial services.

Left to my own devices, I rocked for a while on the ve-randa, watching the cars whip up and down Peachtree. My nearest companion, a gray ball of a businessman, in town for a convention, failed to produce the evening stories I was used to from Ravenna, whining instead and at length about the injustices of the graduated income tax. When I could stand it no longer, I leaped to my feet and with the phoniest Southern accent this side of musical comedy I registered my indignation, "Suh, Senatuh Cahtuh Glass of Vuhginia is the Fahthuh of the income tax. Ah will not heah mah native state insulted bah the lahks of you."

Startled, the complainer began to stutter an apology, but I would hear none of it. I was not a month-old Virginian for nothing. I stamped down the hotel steps and fumed up Peachtree Street. Once I was out of the tax-evader's sight, I slowed to a stroll and my imaginary anger (my real boredom) dissolved in the April evening, the softness of a Southern city spring. After only a few blocks, my walk caught on the edges of a neighborhood shopping center and I crossed the street and headed back the way I had come. Not yet ready for bed, not willing to face the tax structure again in so short a time, I went into a newer, more pretentious hotel and found my way to the bar, which turned out to be —God help us—a cocktail lounge.

It was called the Giraffe Room. Every chair, every banquette, every bar stool was covered with a fabric that was supposed to look and feel like the hide of a giraffe. Not having ever known a nylon giraffe, I was stunned by the shine of the upholstery, but no more staggered than I was by the herd of frisking animals that romped around the absolutely hand-painted mural. I paused just inside the door to make a silent apology to the graceful beast who was being parodied here and then I crossed to the bar where a young man was staring morosely at some ice cubes in an old-fashioned glass, the wreck of a something-on-the-rocks. Except for a hand-holding couple (at least his hand was in her lap) in a dim corner of the room and the hovering bar man, the ice-watcher and I were the only people in the lounge.

I took the stool next to him and prepared to intrude on his despair.

"My name is Carter Glass," I said, settling down. "I'm an income tax man." Fifteen years earlier I could not have got away with that introduction. The young man slowly turned his head and looked at me as though he wished I were dead or in Savannah. Then with a sigh he turned back to his melting ice. "Let me buy you a drink," I offered. "It's after April 15 and I'm feeling almost free."

"No, thank you," he said. Then, before I could insist, he began to talk rapidly, one sentence falling over another, the intelligibility lost now and then in the slur of the liquor and the accent. The gist was clear enough. "No thank you at all. If I say yes thank you, you will buy me a drink and then you will want me to talk and you will want me to talk about me because that's what happens in bars and I don't want to talk about me and about how this girl, this bitch really although she is the best-looking, the really best-looking girl in all of Macon, how she threw me over for the fairiest goddam banker you ever saw with money coming out of his goddam fairy ears and all because that lousy mother of hers wants her to live in this crazyass white house with columns and all where some stinking general or other stole the goddam silver or something back in eighteen sixty-whatever-the-hell because the old lady's been bit by some sillyass history bug."

"On the contrary," I said, "I wouldn't listen to your life story even if you wanted to tell it to me. I'd pick up my drink and go way over to the other side of the room."

He swung around to see where I would have gone had I had a drink and had he insisted on reciting his autobiography. His eyes fell on the busy couple. "Well, will you look at that," he said, his voice too loud. "Will you look at that guy trying to put the make on that perfectly innocent little girl." The girl pushed the man's hand off her lap. "That's a good girl." My neighbor nodded reassuringly, smiled like a drunken father. "That's a good little girl." Then his eyes clouded again. "I had a good little girl once and then this goddam banker . . . I'll fix him, I'll settle him once and for all." He slid from his stool and started toward the couple where, if I had not stopped him, he would probably and with justice have received a good poke in the mouth. I balanced him once again on the bar stool, while the couple (good luck, from a well-wisher) hurriedly left the Giraffe Room.

"You were going to buy me a drink, Carter Glass," said the young man. "Ah-ha, you didn't think I would remember your name. My name is Bragg," and he paused, lifting his hand, and then with alcoholic solemnity, "I am a rambling wreck from Georgia Tech."

"And a hell of an engineer," I added.

"Precisely."

When our drinks were in front of us, I lifted my glass, politely, loyally, a visitor from the North. "To the great day."

"To the great day," he echoed. We each drank deeply, appreciatively, reverently. He put his glass down and turned to me. "What great day?" he asked. "Is it your birthday or something?"

"You're joking," I said.

"I am?"

"You must be. You can't mean that you don't know that tomorrow's Confederate Memorial Day."

"Oh, no," he moaned. "Let's not have any more of that Old South crap. Nobody cares about Confederate Medorial May. Hey," he poked me with his elbow, "that's funny. Medorial May, Medorial May, Medorial May. Get it."

"I get it. So nobody cares?"

"Nobody but a few history professors and a bunch of Civil War bugs from up North"—he hesitated, thinking and then went on sadly, a whine in his voice—"and a bunch of goddam biddies like Gloria's sillyass mother. Did I tell you about Gloria, the really best-looking girl in all of Macon . . . ."

His voice went on, the needle having found its groove again, but without my ears to hear. I slipped away, leaving my empty glass and the patient bartender as company for the wrecked wreck, and walked on back to the hotel.

I had thought that I might spend the next morning locating Annette Despere, the third name on my list, but somehow the hours were used up by a late breakfast and some necessary contemplation from one of the rockers on the hotel gallery. Ravenna habits die hard. By the time I had prepared myself for action, noon was approaching and so was Lester.

In Atlanta, as you must know, there are two Confederate Memorial Day services. One of them is rather pushily social, attracting the monied pretenders and those who want to celebrate themselves as well as the honored dead. It was the other, the one at Oakland Cemetery, that Lester Kenner was going to take me to. "The crowd out at Oakland is the *real thing*," he told me.

When we got to the cemetery, I discovered that *crowd* was a word that Lester used a little loosely. After we had passed through the gate that cuts the handsome old brick wall surrounding the grounds, and had gone roundabout so that we might stop for a moment at the grave of General John B. Gordon, decked for the day with a souvenir Confederate flag, we came at last on a gaggle of folding chairs set up in front of the Lion of Atlanta. (Don't ask me why a copy of the Lion of Lucerne should have been set up to honor the Confederate dead.)

There were not many chairs, a hundred maybe, and most of them were empty. The filled ones held elderly, quiet men and chirping, busy old ladies. One of the chirpers, a gray-haired whisper of woman, sat on the edge of her chair, always on the ready, able to jump up in a wink and flit from one place to another, from one person to another, straightening, arranging, explaining, demanding. She wore no badge of authority for she did not need one; her voice, soft as a razor strop, was all the insignia that she could use.

"Do they call that a wreath?" she snapped at a grave gray man whose ribbon suggested that he must have something to do with arrangements. Like a naughty child, he backed away from her scolding. "Who was in charge of the flowers? I would just like to know who was in charge of the flowers."

"It's going to rain, I suppose," she complained to the harried man. He looked up, praying perhaps, but his prayer was not likely to be answered. I, too, looked up and the bustling little bird was right, it was going to rain. "Well," she went on, "I'm not surprised." The man looked as though he might cry.

"All that I hope," I heard her saying behind me. "All that I hope is that the band can play this year. Last year they were disgraceful." I turned and saw her laying into a pale man in rimless glasses, plainly a high school teacher, the director of the band that had come quietly in behind the rows of chairs. The director was looking worriedly at the clouding sky and trying to assure her, softly, that the band could play, but she had flown away before his words could comfort her and was leaning over a cameo of a lady who sat in the chair next to mine.

"Isn't the governor outrageous?" she said to my neighbor and did not stay for an answer. She caught the sleeve of a man as he went by—a bland young man obviously in politics. or advertising, probably both. "It's bad enough that the governor is not coming today." She shook her finger in his face. "But why is that senator he sent us late? Why isn't he here now?"

"He is," said the young man, and his hand touched her shoulder with such assurance that she was momentarily quieted. She let him lead her to a chair.

"Emma carries on too much," said the lady next to me in a voice as delicate as the look of her, but with strength in it, like a lace that lasts for centuries. Her skin was white and fine, without the marks of age in it; there was still a hint of red in her carefully arranged white hair. She wore a simple blue dress open at a still-lovely throat and around her neck a dark blue ribbon, the kind that I thought no one wore any longer outside of the movies. "You see," she went on softly, "Emma thinks that she is not really doing right by her family unless she makes all this fuss."

By this time the speaker—a nondescript state senator, pretending self-assurance in a white suit—was ready to speak. He stood looking at his audience, resenting that the group should be so small and still so imposing, before he broke into the customary remarks about the day and its meaning for all of us. With the instinctive ineptness of the second-stringer, and bad advice from some source or other, he quickly passed from the rustle of crinoline and the handsome youths on blooded horses riding out to save the honor of the South; he got involved in the tyranny of Washington and school integration and the unfairness of differential freight rates. The placid male listeners took it in stride, but the ladies began to squirm noisily in their chairs.

"The man's a fool," whispered my neighbor.

"The lady's right," said Lester, on my other side.

The fuss-making Emma was noisier in her disappointment. "Who cares about all that?" she asked loudly, her voice floating up to the speaker's stand. "What's he talking about railroads for?"

With Emma's voice assaulting his ears and the visual distress of the wiggling ladies almost bringing tears to his eyes, he went doggedly on with the speech as planned. A practiced politician who could have squashed a red-neck heckler at a North Georgia rally or sidestepped a direct question at a union meeting in Marietta, the senator panicked before an opposition that seemed to say that he existed only on their sufferance, and, having failed them, that he did not exist at all. He stumbled over his words as he had not stumbled since he was an illiterate twenty-one-year-old running for a place on the school board. He ignored or did not see the frantic gestures of the young man who had momentarily gentled the rampaging Emma; his hands, like those of a practiced charades player, were plainly saying *cut it off, stop now, you've lost them,* but the speaker could not or would not go to school to the young adviser and on he droned losing votes the way other men lose direction.

"In my day," said my quiet neighbor, "someone would have recited Father Ryan's 'The Conquered Banner' and that would have been better than this poor man."

At last, red-faced and exhausted, the senator puffed to a finish. Glumly he stepped down from his perch and headed off through the cemetery, not waiting for the services to come to an end, still not knowing how or why he had failed.

Tell me, Senator, on your wedding anniversary, do you bring your wife flowers and a jewel? Or do you go over the housekeeping books?

The first notes of music came with the first drops of rain. The rain continued; the music stopped. Frantically, like a mother hen under pressure, the director raced from student to student, seeing that the instruments were properly covered. Emma was on him in a second, screaming, "A shower. A shower. It's only a shower." Her voice crying, "Play, play," and his lamenting counterpoint, "These instruments are expensive," sounded against a background of scraping chairs and piping indignation, aimed at the heavens. Finally, Emma's shrill accusation, "You are a coward. Think of what these poor dead boys did for you."

Silence—stunned or reverential—dropped for a second. Into it came the director's tight-lipped words, "I don't care what these dead boys are supposed to have done for me. These are new instruments and I'm not going to ruin them for you or for all the dead in Oakland Cemetery."

The dead must wait on the living, or so I have heard, but this was Atlanta, not Galilee, and the ladies descended on the director like initiates on an intruder at a Bacchic festival. He retreated, "But—but—but—," waving his band to safety behind him, and confusion reigned among the gravestones. Rain rained there, too, for Emma's simple shower was thickening; soon it would be a real downpour.

Lester reached across me and said to the lady who still sat quietly beside me, "May we give you a lift somewhere?"

"You certainly may," she said and we quickly got up and out of the cemetery. By the time the drenching rain came, the three of us were bundled into the front seat of Lester's car, looking at Atlanta through the slashes that the windshield wipers made on the glass in front of us.

"I'm sorry, Firth," said Lester (I had reverted to my real name on leaving Ravenna). "I'm afraid this isn't Confederate Memorial Day at its most typical."

"In a way it is," said the lady. She smiled up at me, "Are you interested in Southern history?"

"I'm interested in almost everything," I said. "Lester, here, has been introducing me to the South."

"As long as you're not an enthusiast, you're all right," she said. "Come out to Grant Park with me tomorrow and see the Cyclorama. That will cure you of incipient nostalgia."

So it was agreed. I was to accompany our new friend on an expedition to Grant Park the next day. Only then did the lady mention her name. It was, as you have been expecting ever since she first spoke to me in the cemetery, Annette Despere.

We dropped Miss Despere—it was Miss Despere—at her home and then went on to the hotel where Lester and I fondly said good-by. "You're all right, Firth," he said. "At least, you don't mock all this." The wave of his hand told me that *all this* meant not the hotel lobby that it seemed to encompass, but Lee at Appomattox, Stonewall Jackson dying in the shadow of those Hemingway trees, and Emma hopping along the graveled walks of Oakland Cemetery as though she were stopping Sherman outside of Atlanta.

"Don't I?" I asked myself. Out loud, I said, "Thank you, Kenner, you've been an education." We shook hands and he walked off across the lobby. I looked after his receding back and wanted to say—but that would have been mockery—"There goes the sweetest boyscout I've ever known."

Annette Despere was waiting on the porch when I got to her house. I wanted to play it big—a day on the town sort of thing—and take us out to Grant Park in a taxi. She insisted on a bus.

"I'm not yet eighty," she said. "I don't need to be pampered."

She told me something of herself as we rode along. She was the last of the Desperes, an only daughter, born late in

life to a veteran of the War between the States. Her family
was an old one in the South, Huguenots who had gone to
England after the revocation of the Edict of Nantes and
then, early in the eighteenth century, moved on to America. "I'm not like Emma," she explained. "The Civil War—
you see, I'm not even afraid of your Northern phrase—is
really the only war she's got. It's such a small incident in a
family with a history like mine. I go to the memorial services, of course, but that's for Papa."

She took my arm as we went up the steps of the Cyclorama Building. "We make a handsome couple," she said
airily.

"It's years since I have had so pretty a girl on my arm,"
I said and she knew that I meant it.

"I'm glad your friend, Mr. Kenner, is not along."

"Three's a crowd?" I asked.

"It's not that," she said. "It's just that he's serious about
all this. The Cyclorama, you know, is only what a bunch
of Germans in Milwaukee thought the Battle of Atlanta
must have looked like. I always want to laugh and, if there
were someone being solemn beside me, I'm afraid I would.
You will promise not to be solemn?"

"I promise."

Inside, the officiating automaton—a lady in a flowered
print dress—unrolled her mechanical spiel as she inched
her way around the painted circle, mixing history with improbable anecdote and both with incipient art criticism.
"Notice," she said, "that the wax figures grow smaller as
they get closer to the painting. The workmanship is so
fine that it is impossible to tell where the three-dimensional
figures stop and the painted ones begin."

"A friend of mine really cannot tell the difference between the wax figures and the others," said Miss Despere,
"but poor Adele is almost blind."

"She should set up as an art critic." We giggled like children strutting before grown-up strangers; our jokes were just that good.

The guide, reaching the end of her circuit and her recitation, hushed impressively to remind us just how lucky we were to be able to see the *Battle of Atlanta.* Similar cycloramas of Gettysburg and Missionary Ridge had accidentally been lost.

"I've never believed those were accidents," said Miss Despere.

We laughed our way out of the room, leaving a stricken Atlanta behind us, and paused to consider whether or not we should visit the rest of the museum. We decided instead for tea at Miss Despere's.

When the taxi—this time I had my way—stopped in front of Miss Despere's house, a four-story Victorian mansion, dormers and cupolas and all, I said, as I helped her step down, "This is impressive."

"Papa wanted to avoid the Greek. Cleaner looking buildings, he always said, but too many people put them up out of piety. Nostalgia for the days before the war. When he sold the plantation and got involved with investments and things, he said he wanted a house that looked like the places successful businessmen built up North. He was probably joking, but I *do* like the house. It was a joy to grow up here. A house like this has more secret places than an ordinary child can use up in a lifetime of hide-and-seek."

If I had been your gingerbread boy in the Gingerbread Age, Annette Despere, we would have hidden, hand-in-hand, and escaped growing up and out and old. Split-level and Swedish modern and no accidental wombs to crawl into.

□

"But how do you manage to keep such a large place?" I asked.

"You don't imagine that it's still mine, do you? I lost it years ago—along with almost everything else." I must have looked sheepish, sorry that I had asked the wrong question, for she took my hand and pulled me toward the steps. "Come along, silly, I'm past minding. Very much anyway. And I do have two rooms that are all my own."

Up the steps we went, and past the wicker chairs and potted plants of Southern rooming houses. Miss Despere's two rooms lay on the first floor, in the rear, looking out on an unkept garden. The rooms were packed with fine furniture, large mirrors, heavy silver, handsome paintings. There was no effect of jumble, no suggestion of the junk shop; it was as though the whole house had contracted, pulled itself in and forced its way into these two rooms. "It's crowded, I know," she said, threading her way through her belongings, "but I like to keep my things around me. Besides, the longer I hold on to these treasures, the more I can sell them for—if and when I have to sell them. Or do I just mean *when* I have to sell them."

"Now you sit down," she said, forcing me into a comfortable chair, "and have a look at the Despere history." The chair she had given me was up against a small bookcase full of volumes in which the Desperes figured, often in a large way, in the history of France, England, America. "If you want a capsule history," she said, "try that red leather scrapbook. That's my work."

While she busied herself about making tea, I leafed through her reconstruction of the family chronicles, each page devoted to a single Despere, his time, his position, his importance, his face if a likeness was available. I had not yet got out of France when she began to set the tea things on a small table that stood between my chair and the one that she would take. Then she lifted the scrapbook out of my hands and put it to one side.

"Tea, now," she said. She lifted the cozy and there was an exquisite teapot, its spout a diving bird, its bulk a bit of the sky torn away. I have been conditioned by contemporary ceramics to hate everything cunning and cute, from Dresden figures to Woolworth gewgaws, but I gasped in surprise and pleasure. "It is lovely," she said. "My family brought it from England a few centuries ago."

We talked at first about the teapot and then, laughingly, about the Cyclorama. Finally we came to the Desperes. "Your scrapbook is fascinating," I said. "What an exciting way to fill your time."

"It doesn't fill my time; it *is* my time. It isn't a hobby, Mr. Firth; it's my life."

The ornamental box leaped to the tip of my tongue, but I could not spit it at the gentle lady who sat across from me. Professor Pick was at my back, an admonishing hand on my shoulder.

"I have no children, no profession, no art," she said. "I have only my family. These rooms and I are metaphors, if I may be fanciful for a moment. Just as this whole house has shrunk into two rooms, my family has faded into this one old woman who hands you tea. A second cup?" I nodded yes. She passed me the tea and then she handed me again the scrapbook. "Look at the last page."

The last page was Annette Despere's own page. A birth date (June 26, 1881) was recorded and there was room for a date of death. A drawing of a sweet-faced girl of seventeen or so was fastened alongside a photograph of a sweet-faced lady of seventy or so. On some of the other pages, the list of identifying activities ran to a paragraph or more.

Here there was a single phrase: *the last of the Desperes.*
She leaned across and tapped the words: "It has not been
easy to play that part, but I have done my best. I could not
bring our line to a glorious end. I have at least tried to
keep it from whining its way to dust."

"You are more than enough for them," I said, and then
I could not stop the words that followed, "but how could
they have been enough for you?"

"I said that they were my life; I did not say that they
were enough."

"Is there more?"

"There is always the possibility of more. Even now."
Am I transparent, or did Annette Despere see with special
eyes? "I do not know how you know or how I know you
know," she said, "but you do know something about the
ornamental box. Can you tell me what's inside?"

"I hoped you could tell me," I said.

She shook her head. "All that I know is that it's there;
I do not know what it is."

"And if you get it?" I asked.

Her hand touched the scrapbook that lay in my lap and
then fluttered in the direction of the Despere history massed
beside me. She smiled, almost wickedly, and whispered,
"I'll burn my books."

CHAPTER SIX

I SING THE BODY

AFTER her Faustian whisper, Annette Despere held her mischievous smile, a little girl who *has* done the dishes, *has* swept the floor, *has* run the last errand, and yet disquiets her demanding mother by suggesting that she is more than the washing, the sweeping, the running. I put my cup on the table and, standing up, I leaned down and kissed her lightly on the cheek. "Thank you," I said. "Thank you for giving me tea."

I am not a fool although foolish enough I may be in my way. Miss Despere taught me what I might have learned from Rodney Salvay or Professor Pick if the tears of the one and the anger of the other had not stepped between me and common sense. The people whose names appeared on my list (when had it ceased to be poor Solly Derritch's?) were as ignorant as I was about the contents of the ornamental box that I had lost to the fat man in the Hotel Chevron.

Why then should I have caught a bus for Los Angeles? Why should I have headed for the fourth name on the list, suspecting, as I did, that I would learn nothing? There was always an outside chance that information—the box itself even—lay somewhere along the line of names. That at least is what I let my reason tell me. Knowledge deeper than reason knew better and kept its mouth shut.

It doesn't fill my time; it is my time.

◻ I took Annette Despere's blessing, which I could certainly use, and my one suitcase and set out on what was
to be a longer bus ride than I absolutely needed. The details of the trip have long since faded from my mind; the
scenery has climbed back onto the post cards; the rest stops
and the rest-stop meals have all run together in a kaleido-
scope of warm iced tea, hurried rushes for the men's room,
and cole slaw on the side. I can remember the trip only as
a changing figure in the seat next to mine, a fellow passenger who, whatever his (her) sex or age, was always as
much the same as he (she) was different and who seemed
always to be concerned with the same thing.

The first leg of the journey I spent alone. At Birming-
ham, I was joined by a young lady, neatly, even primly
dressed, who ignored me so pointedly that I felt a sudden
gratitude toward her. Her every gesture reminded me that
I was a male and somehow formidable. Whenever she took
a Kleenex from her purse (God knows what she did with
them; I never saw her wipe her nose) or turned a page of
her *Silver Screen* or straightened her dress, she held her
hands oddly, awkwardly. At first, I wondered if she might be
suffering some kind of mild paralysis, but every joint and
muscle seemed to work. Finally—trust me to take time to
discover the obvious—I realized that the physical gauche-
ness was not physical at all. The girl had a crying need to
make me see her wedding ring and every casual movement
became complicated because she had always to have the
left hand above the right one and, although I did not immediately see why, the left hand had always to be palm
down.

"That's a very unusual wedding ring," I said truthfully.
It was very thin with a ridge all around the center of the

band. My words, I hoped, would gentle her fears, but as soon as they were out of my mouth I realized that they might be insufficiently complimentary. I added, untruthfully, "Very attractive."

She had been sitting like a little girl at an adult party, very straight, unrelaxed, her legs primly together, her feet on the floor in front of her seat. At my words, her body stiffened, an instinctive warding off of evil, and her legs pulled convulsively together. She giggled nervously. She looked at me, a lying smile fighting and losing a battle with the panic in her eyes. She forced a "thank you" through an unwilling mouth.

She tried to get back to her movie magazine, but my words had broken the spell; the cloak of invisibility that she had thrown over me faded. I was present and palpable. Her eyes kept wandering from the conversion (seduction? analysis? divorce?) of the movie star on the page in front of her. Out of the corner of her eye, she watched my innocent hands lying, folded, unmoving, on my own lap. To test, I unfolded them and the expected shiver did run the length of her body. There was (and is) enough of the son-of-a-bitch in me to make me want to send my left hand tiptoeing on the index and second finger—a game I play with children of two—across my left leg and on and along her right. There was (and is) enough of the anti-son-of-a-bitch in me to make me keep my hands where they were. It was hard not to find out whether she would scream or whether she would submit, horrified and fascinated, to an exploratory hand. But I did not find out. I heard myself saying, as though she were some charge of mine . . .

Somewhere—in the New Testament or the eyes of John Donne—I suppose she is my responsibility. A scout *is* loyal . . . and a brother to every other scout.

☐
"If it's any comfort to you, I'm quite harmless. You have nothing to fear from me."

"But I never . . . I mean . . . what I mean. . . ." Her incoherent apology stumbled out of her mouth, pushed willy-nilly into the world by her embarrassment and her relief. She flushed deeply as the words tripped clumsily over her trembling lips and her eyes filled with incipient tears.

"For goodness sake," I said, trimming my exclamations, "don't apologize. You have nothing to apologize for. You're obviously a nice girl . . .

Try saying that with a straight face in this year of our Lord.

. . . and I'm obviously a strange man. Why shouldn't you be nervous?"

"But, I *am* sorry." These words came so emphatically, so loud that half of our fellow passengers looked up to see who could be so sorry for what. "Oh," she squeaked, again embarrassed, but this time the embarrassment was shared (or supposed to be: I had a hard time working it up). Her nervous giggle became conspiratorial and she whispered, "I mean I am sorry," the last words barely audible.

The incident relaxed her, relaxed her in fact into a steady stream of chatter. I got her life history—fortunately short—and her opinions on life, love, and travel—conventionally diffuse. When we began to approach Jackson, she said suddenly, "Shall I tell you my secret?"

"If it's not too secret a secret."

"I'm not married at all," she said.

Well I'll be damned, said something inside me. Conditioning (from novels, movies, and the girl up the block) told me that a young lady only wears an unearned (that incredible adjective) wedding ring on one occasion. How, I wondered, could a girl so obviously afraid have got herself pregnant. I would have gone on to invent a rape, one involving a near relative, I suspect, if her words had not dragged me back to the case at hand.

"You see," she said. She was holding her left hand palm up and there was a glittering stone hooked to the back of the ring. She turned it around on her finger and then held her hand out proudly, as though she were displaying a diamond. "It's not a wedding ring at all. It's my regular ring. Isn't it pretty? It's what they call a zircon. Only it's not a real one."

"Yes, it's pretty." I was willing to like it, but the *why* of the reversed ring still nibbled at the undelighted edges of my mind.

"I always turn my ring around when I ride on a bus," she went on. "Then the men think you are married and leave you alone. Isn't that a wonderful idea?"

"That's a fine idea," I agreed.

By this time we were in the station and she was up and gone, waving a happy good-by. I could have told her that men who molest girls in buses are not respecters of wedding rings, real or make-believe, but why should I knock down her one defense. Let the busy-minded boyos do the dirty work, or, better still, let her grow old and respected and a gray-haired grandmother without ever finding out that a band of gold (or brass) is not a dead certain amulet.

I know, I know. The amateur psychologists and the experienced seducers who read this scene will insist that she really wanted my hand on her leg and the former will call me fool for misreading her and the latter will call me coward for not being the son-of-a-bitch that all of us are. There is enough of the eighteenth century in me, however, to make me, occasionally at least, prefer a feeling to a feel. I am proud she told me the secret of the reversed ring. You boys take your bus trips and I'll take mine.

She was replaced by a round, cheerful man who settled into the seat with much twisting and turning, like a bird trying to get comfortable on a nest. Even before he had come to rest, he tossed me his name ("Call me Harry"), his business ("I'm a traveling salesman, like in the jokes"), his line ("Sampson's Sock. Put your foot in it."). He immediately launched into an apparently endless joke involving a traveling salesman (like in Harry) who asked a farmer for a bed and had to share it with the farmer, his wife, his two nubile daughters, an effeminate hand, and a cocker spaniel. At some stage in the economic history of this country, drummers probably did beg shelter from farmers, but the ubiquitous motel must have long since put that practice to sleep. It seems to have had no lethal effect on jokes about salesmen and farmers' daughters. This one was rich in anatomical detail building emission by emission toward some improbable punch line about the hair of the dog that bit you. Harry finished it in a wild, high snicker of pleasure which bubbled on despite the fact that I sat silent. Wheezing, he returned to comparative calm.

"What's the matter?" he asked. "You don't like jokes? You a preacher or something?"

"I raise cocker spaniels," I said.

"I'm sorry," he said, and with genuine regret. "I didn't mean no insult. I can see where a fellow in the spaniel line wouldn't find the story very funny."

If I had told him I was a farmer or that I raised nubile daughters or effeminate boys to hire out as farm hands, he would not have been sorry, all of which proves I suppose that the way to a man's conscience is through the dog-house.

"I had a cocker spaniel once," he said and he was off on a story about when he was a boy down in Pascagoula and had *this* dog. The reminiscence was full of cunning touches, like the way the dog's ears dragged on the sidewalk and got all dirty, as though his were the only cocker that ever had dirty ears. Of course, the damned dog died, as dogs always do in stories, poisoned naturally by the meanest man in Pascagoula. Tears came into the salesman's eyes and there I sat, feeling silly, commiserating with him for a thirty-year-old canine tragedy and wishing that he had stuck to dirty jokes. It is easier not to laugh than it is not to cry.

Once we got the dog buried, under a headstone with his name, Sport, chipped on it by the boy Harry, we got safely back to sex. I was treated to a detailed chapter of auto-biography involving two lubricous widows, one in India-nola, the other in Mize, both of whom shared bed and breakfast with the old Harry whenever his business took him to their towns. He gave both ladies the appearance of undivided attention, vague talk of marriage, and pictures to set up on their dressing tables. The trouble began when Mary Lou in Indianola asked him for a snapshot to send her sister and when, graciously, he complied.

"A week later I was in Mize," he said, "and I hiked right over to Molly Lou's to get a load off my mind." A titter, a leer, an elbow in my ribs. "I busted straight in the way I always do, hollering, Molly Lou, your hairy Harry's here, and who do you think was sitting right there in the parlor with Molly Lou? Mary Lou from Indianola, that's who. You wouldn't believe it but those two widow women were blood sisters."

He was right. I did not believe it.

Harry left at Shreveport. His seat was taken by a girl who reminded me of Peer Gray's unknown friend in the Ravenna bus station, at least at first glance. A thin little girl of sixteen who had splashed on make-up to prove that she was older, wiser, worldlier. Perhaps she was.

It was night when we hit Shreveport, so it was not surprising that, having stowed her canvas case in the rack overhead, she curled up on the seat, babylike, as if to go to sleep. She rolled restlessly as though she hoped really to find that magic position—the one implied in the ads—that will turn a bus seat into a feather bed. In her tossings, her arm, her shoulder, her leg brushed against me, staying long enough for me to register their presence, and then pushed on, apparently in search of greater comfort. The accidental intimacies of any bus ride were, in this case, not accidental. She seemed finally to have fallen to sleep. She lay doubled up on the seat, facing me, her back to the aisle, her body as close to mine as the seats and her position would allow. Her head nodded toward me and then fell forward onto my shoulder; her face, almost invisible in the dark bus, must have had the look of a calculating angel, but all that I remember is a patch of pale white at my shoulder.

I was caught between father and lover, not certain whether I was to play the protector or the marauder, when her hand moved suddenly, from its place on her leg—oh the aimlessness of a gesture in sleep (all things are forgiven and forgotten in sleep)—and landed on my leg. I was turned slightly toward her, perhaps from the pressure of her head on my shoulder. She inched closer to me and her hand, having caressed my leg, began to move up toward the crotch. Her probing nails hit against my zipper, and she quickly removed her hand, as a person will whose nails have scratched along a blackboard. The hand was back quickly, this time up near the belt, trying to find the tab of the zipper. In her unsuccessful attempt to get the fly open, her fingers pushed and poked, no longer casual, although she tried to hold her imitation of sleep as she worked seriously, intently at opening my pants.

I could have unzipped—perhaps I should have—and given her what she wanted, although I have no way of knowing what that was. Perhaps like a nervous child she simply wanted something to hold while she slept. Perhaps, once I was open to the world, her head would have dipped again, this time from my shoulder to my lap. What do I know of sixteen-year-olds?

I wanted to expose myself to her searching hand. I am, after all, human and—call it a reflex—I could not remain indifferent to the fact of her fingers. Perhaps, like a nervous child, I simply wanted someone to hold me while I slept. And there was one more thing. Her struggle with my zipper reminded me of an eighteen-year-old soldier I once knew well, who tried on a certain April evening to retain the mask of sophisticated worldliness while he struggled vainly with the unfamiliar catches of a brassière and who, failing and frustrated, burst into a little boy's tears.

You do not have to go into rose gardens to meet yourself coming around corners. And in the damnedest shapes.

Perhaps I secretly suspect that the man should be the aggressor. Perhaps I have a lingering respect for laws that set age limits. For whatever reason, the Puritan in me overcame the sybarite and I lifted the child's hand away from the toy it wanted and turned my body away from her.

Her head dropped from my shoulder and jolted her into an imitation of just having awakened. She muttered something and moved to the far side of her seat. There is always something sad in the removal of warmth, bodily or not, but I felt a comfort in the coolness of my exposed side, naked of its drape of child, and I stared fondly into the Texas night making fantasies in which there is never any need for surreptitious reaching.

At the first rest stop, she struck up an acquaintance with a young man, not many years her senior, and when the bus moved on she took the empty seat next to him where, God and the young man willing, her hand closed finally on what it sought. All that I know is that when I passed their seat to step down for the second rest stop, they were both sleeping, lying every which way, an arm here, a leg there, their mouths open in adenoidal defenselessness. At no point, not even at hand or finger, did their bodies touch.

At Dallas, a plump, pasty man, the pretty youth almost obliterated in the man of forty, took the seat so lately vacated by my unlikely love. He was one of the first people on the bus and of all the seats he might have chosen, including double empties which he might conceivably have had to himself, he picked the one next to me which, as things go in this world, is a compliment of sorts. In the busyness of getting settled, he missed a chance to examine some of the passengers who entered after him, but he got himself fixed comfortably in time to watch the last few stragglers aboard.

"I wouldn't mind having her shoes under my bed," were his first words.

Please God, I thought to myself, I have had this bit with

the garrulous Harry (what luck in Shreveport, Harry, boy?), but I was wrong.

The object of his footwear bromide was a harried mother in her midtwenties, attractive enough in an exhausted way, struggling with a shopping bag and a child of four, trying to make her way down the aisle where bag or child caught on the edge of seat after seat. I know enough of the world to know that a tired mother of a four-year-old can be an object of desire, and with cause, but I also know enough of conventional usage to know that the cliché about shoes beneath the bed is reserved for fairly obvious cases, all bottom and bounce. Harry, for instance, would not have made that mistake. "One man's meat is another man's poison," I said, and was surprised to find that my neighbor took an accidental metaphor for a planned joke.

He expressed his appreciation, which I did not need, for the gag, which I had not intended, and then lapsed into silence until the bus had coughed itself alive and begun to purr its way toward the West. As though he had been think-ing over the implications of my sentence, he said, "Your tastes don't lie that way?"

Fatuous exchanges drop away from me without leaving a mark. I had to grope back to the few words we had said to one another. "What way? What tastes?"

"Women," he said, confidingly, as though we were about to hatch a plot between us. "You don't care for women"—he hesitated and then finished the sentence—"like that." He gestured over his shoulder where the mother was struggling to keep the little boy in his seat.

"It's a rare woman who looks seductive carrying a shop-ping bag. A rarer one still who manages to be sexy while dragging a small boy along the aisle of a bus. I don't think that woman makes it, if that's what you mean."

It was not what he meant, of course. He could not say directly what was on his mind, although a simple proposition, concrete and refusable, would have been preferable to the strangely coy feelers which he sent, gropingly, in my direction. Words having failed him, he turned to visual aids. From an inside pocket he pulled a stack of pictures. His introduction: "Are you interested in physical culture?"

No is my answer to that question, even if the speaker means it literally. But before I could use my monosyllable, he had thrust the pictures into my hand. On top was a female nude, attractive in a sunshine-and-health way, sop to the shy man who approaches the male nude self-consciously, protection perhaps for the owner of the pictures who could always use the girl to prove that physical culture was his real concern. She was followed, as naked girls should be, by naked men, but the healthy idyll that my words call up is misleading. The male nudes were conventional shots of simpering muscle-men, like those that stare at you from the covers of Greek-and-health pornography booklets at Times Square newsstands, but with the mailable G strings sponged away.

"Attractive?" he asked, his eyes on my lap.

"Healthy people always embarrass me," I said. "They always look as though they work at it too hard." I handed the pictures back to him.

"Just a minute," he said, feeling again into his treasure pocket. "There's one more. It's the best of the lot."

It was certainly the most remarkable of the lot, fascinating enough in a technical way. It was a kind of montage, a triple exposure, so to speak, in which the model was shown in a naturally relaxed position, in semierection and completely erected in such a way that the still photograph suggested animation.

"Impressive?" my neighbor asked.

"Yes," I said. "It reminds me of *Farrebique.*"

"What's that?" he asked, half afraid that he had missed some kind of sport.

"A French movie. Quite a good one."

"It must have been good if this picture reminds you of it. I don't get much chance to see that kind of movie. What was it about?"

"Flowers. Flowers breaking into bloom."

My analogy escaped him. Glumly he took his prize back and put it away in his pocket. I do not know what the next gambit would have been, whether, the pictures failing, he ordinarily returned to words or passed on to direct action. I was preparing myself to say, simply, I hoped, but firmly, "Relax, sir, it's a long journey," when movement toward the front of the bus spared me the necessity. One of the passengers whom I had seen board while my neighbor was busy with his own comfort got up from his seat and stood in the aisle to take something from a small bag he had put in the overhead rack. He was a young man, probably under twenty, and so softly handsome that he was almost beautiful. Delicate features, dark complexion, a rich curl of hair —he had all the props that so often give a misleading look of innocence to young Americans with Latin blood in them (Mexican probably in this case). His errand finished, the young man sat down.

At this point my neighbor became very concerned with his seat, one that had held so many people comfortably for so many long and garrulous miles. He began to poke at it, to shift nervously. "There's something wrong with this seat," he said. He even went to the trouble to stoop down and look under it. "I can't see anything, but there is definitely something wrong here."

I began to hum a spiritual: *It's me, it's me, oh Lord.*

He went on with his performance. Finally, as if in desperation, "I just can't sit here. You won't mind my finding some place more comfortable?"

By the wildest chance, the seat next to the angelic teen-ager was both empty and in good repair.

At the next rest stop, the young man waited until the first wave of passengers had swept in and out of the men's room and then, walking stiffly, his hands in his pockets with affected casualness, he headed in that direction. He was followed, at a discreet distance, by the man with the private picture gallery.

At Phoenix, the long-vacant seat next to mine was taken by a woman about my own age, perhaps a little older, but certainly not beyond forty. She was so carefully dressed, in dark clothes, so indrawn and apparently unaware of me that I was startled when she suddenly said, "I just buried my husband."

Her words came so bluntly, so much as a surprise that I half expected to hear the next line of an old joke: "I had to, you know, he was dead."

He was dead and it was not a joke. She had just come from the funeral in Phoenix and was on her way back to Los Angeles where they had lived. She talked in detail about her life with the dead man. Her voice flowed evenly for ten or twenty minutes. Then a long silence and a new beginning. I might have been a statue in a church or a photograph on a dressing table. I was not expected to answer and I did not try to say anything, not even an *I see* or an *of course.* By the time the bus got to Los Angeles, I knew the pleasures they shared and the differences they harbored, I knew the pattern of their quarrels from the violence of thrown dishes to the soft reconciliation on bed or couch, I knew the curves and blemishes of his body and of hers and the joining of the two.

She was the first passenger on her feet when we reached the station, but before she hurried to the front of the bus, she held out her hand to me. I took it. "Thank you," she said. "The funeral was in his town and his family kept making me think he was only a dead son. I had to remember that he was a man and my husband." She dropped my hand, but just before she turned away she lifted her heavy purse, her only baggage. "If you had misunderstood," she said, brandishing the pocketbook, "if you had made a pass at me, I would have crowned you."

She stepped down from the bus and disappeared in the crowd. A few minutes later, I too disappeared in the crowd, at least I let myself be swallowed up by Los Angeles, found a place to lay my head and unpack my suitcase, tried to cure myself (this did not work, of course) of kinship with all those whose company I had shared on the trip West and all those who were on other buses, trains, planes, going in other directions.

Call me a tourist. I spent the next few days walking the streets of Los Angeles, wondering if anyone comes really to know that spreading amoeba of a city. Call me a coward. I walked because I could not quite bring myself to approach a person called Candy Stick, the fourth name on my list. I had bused all the way across the country just to speak to Miss (Mrs.? Mr.?) Stick and when I finally got there the conjunction of that name with the city that has Hollywood like a cancer at its heart was too much for me to take—at least without a little conditioning. Finally, an afternoon in Olivera Street convinced me that nothing could be phonier than that quaint bit of old Mexico restored (there is Williamsburg, of course), so I hunted out Candy Stick's address.

I found the anonymity of new glamour. An apartment house, all glass and brick, soaring up out of its tailor-made landscape, wearing its balconies proudly as though they were battle ribbons. A semicircular driveway slashed in from the street so that taxis might dump tired shoppers directly in front of the uniformed doorman.

I was unfortunately on foot. I had taken a city bus to the general area on the assumption that a walk around the neighborhood might give me a feel for Candy Stick. I knew now that I had made a tactical error. It was not my short-sleeved shirt that was against me, for any man might go short-sleeved under the early May sun of Los Angeles; it was simply that doormen cannot be attacked except from a moving vehicle. I retreated. I walked two blocks before I found a taxi unloading a fare.

Slash, up the driveway. The doorman opened the taxi door, watched solicitously as I lavishly overtipped (for a two-block ride, could that hurt?) and received the thanks that I had coming to me. Disentangled from the taxi, I hesitated—just a whisper of distress—before approaching the door that the uniformed guardian had already pulled open. I looked at my watch, frowned slightly. "Damn," I said. "I'm a few minutes early. Has Miss Stick come back yet?"

A stab in the dark, and a connection. "Not yet," he said. Then it *was* Miss Stick and she was out. "Angela's there, I know. I saw her come in. You know the apartment number?" Was he trying to trap me into some kind of admission? I nodded confidently. "That's right," he said, "11A."

The lobby was all clean lines and open spaces. As I moved, exposed, through its impersonality to the elevators and rose toward heaven in splendid automatic loneness, I called down blessings on the garrulous head of the doorman. Was Angela, I wondered, a child, a maid, or an overtrained poodle?

Angela was a maid. She was also an adept at keeping strangers away from Candy Stick's door. A Negro woman, dark, regal, assured, she would have dazzled me completely if she had not been in maid's uniform. In an evening gown, she could have turned back the United States Senate (and may have done so for all I know), but I avoided her Medusa eyes, looked for strength at the silly white frill of her apron and asked for Miss Stick.

"Did you call?" she said.

"No. I came directly."

"Miss Stick receives no one without an appointment. And she never makes afternoon appointments."

"Now that I'm here, suppose I make an appointment."

"I don't intend to be rude, but are you quite sure that you can afford an appointment with Miss Stick?"

"Is anyone sure of anything, Angela?"

A flicker—of surprise? of disapproval? of pleasure?—touched her stone eyes when I mentioned her name, but it did not get through to her voice. She went on, as implacably as before. "You can't make an appointment except by phone, and you can't make an appointment at all until a suitable reference has called on your behalf. Now, if you'll excuse me." She shut the door.

I wanted to lean angrily on the bell. I have done a little house-to-house selling in my day and there is no shutting-out so abrupt, so fatal to one's sense of being human and alive as a final "We don't want any," and the banging of a door. Angela's method may have been more genteel, but the results were the same.

If civilization is not ringing doorbells just because you want to (trick or treat), then I am civilized. Lacking an open-sesame, I left the mouth of Candy Stick's cave and, driven by a kind of logic, went out to Zoo Park to see the animals. None of the guards there, I guessed, would be as impressively imperious as Angela, but neither would they slam a cage door in my face.

A weekday afternoon and the schools still in session: the zoo was almost a private pleasure. Some regulars (I had never been here before, but zoo regulars are the loving same in every city) stood before the cages of their favorites, talking in quiet intimacy or babbling affectionately. I watched a restless lioness pad up and down her cage and felt a little as though I were trying to see Niagara by shaking a bottle of water from the falls.

"I know just how she feels." The speaker was one of those clichés of American girlhood—lightly tanned, brown hair and eyes, delicate but apparent figure, full skirt, flat heels, lightness of stance—the kind that looks out of advertisements for cotton blouses, down from movie screens, over her shoulder as she disappears up the street on the arm of a man as tanned, as brown, as cotton-clad as she.

At first glance I saw only the vitality and youth that the image represents, which is why I said, "I don't really believe that you do know how she feels."

"I've felt that way often enough myself." I looked again. She was not eighteen; she was in her mid-twenties. She had traded the abstract look of innocence, at best a device in these cases, for the face of an individual. Her step—she took two in my direction as she spoke—was not only light, it was wary. "On second thought, please go on believing that I do not know how the lady in the cage feels."

I stood, looking through the bars at her, but there was no reason why either of us should admit that they were there. "Any girl who can identify with a lioness deserves an ice cream on a stick. May I buy you one?"

"Any man who can make so pretty a speech deserves a lioness on a stick. You may buy me one."

Life was a fairly simple matter in the days when the white-coated boys with the white carts had only one flavor to offer. We had to consider variety, but we solved the problem, sensible couple that we were, by settling for the antiquated vanilla with chocolate coating. "This gives us away as old-timers," I said, the last word rising expectantly, my voice ready to settle on a name which, it occurred to me, I did not know. "What do I call you?" I asked.

"Call me Sylvia," she said, and only after her "And what do I call you?" did I realize that we had not asked for identities, only for labels.

"Call me Will."

Will and Sylvia spent the afternoon together at the zoo. When the time came for them to say good-by, I helped him by asking her to dinner. She refused. She also refused to let Will, gentleman that he was, see her to her door. "Good-by, then," I said, holding out my hand.

"You're not very persistent."

"You can't mean that I should coax you."

"I should hope not. But you could say, 'What are you doing tomorrow afternoon, Sylvia?' "

"What are you doing tomorrow afternoon, Sylvia?"

"I have to go to the public library, the main one I mean. If you were to be there around two, we might find something to do."

□   □

I was there, and we did find something to do. We walked for perhaps thirty minutes, but Sylvia seemed not so with me as she had been at the zoo. She could not be amused or touched by Pershing Square; her eyes could not be drawn to a person, a building, a patch of sun on the sidewalk. I guessed why she was ill at ease, but I was almost afraid to act on my guess for fear I was wrong and she would dissolve, in insult and injury, right before my eyes. Finally I said, "Do you want to go home, Sylvia? Do you want me to take you home?"

Her *no* came quickly, but there was no outrage in it. We walked on. Within the block, she said, "Where do you live, Will?"

"In a hotel," I said, "and not a very nice one. But it does have a two-burner hot plate."

"Then you can give me tea."

I gave her tea, but not immediately. Once the door had closed behind us, we kissed. We were excited, but not with that jagged, inept excitement that kills the passion that feeds it. Like explorers, still faint with the shock of discovery, we moved in on each other, tasting and touching, deliberately, lovingly, as though we had all the time in the world. There was no hesitancy, no coyness. We crossed to the room's one important piece of furniture, and, one on each side of it, like an old married couple in which each member has staked his claim to part of the bedroom, we undressed and hung our clothes on chairs. We turned at the same time and each of us placed a right knee on the edge of the bed and there we stood, unlikely mirror images which were actually quite different halves of a not yet completed whole. She lifted her hand warningly and pointed to the bedspread about which I did not care, but I found myself following her silent directions. I took one end and she the other and, as we folded the ends in until they met, our bodies touched and parted, touched and parted, touched and parted, until the spread was a tiny square (never so well looked after) and we stood naked in each other's arms. This time no warning hand stopped us at the edge of the bed.

Later, as we lay alongside one another, she reached over and rubbed her hand across my belly. I was settling in to her caress when her thumb and forefinger closed on a pinch of body hair and she yanked suddenly. I shouted and swung at her, as much in defense as pleasure, but she had rolled quickly to one side and was standing now at the edge of the bed, laughing down at me. "You're fat, you know," she said. "That hair pull is what you get for letting yourself go."

"Don't you occasionally let yourself go?"

"That's not what I meant," she said. She climbed back on the bed and settled herself, sitting cross-legged, near my head. She bent down and kissed me. "That's to make up for pulling your hair." She sat up again and I was just reaching to pull her back down, when she caught my arms and said, "You promised me tea."

"I suppose I did," I said. "I'll bet you a quarter that I can get dressed and get the tea ready before you have your clothes on."

"That's a bet you'd lose, but I don't want to make it. Is there a house rule—no clothes, no tea? Can't I drink it like this? Must I be modest?"

I rolled over and put my head where her lap would have been if her legs had not been folded one under the other. I brushed my cheek across the down of her belly and then kissed her once, as though I were planting a flag and claim-

ing the land as my own, just below the navel. I looked up
through her breasts, into her laughing eyes. "Be as im-
modest as you please. I like what I see."

"I'm glad," she said. "I like my body too."

"And mine?" I asked. She wrinkled her nose. "O.K.,
O.K., but you'll just have to get used to it." I touched my
waist, where there is flesh enough that I do not need. "Let
this be a lesson to you. Don't be piggish at tea."

I would not choose to watch the naked male body while
the naked male is making tea, but Sylvia, more amused
than reverent, I'm afraid, kept her eyes and her smile on
me while I busied myself with the hot plate and the tea
bags. I looked up often enough from the watched pot which
finally boiled to assure myself that she really sat on my bed.
I joined her there; each of us drank two cups of tea and we
shared a box of animal crackers. We quarreled over the last
animal, a lioness with a missing leg, each of us insisting
that he should eat it to save the figure of the other. I was
in actual possession, but, as I brought it to my lips, Sylvia
snatched at it, knocking it from my hand. We both scrambled for it and our scramble became a physical struggle
which, crumbs and all, became something else again, and
the tea ended as it had begun.

Later, after Sylvia had gone, I remembered that this was
the first time I had had tea with a lady since that afternoon
with Miss Despere.

Not every afternoon, but most afternoons, Sylvia and I
met. Tea became our ritual and our euphemism. We met
somewhere in the city—the ostrich farm, say—and played at
being tourists before we returned to my hotel and played
at being lovers. We seldom got as far west as Hollywood
and Beverly Hills, but once we did go to the beach at

Venice where, if I had persisted, we might have managed a fine quarrel. A group of young people, truants from one of the city colleges, were romping all around us; both boys and girls were bursting, struttingly, from their suits in obvious directions. I found myself feeling fifteen years their senior, which I was of course, but that did not make it any easier, and I was harshly aware of the paleness of my skin and the unnecessary circlet of flesh that I wore like an amulet around the top of my bathing trunks. "My God," I muttered, "these peacocks love their feathers."

"Why shouldn't they?" Sylvia's question was accusation, not conversation.

"Being body-proud is like being purse-proud."

"There speaks a poor man."

Then, thank heaven, I laughed. "There speaks a rich woman." I held out my arms toward her. "Alms, for the love of Allah."

She kissed me. "What can I do for the poor little beggar?"

"If wishes were horses," I said, "beggars would ride."

She punched me softly with her doubled fist. "You will, you will."

Who is Sylvia? What is she? I asked the question from time to time, but you cannot grill an idyll and expect it to remain forever green. Besides Sylvia knew no more of me than I knew of her and seemed to care not at all. She insisted that we meet only in the afternoon, which made me suspect that she was a childless wife with no claim on her daytime hours; if there was a husband somewhere I did not care, but I did not care to know.

Our one evening together was a failure, proof enough that the aesthetics of our affair—we were an afternoon couple—if not its politics demanded that we turn into pumpkins at the dinner hour. I do not remember now which of us decided that it might be amusing to spend a conventional evening on the town, but spend one we did and spend spirit too. We went to one of the overdressed and expensive night clubs where out-of-towners flock, hoping to see the stars at play. There was one bona fide Hollywood couple—a romance made not in heaven, but in the studio publicity offices—who had been sent out, like show dogs, to attract eyes and cameras, but who had slipped their leashes. The girl sat at their table pouring drink after drink into her pouting mouth, fingering but never lifting to her lips a cold cup of expresso that sat primly in front of her; at last, she fell forward, unconscious, across the cup which tipped toward her, sending the Italian coffee spilling over one of the most publicized breasts in Hollywood. Her escort, meanwhile, spent most of his time at the bandstand trying, with no success, to keep his hands off the trumpeter. The spectacle of royalty relaxed so depressed us that we parted without even a chaste kiss between us.

It took two afternoons to revive us. Or perhaps we never really revived, for it was not many days after that night's excursion that our Maytime romance ended. Sylvia said one day, after tea, that she had to leave town and that it would be better if we parted for good. My instinct was to cry out, to protest, to insist, to use a phrase that I had carried from my childhood, that we were made for each other. But I did no such thing. I simply, sadly said good-by. Something in me, I suppose, preferred the shock of a full break while we were still storybook lovers to the possibility of change, of indifference, of incompleteness.

After Sylvia had gone out my door for the last time, I had trouble getting back to Connie Firth. I had been Will willingly for less than four weeks, but it had been long enough for me to forget that I had come to Los Angeles to find a confection named Candy Stick. The best way to come home to myself, I decided, was to go back to where I left me. I had escaped from the forbidding Angela to the shelter of the zoo and Sylvia; now it seemed logical to go from Sylvia back to Angela. I skipped the zoo step this time.

I also skipped the confiding conversation with the apartment doorman. I went directly to Candy Stick's bell and rang it as if I were wringing a neck. Angela appeared accusingly. "It's you again."

"That's right. I want to see Miss Stick."

"I told you before and I will tell you one more time. Miss Stick sees no one without an appointment."

"I will lean on this bell until she sees me," and I did lean on it, setting off a muted racket in the rooms that gave off the chaste, cream-colored hall into which I had not yet set foot.

A door opened on the hall and through it stepped a familiar figure dressed in an unfamiliarly fragile dressing gown.

"Sylvia," was all I could say.

"Will. How did you find me?" Almost tears. "Why did you find me?"

"I didn't want to find you. I wanted Candy Stick."

Angela had disappeared, leaving us standing alone in the hall.

"Did you want to see Candy Stick on business?" she asked finally.

"Not in the way you mean," I said. "I just wanted to find out why she should long for the ornamental box."

If my words surprised her, she did not show it. She hesitated for just a second and then took a step toward me. "Don't you know?" she cried out. "Don't you know?"

"Yes, I know. Now I know." I backed the few steps out
of the apartment, my eyes not leaving her face. As I closed
the door on Candy Stick I said only, "Good-by, Sylvia." I
did not say what I knew: that there is no permanence in
peacock feathers.

CHAPTER SEVEN

MONEY MAKES THE MARE GO

 SOMEDAY, I can tell my grandchildren that I once had a tame lioness as a pet.

When I closed the door on Candy Stick, I left Sylvia prowling her cage once more. It would be damned funny, I said to myself, if she finally gets that box and gets it open and I step out. Do not ask how such a thought came into my head.

The bar in the lobby would have been the nearest place in which to slip quietly into alcoholic unconsciousness if, like my friend in Atlanta, I had wanted to forget the really best-looking girl in Macon who had married a banker. All that I wanted to do was to arrest the centrifugal force that was spinning my thoughts off in all directions. I might have done it by walking, but the all-glass door of the sanctuary-lounge caught my eye as I stepped out of the elevator and I went in instinctively.

I finished one drink and decided that my name was C. M. Firth and that I might as well run off and join a circus or the Foreign Legion as to keep chasing my tail (my tale) by following a list of names that kept folding me back in on myself. I drank a second drink and decided to go any-where (Oklahoma City, Kansas City, Mexico City) instead of San Francisco where the next name (P. R. Eferred) and the next address waited for me. I ordered the third drink, but it was still in front of me untouched when Fate, in the person of a drunken millionaire in a white coat, blundered up to me and let me know that, whatever other plans I might have, I might as well finish the game that I had begun in Providence when I tore the page from Solly Derritch's diary.

The coat was evening white, with a black tie, held over from the night before, although it was now late in the morning. The drunkenness was the safe side of the coherent and the operational. The millions were genuine apparently, although Theodore Fineline III ("my friends call me Teddy": every freeloader on the West Coast called him Teddy) did not know what to do with them. His first words were, "Can you drive?"

"Yes, I can drive."

"How much would you charge to drive me to San Francisco?"

"Five hundred dollars."

"Done," he said and held out his hand to shake mine. We shook. I drank my third drink and was thinking that I could just do with a fourth when he put his hand on my arm. "No more of that now, buddy. You probably wouldn't think so to look at me, but I am a moralist. I believe in drunk passengers, but I do not believe in drunk drivers." He tugged at me. "Come on, let's go."

Let me remind you that I am a peaceable man, which means that from time to time I want to hit someone.

I did not hit Teddy. Love, the near-cure for longing, had been so recently a sure thing that I had no inclination for that other panacea, violence. Besides, drinking makes me sad, not belligerent. All that I did was shake my arm loose from his grip and say, "Don't you want to go upstairs and take a nap?"

"We made a deal. I asked you . . . ."

I interrupted him. "A joke loses a great deal in recapitulation."

"Joke," he shouted. "Joke." And then he broke into an angry mutter in which the word *joke* shared space with a variety of obscene epithets, aimed, as nearly as I could figure, at jokers in general and me in particular. He accompanied his plaint with an elaborate attempt to get a wallet from his inside pocket, a struggle that looked at first as though it would crash on the twin rocks of his anger and his failing coordination, but he succeeded. Opening it, he took out a stack of bills and, counting loudly, "ONE . . . TWO . . . THREE . . . FOUR . . . FIVE," he piled five one-hundred-dollar bills on the bar in front of me. "*There*," he shouted, "does that look like a joke?"

"Are you crazy?" I asked.

"No," he said, quite calm now. "I'm rich."

"If you're so rich, why haven't you got a chauffeur?"

"I had one until five minutes ago. He quit."

"Why?"

"How do I know why? He was mad or something. Just because I called him a lazy black son-of-a-bitch."

"Did he hit you?"

"No, he just quit. Should he have hit me?"

"I think so. If you call me a lazy *white* son-of-a-bitch, I'll hit you. And quit."

"Well, maybe he should have hit me then." Momentarily doubt settled on his shoulders, but he shrugged it off quickly as he thought of the perennial solution to his problems. "Oh well, I know where he lives. I'll send him a check."

"What is the going rate for permission to call someone a lazy black son-of-a-bitch?"

"I don't get you," he said.

I had lost my pupil somewhere between perceptible personal guilt and the implication of rot in the economic and social structure. If I can't save his soul, I thought to myself, perhaps I had better drive his car. The five bills still lay on the bar between us. I have a natural protective instinct toward currency and I would gladly have given the five hundred dollars the shelter of my pocket. But for the word *lazy*. "How lazy? I do not like to be worked to death myself."

A novelist would probably make something monumental of Teddy Fineline's story, knowing that the reader, to whom a double feature at Loew's and a glass of beer is a night on the town, longs for a vicarious Rabelaisian romp, a debauch in which no one slips in his own vomit, and there is no hangover to carry, like a hump on the back, through the paycheck-necessary work of the morning after. Teddy was matter-of-fact enough in his own recital. At lunch the day before, in San Francisco, he had heard about a Los Angeles girl of great charm . . . .

"Candy Stick?" I asked.

"Do you know her?"

"No," I said. "I've heard about her."

He had had himself driven, drinking, down the coast and had got into town, drunk and ready, only to be turned away by the fastidious Angela. He had shrugged off the snub (no bell-leaner, he: if you cannot buy the bell or hire someone to lean on it, why bother?) and had spent the evening, the night, the morning systematically scouring the town for the music, the girl, the drink that would finally convince him that Theodore Fineline III was, after all, one of the immortals. Settling at last for mortality (not yet, not yet) he had demanded that his chauffeur, who had carried the night on his back and was dead tired, dog tired from the burden, turn the Mercedes around and head again for San Francisco. The epithet, the resignation, the approach.

"Two stipulations," I said. "I will drive you to San Francisco . . . ."

"To my house," he interrupted.

"All right, to your house, but not on a hide-and-hair treasure hunt of San Francisco." He nodded. "Second, I will first go past my hotel to pick up my suitcase. I'm leaving Los Angeles for good."

"Are you wanted?" he asked, having seen too many TV shows.

"Who is?" I asked and found myself yearning for the eleventh floor. I scooped up the money. "Let's go."

"Shake hands for a deal," he said. "I'm Teddy Fineline." Easily the fifth time I had heard the news.

"My name's Eddie Anodyne," I said.

"That reminds me of an old night-club act."

"Me too," I said. "Let's go."

The trip was not as painful as it might have been. Teddy slept most of the way, snoring noisily in the seat beside me. He had insisted that we ride together because I did not have a chauffeur's license and was therefore technically incapable of a pure employer-employee relationship. That is not exactly the way he phrased it. "I can't see you calling me *sir*," he had said.

"Or tipping my hat to you," I had agreed.

The most difficult stretch of the journey came when my impure employer stayed awake for thirty or forty minutes by telling me, in detail, about a coach dog he had had when he was ten. Champ (the name was actually Fineline Champion VI) had drowned in the ornamental fish pool and broken the boy's heart. "Teddy," I wanted to say, "I know a guy named Harry who has been looking between the legs of widows for thirty years in search of a dead cocker spaniel. You don't really hope to find a coach dog in a bottle, do you?" Want or not, I said nothing. I kept my eyes on the road and Teddy, sniffing back his tears, went off to sleep again.

I wonder if the psychiatrists in this country know how many compulsive neuroses are the result of puppy-dogs under the wheels of passing cars.

Teddy's amendment, "to my house," turned out to be less innocent than it had sounded when he proposed it. When he woke up to stay, twenty-five miles or so outside of San Francisco, he began to give careful directions—turn here, turn there—which brought us finally to his estate, an endless expanse, somewhere on the coast south of the city. I had no idea exactly where I was.

"You'll never get to town tonight," he said. "You might as well stay for the party."

"What party?"

"Tonight's party."

There was a forest of cars in front of the Fineline mansion—a rococo eruption in the San Simeon tradition. We threaded our way through the clusters of immaculate sports cars which shared space with aged American models, held together by rust and faith, middle-class, middle-sized elephants that had apparently come to the estate to die.

A jangle of noise came around the corner of the house, coaxing, like the distant sound of a calliope, but Teddy said, "Come on," and led me into the mansion, across the marble entry, up a Penn Station stairway, into a study in which the walls were books, broken on one side by French windows. He threw open the windows, and sound poured up from the lawn assaultingly. "There's the party," he said, gesturing.

There it was indeed. The vast lawn, pampered by platoons of gardeners, fringed by complacent trees, had been invaded. Chaos was making itself at home where once the crack of croquet balls would have been the wildest sound. It was an English garden party with the vicar reeling drunk, singing obscene lyrics to "Rule, Britannia." It was a Fourth of July picnic where the visiting senator, having shredded the American flag, was leading a boy scout into the bushes. Floodlights slashed the lawn and by their light I could see that the deep green grass was turning brown under the nervous heels of the guests as they sat, tapping, at the scattered tables. Facing us, like a band shell on the skids, was a makeshift stage on which a jazz combo felt its way along the intricacies of a cool composition. In front of the musicians, a stripper, down now to nothing at all, was contemplatively grinding, pushing an occasional, intellectual bump into the maze of the music. On the other side of the stage front, a young man with curly hair, dressed in black corduroys and a dirty T shirt, was undulating with the band and the stripper, moaning a message into a microphone: *o bitch mother America why have the milk shakes gone thin in the balls of time and amalgamated cesspool gone up four-and-a-half points.* I may not have got the message word for word, but that certainly was its gist.

"Poet," said my employer-host.

"The boy or the girl?" I asked. He ignored my question.

"Girl I know talked me into going to one of those arty night clubs. Bad booze, bad air. When she wanted to go again, I said what the hell and hired the whole thing to come out here."

"Your guest list seems a bit mixed." White coats and formal gowns shared table space with blue jeans and black slipover sweaters.

"Oh, I hired the customers from the joint, too."

"I thought that crowd was in revolt," I said. "I didn't know they were for sale."

"My grandfather used to say that a revolutionary is a guy who hasn't found out how to package what he wants to sell."

"I plan to like your grandfather," I said. "Where is he?"

"Oh, the old boy's dead."

We stood looking into the confusion below. My mind had pulled away from our conversation and had begun to prowl around the lawn, which was strewn, I noticed, with paintings, probably the ones that had hung on the nightclub walls before Teddy had bought the revolution out. His mind had gone its own way. "An impressive old gent," he said. I looked at him questioningly. "My grandfather, I mean. I was thinking about him. The only thing remotely like him is his old partner. Fineline and Eferred, did you ever hear of the firm?"

"P. R. Eferred?" I asked.

"That's the one. Old Eferred is still alive, you know, and still runs the firm. You ought to see him."

"I'd like to see him," I said.

"Really?" He was asking a genuine question.

"Yes, really." I was making a genuine answer.

"I'll give you a letter to him. Remind me tomorrow."

"Why not give it to me now? I may not see you tomorrow. At least," I gestured toward the lawn, "judging by the arts-and-crafts clambake going on down there."

"You mean you're leaving me?"

"Sure, I'm leaving you. I'm not a chauffeur. Remember what Voltaire said about once a philosopher, twice a pervert."

He went to the desk and perched tentatively, half sitting,

half leaning, on the edge of it, as though he were afraid that if he ever got squarely behind it he might be sucked by tradition and liking into his grandfather's shoes and offices and never again be free to piss his years away. He scrawled a hurried note across a sheet of paper which he sealed in an envelope that had come from its destination. "Fineline and Eferred, Investments" was written in the upper left-hand corner; there was an address, too. He wrote "P. R. Eferred" across the front of the envelope and handed it to me without a comment. Returning him silence for silence, only looking my thanks, I slipped the introduction into my pocket.

Only then did he speak. "Once we get downstairs, it's every man for himself. I'll say good-by now." Smiling, I took the hand he held out to me, but his thoughts were as dark as an old epithet. "You're still thinking about my calling that guy a lazy black son-of-a-bitch," he said. "I'm not as bad as that crack makes me sound."

Who's still thinking about what, I wanted to ask, but all I said was, "No one is as bad as their acts, but what else have we got to go on?"

Those were the last words between us. I walked downstairs with him and out of and around the house. Teddy stepped directly into the party. I stood at the corner and watched, preparing myself for a plunge that I did not take. I was filled suddenly with panic, like a man at the door of a department store on the first day of the white sales, and I turned away to save my life, my soul, my sanity. I was on my way back to the front door when I remembered my suitcase in Teddy's car. I retrieved it, went inside and upstairs. I looked until I found a room which seemed to have no regular inhabitant. I sank, naked, into the soothing soft-

ness of silk over down and found my own peace while outside the search for beatitude racketed into the morning.

When I swam up out of the dreamless down into being
awake, the sun was already bright at the window and the
only sound from the lawn was a muted murmur, rising, like
an inarticulate complaint, from the small army of workmen
busy collecting the debris from the night before. I was met
at the foot of the stairs by a man who seemed to be in
charge—obviously high in the hierarchy of service, but I
cannot put a name to his rank. He was not at all surprised
to see me; he simply called up some eggs and coffee from
somewhere in the guts of the mansion, smiled me into them,
and then went out to command the salvaging operation.
  I was glad that I had thought of my suitcase the night
before, for Teddy's car was gone with those of his guests—
except for a 1947 Dodge which someone had crashed against
the gatepost where the driveway led out into the road. I
passed it there, deserted, when, fed and informed (turn
right for San Francisco), I began my hitchhiking way into
the city. By the time Teddy got back from wherever he
had gone—perhaps he had heard about a girl in Seattle—I
knew that the wreck would have disappeared, neatly policed
by the organized lint-pickers already at work on the lawn.

Another city, another hotel room. This time, the St.
Francis, thanks to Teddy's five hundred dollars. I dumped
my suitcase on the floor of its new home and headed immediately for the offices of Fineline and Eferred. I had
made such a practice of the hesitant approach, dancing
around each of the names on my list (my list?) like a big
bird in courting season, that I was vaguely startled by my

own sense of purpose. San Francisco is, after all, such a fine town to kill time in that I might have dawdled away a harmless week or two if something had not nagged me into action.

It was Teddy's note that did the nagging. I felt as though I were sealed in that envelope and that I had to deliver it to P. R. Eferred so that he could let me out. I was tempted to open it myself, to find out who I was, but I restrained myself on the theory—unarticulated, God knows—that identity could only be established through the intervention of the recipient, the catalyst—the notary public as magic agent.

If I had not been so intent on what I was doing, like a genie trying to push the cork out of his bottle, I might have noticed the crowds around me. I might have seen that they were secretaries who had already downed their cream-cheese-and-jelly sandwiches (on diet bread) and were rushing to lose the rest of their hour shopping, that they were stock boys taking the June sun before they disappeared back into the bowels of stores, that they were clerks crowding into bars where they could pick up news of the ball games already under way on the East Coast. I was aware only of activity, but as far as I was concerned it might as well have been the morning bargain hunters or the suburban afternoon-killers as the lunch-hour crowd. In short, I had no idea that it was almost one o'clock. If I had, I might not have pushed on with such assurance.

Business, so current mythology tells us, is carried on only over the luncheon table; contacts are made through the martini glass darkly. Once the lower-echelon feeders, the secretaries, the clerks, the stock boys through whom I was walking unheeding, have poured back to their desks and counters, the executives fan out to the swankier restaurants and close deals over their expense-account Hollandaise. By

rights, no P. R. Eferred should have been on hand to receive Teddy Fineline's message.

Ignorance, as it turned out, served me as well as knowledge would have, although the girl at the reception desk
plainly expected that such would not be the case. As I came
in she smiled at me and said, "Whoever it is, he's out."

"It's Mr. Eferred. I've a note for him."

"He's in, of course. Who's the note from, please?"

"Theodore Fineline III." I held it out to her.

She looked at me. "Well, you never know who will turn
up running his errands for him." I stood waiting for what
would happen next. "You don't have to stay; I'll see that
he gets it."

"He may want to see me."

"He never talks to the messengers. He always calls Mr.
Fineline and talks to him directly."

"Are all kisses the same?"

Until I asked that question she had been playing her part
well. There are only a few variations on the role of the receptionist. Hers was the most difficult, the relaxed, almost
joking near friend of the outsider who is pulled in and held
off at the same time until his acceptability has been
checked. I had been weighed and found wanting and so I
was being jollied into the street where, according to the
script, I should have walked off feeling that the girl who
had shown me the door really felt toward me like a sister.
Although her lines were ad lib, she played ordinarily within
a given set of cues, and, alas, her duties provided no stock
answer to the question I had asked. She dropped her mask.
No longer able to be a receptionist, she became an annoyed
girl, uncertain whether or not I was making a pass at her.
"What did you say?"

"I said, 'Are all kisses the same?' That may be a misleading question. Let me put it another way. Do all pieces of chocolate cake taste alike?"

"I don't know what you're talking about."

"What does everyone talk about? I'm talking about myself. Have you ever seen me before?" She shook her head. "Do you really know that I'm a messenger?" She gestured helplessly with the envelope I had handed her. "I may be a bookie, or a hypnotist, or a dope pusher, or a Swedish masseur. I may be the bar sinister on the Eferred escutcheon. I may be Judge Crater."

She was in retreat. Her confusion was so genuine that I almost regretted my pretense of outraged innocence.

Any man in heavy shoes can storm a sand castle, but where's the percentage in being a sand-castle stormer?

She backed out of the room, stuttering her promise to deliver my note, and left me to the solidity of Fineline and Eferred. The dark paneling and heavy furniture of this one room gave the impression that the firm would last forever, a hint of permanence that increased almost to certainty as I followed her—"Mr. Eferred will see you, sir"—along a deep-carpeted hall and into a room which could have been moved bodily into the Edwardian wing of any museum. In the center of the enormous room was a desk the size of a small playing field and behind it sat a cadaverous man whose presence screamed out, contradicting his surroundings, *This, too, will pass.*

"Mr. Anodyne?" asked P. R. Eferred. His voice was firm, but there was a dryness in it that suggested that all expression had long since evaporated. The words came through a thin slash of a mouth, just one more sharp feature in a face of sharpness. His hands, the blue-white of age, were folded on the desk in front of him. He did not move them, made no gesture of welcome. After I had nodded my acceptance of the name that he had given me, he said, "Sit down." I sat.

The note lay open in front of him. "Hand the letter to Mr. Anodyne," he said as though the desk were so long that I could not have walked from my chair to his. The receptionist brought it to me and then, on his nod, left the room.

The note was as short as the time Teddy had taken to write it:

Dear Uncle Perry:

You will probably like Eddie Anodyne. He's not much like me.

Theodore

"How are you most unlike Theodore, Mr. Anodyne?" he asked.

"I'm poor."

The answer apparently pleased the old man, for something remotely like a smile touched the line where his lips should have been. He pressed a buzzer and a girl appeared from one of the doors behind him. "I'm going to have my lunch, Mr. Anodyne. Will you have something?" His words reminded me that I had not eaten and hunger followed on the knowledge. I accepted. "What would you like?"

"Whatever you're going to have, sir."

"I wouldn't if I were you."

"Please," I said, "anything's all right. I don't want to be a bother." I found myself being conventionally polite and knew that the old man had somehow turned me into a child on his good behavior.

"All right," he said. The girl disappeared. We sat in silence for a full ten minutes. Most of the time he stared ahead, looking at nothing or at the lithograph of a bird, a fat worm in its mouth, which hung on the wall in front of him; occasionally he glanced at me. I sat, shrinking in my chair, wondering if I would not have got so small by the time the girl came back that I could not reach up to the edge of the desk to feed.

It was the lunch that saved me. Not that it gave me strength or anything like that; there could not have been much in it. Tea and dry toast—that is all there was. His words, "I wouldn't, if I were you," echoed mockingly from the cup as I poured the steaming tea into it. P. R. Eferred, sly by instinct, had warned me in his cryptic fashion that I should not (could not?) eat as he did. The dry toast scraped the roof of my mouth and, as I sent tea in to wash the taste-less crumbs away, I thought to myself, P. R. Eferred is an old man with a bad stomach. And, as sure as I was Eddie Anodyne, I was ready for anything he might say.

His first words were simple enough. "How do you come to know Theodore?"

I edited—for space, not for style—the story of our day to-gether, told him briefly how Teddy had hired me to drive him to San Francisco and how that small chore had been accomplished.

"And when you got here," he said, "there was a party in progress."

"Surely you weren't there, sir?"

"I am eighty-seven years old, and I was not there. Still, there has been a party in progress at the Fineline estate every night for the last two generations; so why should last night have been different? There are only two ways to en-joy money."

He turned back to his tea and toast. His speech sounded unfinished to me, but I thought it likely that he needed a sip and a bite before he could go on. He bit and he sipped, and still silence. Finally I asked, "Two ways?"

"Spending is Theodore's way. It was his father's, too. Only old Ted knew that the real way to enjoy money is to make it. If I had lived the way young Theodore does, I would be as dead as his father."

"And his grandfather."

"And his grandfather," echoed Eferred. I could not tell whether he was contemplating the error in his reasoning or whether he was back in the San Francisco before the earthquake and the fire when he and young Ted Fineline were to West Coast finance what the Barbary Coast was to sin.

"I kept busy and I kept alive," he continued. I said nothing. I just sat, watching him, waiting for him to go on, but something of what I felt must have shown in my eyes. "You don't think I'm very much alive, do you? What was it Satan said in *Paradise Lost?* Better to reign on tea and toast than to serve in Heaven."

What was I to do? If I had had a sky rocket in my pocket I might have fired it in celebration of Uncle Perry Eferred. Instead, I smiled my admiration, kept my mouth shut, and left him free to walk the fine line between strength and corruption.

"Did you ever steal anything?" he said suddenly.

"Of course," I answered. "Nothing much, and not for years."

"If I paid you enough, would you steal something for me?"

"Why don't you simply buy it?"

"I've tried, but it's not for sale."

"Then it probably can't be stolen, or if it can it loses its magic power?"

"What loses its magic power?"

"Whatever it is you want me to steal." We had finally come face to face, but we retreated. He to silence. I to the question, "What is it that you want stolen?"

"I collect carved wood of all kinds," he said, conversationally, "and I once saw an ornametal box . . . ."

"Held it in your hands?"

"Yes, held it in my hands, but what difference does that make?"

The difference of months and miles, I could have told him, having held it once myself, but I simply shrugged.

"The agent who let me hold it . . . I mean who showed it to me . . . refused to sell it. Not that Mr. Derritch was completely incorruptible."

Oh, God, I hope I'm finally going to find it, cried Solly into his diary.

"Would you mind wheeling me over to the fireplace?" the old man asked and for the first time I realized that his desk chair was on wheels. The legs as gone as the stomach, he still wanted to set me stealing. I wheeled him to the spot he pointed out and he pulled aside some false brick to show a safe underneath. "Yes, Mr. Derritch was not a pure knight of incorruptibility," he said, working the combination; "he would not sell me the box, but he did sell me a list of people who are interested in it." He held up a sheet of paper. "One of them may have it."

"Perhaps your Mr. Derritch wanted the box himself." Perhaps . . . of course. As I said the line, I realized why the fat man in the blanket had turned up at the Hotel Chevron. Whoever or whatever was behind the box knew that by the time Solly Derritch had carried it to nine cities he could not give it up.

"Why should he want it?" snapped Eferred.

"For the same reason that you want it," I said, truthfully, but I added, "He may be a collector."

"Would you be willing to visit the people on this list?" he asked. "I would make it worth your while."

"I would be willing, yes." Here was my chance to finish the circle, all expenses paid, but when he held the list out to me I killed the possibility of traveling on Eferred's money, by saying "I don't need the list."

"What do you mean?"

"Rodney Salvay, Edward Pick, Annette Despere, Candy Stick, P. R. Eferred . . ." I intoned, calling stations, or reading off a roster of those picked for dangerous duty.

He shriveled as the names pounded against him, the shell of a man become the shell of a shell of a man. "How?" was his only word.

"I have my own list. Solly Derritch left it to me when he died."

"The box?" the words strangled out of his throat. No sad songs for Solly.

"If I knew, would I follow the list? The box has gone back to where it came from, I suppose. Don't you know who sent Derritch?" He shook his head. "Don't you know the source?" A different question, and the same, but he shook his head.

"Help me," he whimpered like a child. "What can I do if you don't help me?"

"What were you supposed to do?"

"Wait; the word was wait. How long can I wait? How *can* I wait?" The plea had turned in on itself. He sat, hunched, muttering, "You can't buy time, you can't buy time, you can't buy time."

CHAPTER EIGHT

ART FOR GOD'S SAKE

THE EFFICIENCY of the rich always surprises me. I supposed that I had heard the end (forgive that noun, Uncle Perry) of P. R. Eferred when, having pushed every button on his desk, I left him in the solicitous hands of four secretaries and a male nurse, all trying to force restorative pills between his still-moving lips. I was wrong. The old man knew me only as Eddie Anodyne and, yet, within a week, the desk clerk at the Francis handed me an envelope addressed to C. M. Firth.

The foolishness of the rich always surprises me. Why a man who could afford to hire detectives capable of finding a Firth in a haystack should want to butter me up is beyond me. There were ten one-hundred-dollar bills in the envelope and a note, unsigned: "Please accept this gift. Good luck in your travels."

I still do not know what the old man had in mind. Perhaps he imagined that the thousand dollars was some kind of a binder, a moral obligation that would force me to steal the ornamental box, supposing that I finally found it, and drop it one happy day on that half-acre desk of his. Perhaps he simply wanted me to send him a post card from each of the last four stops on my accidental itinerary; or he may have wanted me to write on one of those post cards, "Here ends the search"—and so mark the spot to which he could send his own anonymous fat man in blankets to do the box-lifting. He may have hoped that the sight of those bills would wipe from my eyes the picture of the crumpled giant, the fallen angel in the wheel chair, muttering that his god had failed. Perhaps he simply wished me well. On that unlikely prospect I took my stand. I took the money and, shortly after that, I took to the road.

I first had to decide where—with my new riches—I should go. The list, up to now, had been laid out neatly, as though a travel agency had planned a peripheral tour of the United States. After E ferred the orderliness disappeared. The last three names were clustered in the Midwest—Detroit, Chicago, Indianapolis—and logic should have taken me to them first. But logic had as little to do with my journey as common sense did. Call it sentiment, call it superstition, I chose to take the names as they came, which meant that I had to get from San Francisco to East Ariel, Massachusetts, where Arthur Krafft—my next oracle, my next victim— waited for me. Not that I am quite as feckless as my loyalty to the list makes me seem. I had looked East Ariel up on a Massachusetts map and had found that it was on Cape Cod, somewhere near the center of a clot of Truros, and to head for the Cape in midsummer is not such a bad idea, although most people who are not sunsick or art-happy would probably avoid it.

After the destination, the means. I used one of Uncle Perry's gift bills to buy a 1950 Studebaker, a purring pet of a car that got me all the way across the country, served my brief purposes in and around East Ariel, and only came coughing to an end when I tried to turn her nose west once more.

But I am rushing things. I should say a word about my habits as a driver. I do not mean my skill, although I am proficient enough in an unflashy way. I mean the community spirit . . .
☐

That phrase is the socially acceptable way of designating the personal loneliness that forces men together to organize Red Feather drives or to form lynch mobs.

. . . that makes me pick up hitchhikers on the road. Whenever I own a car—infrequently, thank God—I turn it into a kind of free-loading bus. I am constitutionally unable to pass a man (woman or child) who stands, thumb out, on a road. Alarmists who insist that all hitchhikers are psychopaths. . . .

Statistically, the percentage of psychopaths among hitchhikers is appreciatively less than that among clergymen, dentists, and concert baritones. I cannot remember just now who it was who carried out the study, but any abnormal psychologist should be able to put you onto the material.

. . . keep warning me away from the thumb-wagging mendicants.

"If I've told you once, I've told you a hundred times," his best friend said when he got home to Samaria, "you should leave strangers lying in the ditches where you find them."

A few of the alarmists who read too much assume that I subconsciously share their suspicions and that I am really suffering from a death wish. Who isn't, I would like to know, but that does not mean that I intend to implement it. Actually, there are two sensible reasons for picking up hitchhikers. The first and most metaphysical is that the hitchhiker is the driver in a manner of speaking. The second and more natural is that the hitchhiker is not the driver and is therefore company for him. The hitchhiker is, then, both You and non-You. Is any other justification needed?

□ □

With all of the unofficial unemployment in the country, I expected to find the roads full of men moving from one town to another in search of work. Perhaps I chose the wrong (or the right) moment to get on the road. I was well into the Dakotas before I saw my first hitchhiker, acquired my first passenger.

At a distance, there was something vaguely familiar about the man in the road. The black corduroys, the T shirt, the curly hair, they might have been on almost anyone. It was something in the way that he stood, not with the careful dignity of the hitchhiker who wants to impress the driver with his respectability, nor with the careless slouch that declares, like a name tag, college boy on a summer's bumming, but with a weaving bob to no audible music. When I stopped in front of him, the face, one borrowed from a mischievous small boy and kept for thirty years in a reasonable state of preservation, was unknown to me—except as a type. He pulled the door open with a gesture of manly violence (a child could have opened it without a strain), bounded into the seat beside me, and slammed the door behind him. He lifted his left foot, in a white sneaker of course, and tapped it three times, "One . . . two . . . three," like a conductor about to get the brass band ready, and lifting his arms toward heaven or the roof of my car, called out, "WHOOIE, man, We're off."

That was enough. I knew then that the long-distance hint of familiarity was not the optical illusion (a heart condition) that makes all of us see our acquaintances in strangers who are not close enough to be unknown. I had only seen this man at a distance. He was the poet who had sung me into San Francisco, the real toad in Teddy Fineline's imaginary garden.

"I'm sorry you're not the stripper," I said, by way of greeting.

He wooshed an inarticulate answer which seemed compounded of surprise and pleasure, and, stumbling over an occasional *man,* rolled at last into a simple question, "You've heard me read?"

"Not exactly," I said. "I've seen you read."

"Let's not quibble about the senses, man."

"Spare me the *man,* man," I said, "or you'll be back on the Dakota roads with your hand in the air. *Sir* is an admirable noun of address. *Mac* is possible, particularly in taxis. *Mr. Firth* is accurate."

"A pleasure, Mr. Firth," he said, holding out his hand. "My name's Johnny Bucks. But then you know it."

"A pleasure, Mr. Bucks." I took the hand. "The name—I'm sorry—I did not know. Teddy Fineline neglected to give out programs." After a silence, I added, "By the way, what happened to Fineline that night?"

"Damned if I know. A bunch of us were heading for Seattle, but I ran my Dodge into the gatepost and ended up walking all the way to San Francisco."

"Why didn't you steal another car?"

"Whatsamatter? You crazy or something?" Understanding filtered into his eyes. "Oh, that. You don't believe all that stuff do you? That's for the public."

My experience of poets is limited. If I do not count the late Eddie Anodyne, and I don't suppose I should, or Mrs. Billings, and I don't suppose I should, then Johnny Bucks is the only poet—or the only two poets—I ever met. Mrs. Billings was a lady I ran across when I was in the army. She wrote verse about the seasons and printed them in her husband's newspaper. She was not really what the professionals would call a professional, I suspect, but she did collect her poems into a volume which sold steadily and well within twenty-five miles of the Midwestern town where she lived. I still have a copy of it—*The Turning Year* or something like that—which she forced on me after she found me sitting in the USO reading Blake. The two of them never had a great deal in common.

Not that Blake and Johnny Bucks were really brothers under the skin. As a matter of fact, Bucks reminded me of my old *friend*, Peer Gray. When I said up there that he was two poets, I meant it, although he had just one flesh to both, and not much spirit to either.

His speech lost its skittering inauthenticity after he got comfortable in the seat of my car. "You're talking like people," I said.

"I don't wonder," he answered. "I get damned tired of talking that crazy jargon, but they expect it of you."

"Who expects it of you?"

"The people who expect it of you, if you know what I mean." I didn't, but I let it go. He had his problems. "Look at me. How old would you say I was?"

"About thirty?"

"On the nose. Thirty years old. I'm too old to go running back and forth across this goddamned country like a crazy kid. And those parties. Those parties, for God's sake. Dope and all that. I wouldn't touch a fix with a ten-foot needle. I'd be scared shitless I'd get caught. I can't even drink. Makes me sick to my stomach. And just because I use the word *fuck* in my poems every damned juvenile delinquent in black stockings expects me to screw her. And the boys. They're just as bad. What am I, a queer or something?"

"You should know."

"Do you know what I want? Do you know what I would

really like to have?" I had no idea, so I left a silence for Johnny Bucks to fill. He filled it. "I would like a hot bath. I would like to soak in a hot bath for hours on end. Look at this." He pulled out the front of his T shirt. "What do you think of that?"

"It's filthy, if that's what you mean."

"That's what I mean, that's exactly what I mean. It's filthy. I'm filthy. It's a wonder I don't have lice as little as I wash. It's for Christ's sake antisocial."

"I thought that was the point. I thought all you boys were protesting the sterility of our civilization or some such jazz."

"I am one dirty poet, I can tell you, who would like to turn in his lice-ridden jock for a split-level somewhere. My problem was that I figured wrong."

"Figured wrong?"

"That's right, figured wrong. You don't think I always wrote this stuff do you: *I sucked at the dirty dugs of my America and galled to the balls rode hop-head-happy into the last ejaculation of rue.*"

"I hope not," I said truthfully.

"Nah, I used to be one of those academic poets. You know, the kind that describes everything in sight to prove they love their wives. I was married then, of course.

> The toothbrush in the glass, lime lined
> At the bottom, your hairs in our
> Common comb, the tick of the calm
> Alarm. I turn to you, my love.

You know. Naturally enough, I assumed that those boys couldn't last. When the WHOOIE crowd turned up, I kicked over the metrics, divorced my wife, quit my teaching job, and took to the road. I must have been nuts. Turns out the toothbrush-in-the-glass boys got the staying power. Now what have I got? A dirty T shirt and a suspicious rash in my crotch."

How is it that just anyone at all is likely to come up to me and tell me that I'm getting fat or that I've lost the button off my overcoat or that my fly is not fastened? And that I am so shy about passing the same information along to another man who doesn't want it?

It was that kind of message I had for Johnny Bucks, or I thought it was. Something that he knew or could easily know if he wanted to.

He was only riding as far as Chicago. "There's a new joint in Near North that needs a howling poet. I can pick up a few dollars."

We were at the end of the Bucks lap of my journey east, had dropped as far into spreading Chicago as Skokie before I brought myself to say, "You know, don't you, that you don't have to be a poet at all?"

"What?"

"You don't have to be a poet at all."

"I'm afraid that you don't know much about poetry, Mr. Firth."

I had not told him about Mrs. Billings because who wants to force on a man an image of himself, especially when the image is a middle-aged lady with a printing press and a fondness for *snow-glow, ice-nice* rhymes. "A man cannot choose to be a poet. Poetry chooses the man. The genuine poet is driven by necessity. With the real poet there is no possibility of choice."

"That's what I mean, Mr. Bucks. You don't have to be a poet at all."

"Oh." Just *oh* and then silence. I felt as though I had

taken away his cap pistol and the Fourth of July not even half over. When I let him out of the car and wished him, really, "Good luck," he lifted his hand and nodded, an automatic smile on his lips, but his eyes were off somewhere—inside himself maybe—and they never even saw the apology in mine. What have I to do with trying to keep a poet from making a *manqué* of himself?

It really was the Fourth of July, which is why the cap pistol came into my mind. All the way into the city, small boys in big hats, wearing heavy holsters, had fired at the car, killing us dead—if they had only known—in revenge for the laws that would not let them set off cannon crackers under tin cans or throw strings of lady crackers behind frightened members of the sex that gave their name to the dainty explosive. I was tempted to pull into one of those lush motels—swimming pools, cocktail lounges, doormen—that have elbowed their way in among the hotels and apartment houses on South Shore Drive to escape the holiday roads leading out of Chicago. I overcame the temptation. I was afraid that if I really stopped in Chicago I would be unable to resist the pull of the local address on my list of names, that I would be sidetracked from East Ariel and Arthur Krafft, that I would break whatever magic lay in the sequence of the names. I went on through the city, up and out along the Indiana Turnpike, which I found pleasantly uncrowded, since so many drivers had wisely stayed home to avoid the holiday traffic.

It was late on the afternoon of the fifth when I read correctly the conjunction of the Cape and July and knew that, even if I kept my foot on the gas pedal and reached East Ariel by night, I would have no place to sleep. I stopped comfortably west of the art-and-antiques belt and

turned up the next morning at one of those municipal information booths that tell you which beaches are sandy and
where to find the nearest drive-in movie. The woman in
charge was friendly enough, but she was incapable of accepting the fact that I had walked in at the height of the
season and asked where I could rent living space for a week
or two.

"You might find a room in a house that takes tourists,"
she said. "But even that's not likely."

"Not in East Ariel," said another voice. "Artists seldom
take tourists." The other speaker was a man whose voice
prissed slightly, whose tongue licked his words into shape
and pushed them toward me as though they were *objets
d'art* that I had better snap up before the museums outbid
me. He was meticulously overdressed, as though he were
trying to parody an international playboy from some movie
of the thirties—*The King and the Chorus Girl* maybe—
with white trousers cuttingly creased, a blue blazer, a silk
scarf. "I came in for one of your little area maps, Mrs.
Gaines," he said, holding up the fold of paper as though it
were a treasure that he hoped to put on display. "I want to
send it to a friend of mine who is coming up in a few weeks
and *he* is the kind of man who gets lost so easily."

Instead of taking the map and heading back to the yacht
and Joan Blondell, he walked over to me and looked at me
as though we were playing a game of stare-me-down. His
words were a warning that I had better get my cattle off his
range. "We're all artists around here."

"Except the natives," muttered Mrs. Gaines, but little
boy blue never heard her. He was listening probably to the
echo of his own horn which, I was to discover, he never
forgot to blow.

"That's why I'm here," I said.

"*You* are an artist? But I *know* all the artists in America."

"I'm not an artist. I'm writing a book on contemporary American painting."

"Oh, you are." He swayed slightly toward me, his mouth open in acceptance. I stepped back to keep from being swallowed. "Well, then you will certainly need my help. I'm Adrian Foze. Of course, you know my work."

"Of course, I do," I lied. "I'm C. M. Rosmer, from Ravenna College." We shook hands. "I'm something of a stranger among the contemporaries. Most of my work has been in pre-Renaissance. I suppose you know my book on the Clementine school—*Haring Bachses and his Circle.*"

"An excellent book," he lied. "The best work on that school, I think."

"The only one, I'm afraid," I said placidly, and waited for him to talk his way out of that. Which he did.

"How silly of me. I meant on the *period,* of course, not on the *school.* The remarkable thing about your book, I think, is that you make that time so alive." Adrian Foze may never have read a book, but he had certainly known some authors. I was so touched by his praise that I almost wished I had a copy to give him.

His admiration for the mythical C. M. Rosmer had its practical side. "Perhaps I can help you," he said. "Are you looking for a place for the whole summer?"

"Oh no," I said. "Just for a week or so. I have to see a great many people this summer. Gathering material and all that." I waved out *all that* because I am damned if I know what authors do when they are supposed to be getting information for a book.

"Then you are here to see someone in particular?"

"Yes." Before I could bring myself to say the name, I offered up a prayer to the God who watches over liars and

travelers and seekers after ornamental boxes that seem almost alive, asking him to make Arthur Krafft—please, Lord
—an artist and not a fisherman or a hotelkeeper. Finally, "I
hope to see Arthur Krafft."

The prayer—thank you, Sir—was answered. Adrian Foze
became beatific. "Arthur Krafft! Why, Arthur is one of my
dearest friends." He read that line as though it were a
compliment rather more rewarding than a retrospective at
the Whitney. "And I must say," he went on, "that I am
more than pleased that it's Arthur you want to talk to. I
must confess a tiny fear I had—that an old Renaissance"—
I looked at him sharply; he caught the look—"an old pre-
Renaissance hand like you might be interested in the
representational painters here. But Arthur . . . well, now,
that's more like it."

So Arthur Krafft painted abstractions. Thank you,
Adrian Foze.

He talked on into my thoughts. "I see absolutely no
reason why you shouldn't stay at my place. I have an extra
room that isn't promised until next week. Be my guest, Mr.
Rosmer . . . but I can't go on calling you Mr. Rosmer. And
I absolutely cannot call you C. M. What do your friends
call you? We will be friends, I'm sure."

I wanted to tell him to call me Professor Rosmer, but the
politics of the moment suggested that I invent a nickname.
After all, Foze meant a place to sleep and an introduction to
Arthur Krafft. Never look a gift horse's ass in the mouth, I
always say. "I'm called Roz. Short for Rosmer. The *C* and
M stand for names too terrible to mention."

"Call me Adrian." We shook hands for the second time.
"Do you want to come along with me now?"

"I do have a few errands I should run," I said.

He took a pencil and a scrap of paper from Mrs. Gaines's

desk and wrote down an address. "Here it is. Come when-ever you're ready." Waving his hand in a child's bye-bye, he disappeared through the door. Before I could turn to Mrs. Gaines, his head came back around the corner. "I'll call Arthur. I'll call him right away. Anyone else I'd just drop in on, but *that man*—how he hates to be disturbed while he's working. Don't worry, I'll call." The stunted wave again and this time he was really gone.

Mrs. Gaines had sat through the meeting of the Rosmer-Foze mutual admiration society without attempting to take part, masking any desire she might have had to scream or to throw up. When we were alone, she said, with the smallest touch of acid in her voice, "Well, you found a place to live at least."

I stepped around the bite in her words. "What does that guy do anyway? What does he paint?"

"I thought you said you knew his work."

"Tell me, Mrs. Gaines, when you meet a friend of yours on the street and she says, Eleanor . . . I'm pretending your name is Eleanor . . ."

"You don't have to pretend. It is Eleanor."

"It figures. And your friend says, Eleanor, how do you like my new hat? Now, what do you say?"

She laughed. A genuine laugh. "You win, Mr. Rosmer. You want to know what Adrian Foze paints? Nothing, that's what he paints. You want to know what he does? He runs around in those white pants and that blue jacket and prisses as though he owned the whole town. And he doesn't, I can tell him that. All the artists around here put up with him because he's what they call an art critic. I don't think they like him very much, but maybe they need him. I don't. I wouldn't let him in my kitchen. Even if he took off those white shoes of his."

"You're something of a painter yourself, Mrs. Gaines. At least that picture's clear." I gave the sketch of Foze time to settle before I asked, "What about Arthur Krafft?"

"Oh, I like Mr. Krafft."

"I mean his painting."

"What do I know about painting?"

"You mean you don't like them."

"There's nothing to like. They're big and they're all colors. Sometimes I see one kind of by accident and I think it's pretty. Not pretty, really, but I stop and look at it. Like when a kid scratches lines in the gravel, you know, and you look at them for some reason."

"I don't know Mr. Krafft, but I guess maybe he'd like that kind of look at his work."

"Maybe he would, maybe he wouldn't. I quilt, Mr. Rosmer, and I wouldn't like people to admire my quilts if they thought I just got those blocks in by chance, like those kids I was talking about."

"What makes you think those kids work by chance, Mrs. Gaines? I've seen a kid sit for hours drawing lines in dirt and stamping them out. Accident and plan, I think. Like with your quilts. Accident what color blocks you got; plan the way you use them. It's probably the same with Mr. Krafft."

"Well, at least you make more sense than that Foze does. He talks about 'chaos in the contemporary soul' and stuff like that. Just between you and me, Mr. Rosmer, I like pictures in my pictures. Not that that matters I suppose."

"In the long run, Mrs. Gaines, I suspect that it matters very much. Just between you and me, I like pictures in my pictures, too."

"Still, you know what my husband says. He runs the garage here in town. He says Arthur Krafft doesn't tell me how to fix cars and I don't tell him how to paint pictures. Fair's fair, he always says."

"A sensible way to look at things, Mrs. Gaines. Still, if your husband's repair jobs didn't suit Arthur Krafft, he wouldn't bring in his car, would he?"

"We've got the only garage in town."

"I didn't think of that. It doesn't work that way in art. At least not yet."

The class in art appreciation was over. Professor Rosmer had other things to do. Our conversation slipped (climbed?) from the aesthetic to the practical as Mrs. Gaines told me how to find Adrian Foze's house. As I was going out the door, she called after me, "I'll bet five bucks that Foze never read that book of yours."

I stopped and grinned at her. "That's all right, Mrs. Gaines. I never wrote it." I heard her laughter on the far side of the door as it closed behind me.

According to popular myth, people are supposed to become like the homes they live in. Let me make my report here. Houses sometimes become like their inhabitants. The farmhouse that Adrian Foze lived in was genuinely pre-Revolutionary. It looked as though it had just been built by union carpenters on a studio lot in Hollywood.

I spent two days with Adrian Foze. We sat for hours on end in the room of the house that he—out of environmental necessity—called his *studio,* drinking and talking, while I waited for the wall to fall away and the camera to truck in for close-ups while the sun-shaded director, in puttees of course, shouted for tears. The atmosphere was so phony that I had a difficult time remembering the lies that I had made up about myself.

It was a parole to get on to Arthur Krafft's studio, a big,

plain building, like a garage with a glass roof. It was a pardon to meet the man himself. Krafft was massive, tall, and big-boned, given now to fat, although he still walked with the deceptive amble that masks the man who can (or could once) move suddenly and surely. His head was big even for so large a body. His hair, cut short, was streaked gray and black, and the beard—several days—was all gray. He wore shapeless, paint-smeared pants and a shirt to match. He met us, glass in hand, at the door of his studio and with unwelcoming cordiality asked us in and offered us a drink. "When Arthur doesn't have a brush in his hand, he has a glass there," Foze had said earlier.

At Krafft's offer of a drink, Foze's hand came up in refusal; I expected to see him extend the index finger and shake it—shame, shame—in Krafft's face. His proprietary step took him past the artist into the center of the studio. I stood at the door; Krafft stayed near me, leaning on the high back of an old rocker, and watched Foze over the rim of his glass. There was amusement in his eyes, and disgust, and a kind of patience. The critic stood in the center of the room, unmoving, purposely ignoring the painting that hung on Krafft's working wall. He began to circle the studio. He ran his hand along the tops of the canvases, stacked, their faces to the wall, against one side of the room, as though he were checking to see that none had been sent away without his permission. He leaned over the table full of paints, lightly putting a finger against one tube (ochre, I'll bet) and wrinkling his nose. He paused in front of the battered dresser on which sat several whisky bottles and shook his head sadly. Catching sight of himself in the dresser mirror, he shook his head again, watching to see if he were communicating the correct degree of personal pain. He stopped finally in front of the picture. "Arthur," he said, the housekeeper reprimanding the upstairs maid, "you haven't done any work for a week."

"So what's that to you, you nosy old woman?" said Krafft.

"Don't snap at me, Arthur."

"I don't snap, Adrian. You snap. I growl."

"Very amusing. Funnies don't get pictures painted, though. You haven't touched this thing for a week."

"Don't let me interrupt a private quarrel," I said, "but hasn't that patch of blue on the upper right just been put on?"

"Thank you for your eyes, Mr. Rosmer," said Krafft. "If there's ever anything I can do for you. . . ."

"You can give me that drink you offered."

"In the morning?" prissed Foze.

"In the morning," bellowed Krafft.

That is how Arthur Krafft and I became momentary allies against Adrian Foze. My remarks look innocent enough, I know, as they stand on paper, but I knew what I was doing. I am still not certain why I was doing it. Perhaps I was jollying Arthur Krafft, the painter, so that I could be ready for Arthur Krafft, the box-seeker. Perhaps I was simply sick of my host and his way of moving in on my every thought and speech, claiming it as his, as he claimed Arthur Krafft's paintings. I may have hoped, somehow, to make a fool of him.

It was impossible to make a fool of Foze. He could not be ruffled. By the time I had my drink in hand and had begun to work up a little enthusiasm for it, he was in command again. "Imagine *my* not noticing that blue," he said.

"You *are* an art critic after all," said Krafft.

"That's just what I mean, Arthur," said Foze. "Well, it looks to me as though it is almost finished."

"Not almost, Foze. Is. Is finished."

A mouth-pursing moment of silence while Foze studied the picture. "It's a fine one, Arthur." He motioned to me. "Come here, Mr. Rosmer. No, stand here." He pointed; I stood. "That's where you can see it best, I think. Now, look at that painting. I call it 'The Caged Bird.' Doesn't that reflect the chaos in the contemporary soul?"

Dear Mrs. Gaines.

I pursed my own lips, thoughtfully, playing his game. Finally I said, "I don't think so, Mr. Foze. The chaos in the contemporary soul is as concrete as a bowl of fruit and I think Mr. Krafft had something else in mind. Nothing else, in fact."

"He's got you there, Adrian," said Krafft. "Why don't you go annoy someone else and let me talk to him? If he's really going to write a book, he might as well make his own mistakes about my work."

"Always the card, Arthur," said Foze, laughing, like ice on a drainboard. But he did leave us alone.

I continued to stand, looking at the picture. Krafft came and stood beside me. "Everyone who writes about art is full of crap," he said.

"Including Foze?"

"Especially Foze."

"Then why do you put up with him?"

"There are all kinds of crap, you know. Foze writes friendly crap about my work and the crap-swallowers swallow it and it does my painting more good on the market than it does it harm on the canvas. So let him go. Besides, he's kind of pathetic. He likes to be around artists and paintings. Sex is mixed up in it, I suppose, but I don't know a damn about all that stuff."

With Foze buried, we turned our attention again to the

painting. "You know, I don't understand this at all," I said. "Why did you put that blue patch in the corner?"

"The picture needed it. It was too light in that corner. The white was pulling the eye up in that direction and finally off the canvas."

"You call that composition?"

"I don't call it composition. Art teachers call it composition. Critics call it composition. You would call it composition. It is composition. But I don't call it anything. I just put the blue in where I need it. Do you want another drink?"

"Yes, I want another drink." He went to the dresser, poured drinks for both of us and joined me again in front of the canvas.

"Let's start out simply," he said. "Do you like it?"

"No," I said. "I don't like it. Do you like it?"

"No," he said. "I don't like it either."

"Then why did you paint it?"

"Because I hoped I would like it. You don't like it because you don't like this kind of picture. You want nudes or flowers or Rembrandt's sad old eyes."

"Those are fine old eyes."

"Granted. But that doesn't change the fact that this is possible too." He pointed to the picture.

"For the moment. But what happens to this in fifty years?"

"I don't know. It would be nice to think that it would become as respectable as Renoir. That all the art-happy students in Eastern girls' colleges would have Arthur Krafft prints on their walls. But I can't worry about that, can I? I have to paint today and this is the way I paint today."

"You never said why you don't like it."

"I don't like it because it didn't do what it was supposed to do."

"You mean it isn't good?"

"Of course, it's good. I don't paint bad paintings. I just mean it didn't do what it was supposed to do for me. Do you know anything about my work over the years?" I shook my head. "I've painted more styles than Picasso. In the thirties I used to paint bread lines so real you could stand in them and real pigs eating real corn on imaginary farms. Good paintings if you like that kind of stuff which nobody does any more. But it didn't do it for me. So I looked around. I have been impressionist, expressionist, surrealist, cubist, and God knows what else. And now I'm one of the authentic voices of the American abstraction movement. That's the way Foze would put it. Do you know why I shop around?"

"I think I do," I said.

"There speaks the art critic."

"I wasn't speaking as an art critic," I said. "I was speaking as a human being. You shop around for the same reason that we all shop around."

"That's more like it." He caught his train of thought where he had dropped it. "You know, every time a smart aleck goes into a gallery and sees a picture he doesn't like, he decides the artist is just being fashionable."

"Some are."

"All right, all right. The jerks are. And there's a lot of jerks painting these days. Any days. But not as many as the jerks outside think there are."

"So you're shopping."

"See this." He held up his glass. "Every time I pour a glass of whisky, I think this is really the glass that is going to quench my thirst." He pulled the glass back as though he were going to throw it at the painting and then turned slightly and smashed it against the wall. "That's a thirst that never gets quenched. Everytime I pick up a paint brush

and move in on a canvas, I think, by God, this is the painting that's going to quench that thirst. It never is. It never
is. That's why I don't like that painting even though it's
a good one."

He grabbed me by the shoulders and shook me as though
I were a small child. "Put that in your book. Put that in
your goddamned book, professor."

He let me go. He slumped, limply, as though he were
completely exhausted. He went to the dresser and took up
another glass. He pointed to mine which had fallen in the
shaking and rolled across the floor. I shook my head. He
held up his new drink, grinning, as if making a toast. "This
may be the one." Then, very softly, "Put that in your
book."

"I'm not writing a book, Mr. Krafft. I came for something else."

"Something else?"

"I came to ask you a question." I walked to the door of
the studio and started to go out.

"So ask it."

I turned. "Not now. I don't need to ask now why your
name is on the list for the ornamental box."

CHAPTER NINE

LONGING IN THE LABORATORY

I HAVE READ enough novels to know about the cleansing effect of the sea. I have seen enough movies to know the efficacy of a wild ride through the night. Having looked into a man's soul, I knew what was expected of me. I should have thrown myself into an automobile, a late-model white convertible, any respectable make—certainly not a 1950 Studebaker sedan—and driven blindly to the ocean, where, stripping (the act symbolical), I should have dived into the waves as they pounded against the shore and emerged later, a tired Odysseus or Huck Finn, all physical exhaustion and innocence.

I could not drive through the night, for it was day. I could not drive at all, not even in my old Studebaker, because my car was back in Adrian Foze's driveway. I could and did walk, because I was not yet ready to fall into Foze's simper and wade with him through the muddle of metaphor and the slough of syntax that filled the landscape of his private world of art. I walked through East Ariel where outsize ladies, in undersized shorts, dragged children and shopping carts through the sun-bright streets, saying, with every familiar gesture of fatigue or exasperation, the holiday is the everyday, the special is the ordinary. A child of five fell headlong over an imaginary obstacle outside MacCarthy's Drug Store, cutting a neat red gash in his right knee, and his mother let go the handle of her shopping cart to scoop him up, like a dipper of ice cream, and race with him into the air-conditioned sanctuary of the drugstore where a touch of Mercurochrome and a Band-aid might work their magic. The abandoned cart tipped over and spilled the top groceries onto the sidewalk. A roast of beef, oozing red through its butcher's paper, rolled into my path and demanded attention. What would Arthur Krafft do, said the roast beef, if he had to prepare three meals a day for a family of five? "He would do what he could," I said, picking up the roast beef and dropping it back in the shopping cart. "He would go on hoping that every meal was going to be the perfect one," I added, dropping the scatter of groceries—a loaf of whole wheat bread, a package of frozen asparagus, a box of Jello—on top of the roast beef. "We all do what we have to," I said into the mouth of the cart as I settled it against the wall of the store, carefully, so that it would not tip again. "Although some of us have a stronger *have to* than others," I finished to the astonished crowd that had gathered to watch me retrieve the worried mother's groceries. "Don't look at me," I said as I walked away. "The roast beef started it."

I must have passed half the population of East Ariel between the drugstore and the beach. I remember only four people. A very old woman stood precariously on a step ladder washing the windows of her cottage. Two boys pitched pennies at a crack. A little girl, a look of complete concentration on her face, skipped her rope, counting . . . 108 . . . 109 . . . 110 . . . 111 . . . . The beach could not have been deserted of a July morning, but I remember only sand and the sea. I looked at the ocean and I had no inclination to strip, symbolically or actually. I had had my plunge and was innocence again. I shrugged at the ocean to show that I knew it had been invented by poets. As I turned back toward Adrian Foze's house, I passed the little girl, still skipping, still counting . . . 78 . . . 79 . . . 80 . . . 81 . . . . How many times had she skipped before missing? I wondered, but I did not stop to ask. Her eyes told me that the last record was not so important as the present attempt. I nodded my applause and went on.

"Where have you been?" demanded Adrian Foze when I got back to his place. I might have been a wandering child or a cheating wife. "I took you to talk to Arthur Krafft and this just came to you . . . from Arthur Krafft. Now, where have you been?"

"Don't ask," I said. "It's all too sordid." His eyes lit up at the possibility.

"But where?" He wheedled a little now, hoping for a story that he might use later. "Did you have a fight with Arthur Krafft?"

"A physical fight?"

"Oh, for heaven's sake, don't beat about the bush. A fight. A fight. Physical, verbal, who cares?"

"No, I never had a fight with Arthur Krafft."

"Then where have you been?"

"You *are* determined. Well, here goes. When I left Arthur Krafft, I took a walk. I had a conversation with a roast beef and watched a little girl skip rope."

"Did you touch?"

"The roast beef, yes; the little girl, no."

"Then what's so sordid?"

"Your questions." He snorted his hurt. "Can I have my message from Mr. Krafft?"

The *this* which had come from Krafft was a large manila envelope with my name . . . oh, well, a name . . . written on the outside. It was for me.

"It's sealed," said Foze. I looked at him over the edge of the envelope. "Oh, well, I just happened to notice."

"Of course," I said, running my finger under the flap.

"Do be careful. There may be a drawing in it."

Foze was right. The envelope did contain a drawing. A cartoon, at least. The heavy head of Arthur Krafft, easily identifiable—no abstraction this—had been hooked onto a tiny body, little more than a stick figure, which was running desperately to catch up with two inanimate objects that had been given legs like the fork and the spoon in the old nursery rhyme. A canvas on two legs and the ornamental box on four were running side by side just out of reach of the straining artist. Underneath the figures Krafft had written, "I call it 'As Well As Not Instead Of.' "

"Of all the idiots," Foze muttered into my ear. "He forgot to sign it. It won't be worth nearly as much unsigned."

"It's a message, not an investment," I said, slipping the picture back into its cover.

After I had put the picture to bed, I had a struggle on my hands—a mild one that I was plainly destined to win. I was ready to leave East Ariel. Foze insisted that I stay the rest of the week, but I pleaded commitments. I could at least stay for lunch, he demanded, and tell him *everything* that had passed between me and Arthur Krafft. I pleaded the creative process: I did not want to talk my book out. Grudgingly, he let me go, making me promise to send him a copy of the book as soon as it came off the presses. And he shall certainly have the first one. That I *did* and *do* swear.

C. M. Rosmer backed his Studebaker out of Adrian Foze's driveway and headed south along the Cape, hoping for the mainland and finally the Midwest, but before he had gone very far the motor coughed despairingly, sputtered once or twice, and stopped completely. Connie Firth was forced to catch a train to get to Detroit and Harvey Williams.

Dr. Driver, whom I met on the first lap of my journey, was a psychoanalyst by trade. He, too, was returning from Cape Cod.

Experts tell me that the psychoanalytic crowd is getting so thick on the Cape that you cannot throw an abstract expressionist without hitting a Jungian. But enough of the folklore.

He was a large, florid man, collapsing into his early forties, with a booming whisper that might have knocked an unwary patient off his couch. He had set up housekeeping in the club car where he greeted me as though I were a newcomer in town and he belonged to Welcome Wagon. "Sit," he said, pointing to the chair next to him. "Sit and make intelligent conversation."

"I'll sit, but you'll have to make the intelligent conversation."

"If I must, I must. What'll you have?" After the drinks were served, he decided to get to the point immediately. "Do you know anything at all about psychology, psychiatry, or psychoanalysis?"

"Not much."

I do know a man who once tried to build his own orgone box out of old beer cans, but I thought it best not to bring him up. Besides, he was badly burned.

"Thank God," said the man. Then he introduced himself, "The name is Driver. Dr. Anthony Driver."

"Charles Seeker," I said. I had not been Charles Seeker for months.

"The trouble with being an analyst, Mr. Seeker, is that everyone wants to talk analysis at me."

"I wouldn't have known you were an analyst, if you hadn't mentioned it."

"You would have guessed. As soon as I said doctor you would have guessed."

"You didn't even have to say *doctor*. If you'd said, *I'm Tony Driver,* I would have supposed you were on your way to a convention."

"After all the years I spent in medical school, I'm supposed to keep it a secret?"

While the introductions were going on, a middle-aged woman came into the club car and took one of the chairs across from us. She was wearing a cloth coat with a fluffy fur collar, the kind that I thought no one wore any more, and carrying an enormous black leather bag. She slipped out of the coat, turning the right sleeve inside out as she withdrew her arm. She let the coat fall over the left arm of the chair once she was completely free of it. The fur collar dragged on the floor. She opened her purse and rummaged inside for cigarettes and matches. Having found them, she set the purse down, unfastened, on the small metal ash tray table in front of her and the contents poured out. She went unconcernedly about the business of lighting her cigarette, while the lipsticks, coins, pencils, Godknowswhat spilled across the table and dropped into the holes that were waiting to receive drinks from the bar.

"Look at that," muttered Dr. Driver. "What kind of toilet training do you suppose she had?"

I could not say. I never remember whether rigid training makes you sloppy and sloppy training makes you rigid or rigid training makes you rigid and sloppy training makes you sloppy. All I knew for certain was that whatever kind of training the lady had had, Dr. Driver had had the opposite in spades. He chafed visibly at the clutter of her spilled purse. Finally he said, "Pardon me, madam, may I help you retrieve your belongings?"

"Oh, don't bother," she said with a wave of her hand that said *oh don't bother.* "I'll just spill it all again." She pulled the coat out from under her and made a stab at putting it across the back of the chair. It slipped off and settled in a heap on the floor. A look of real distress crossed the psychoanalyst's face.

"I don't think I can stand it," he whispered to me.

"Don't look. Pretend she's not there. Aren't healthy illusions allowable in your trade these days?"

He turned toward me and kept his eyes on my face, talking animatedly about the necessity of social adjustment or some such nonpsychological matter, until I warned him that the lady had retrieved her property and gone back to her car.

Her place was taken by an attractive woman who worked obviously at the business of attraction. Her accidents did not expose the contents of her purse. When she slipped out of her coat, she held her arms far behind her, thrusting her ample bosom up and out, straining her breasts against the top of the dress that barely covered them. When she, having found her cigarettes, put her purse on the table, she did so carefully, leaning far forward so that the doctor and I could look down the front of her dress without straining. Of course, she had no match, so she had to lean forward again, a cigarette provocatively on the edge of her lips, and to murmur, like a bad movie, "May I have a light?" The cigarette lit, she sat back, inhaling, and crossed her legs, pausing long enough before completing the cross to give a glimpse of the dark at the top of the stairs. I was in no mood to go climbing and Dr. Driver was off sliding down some banister of his own.

"Compulsive need to expose herself," he whispered. "Bad case."

"Economic need to expose herself," I whispered back. "Professional."

"Oversimplification," he insisted and went on to explain why his analysis was correct. While he talked, an executive type, apparently with an expense account compartment and without Dr. Driver's doubts in the matter, walked over to the woman, leaned down, and said a few words. After which, the two of them left the club car together.

"One for Marx," I said. "Maybe Freud will mark in the next frame."

The chair across from us remained empty. Dr. Driver with no new outside material turned his attention to me. I wondered momentarily if I should invent a good story to titillate him, but I could think of nothing on the spur of the moment quite so provocative as the truth. When he wanted to know what I was up to, I said quite honestly, "I'm looking for a box."

"My God, a coffin. Death wish."

"How about a womb?"

"Same thing. You obviously want to get away, to escape reality."

"Of course, I do. Don't we all?"

"Don't confuse the issue. The problem here is you and your failure to adjust. Have you ever been analyzed?"

"No." I thought a moment. "My handwriting has if that's any help."

"Don't be facetious. This is serious. Here you are a man

in middle age"—that crack did not go down too well with me—"refusing to accept your place emotionally, in the world in which you are forced to live. Analysis would help you adjust."

"There are two possibilities, it seems to me. I can adjust to the world, or the world can adjust to me. The last seems more sensible."

"That way lies madness."

"It's the way of the revolutionary. And of the poet."

I was on the point of making a speech, but I was saved by the reappearance of the fur-collared lady with the inappropriate toilet training. She scattered her belongings like seed. Before she had time to settle amid her debris, Dr. Driver leaped to his feet crying, "I can't stand it," and ran out of the club car.

"What's the matter with that guy?" said the lady, letting the contents of her purse fall to the floor, as she watched him disappear. "He ought to see a psychoanalyst."

I never saw Dr. Driver again. He is safe, I suppose, in his office, which is almost certainly kept spotless by a compulsively neat nurse whom he hires for her neurosis.

I met John Karome in the diner, over breakfast coffee, when Detroit was barely an hour away. He had that washed and pressed look that goes with men in the advertising business, but, disconcertingly, he was reading a chemical journal.

He spoke first. "I try to keep up." He held the journal out in front of him and lightly turned his wrist, waving the magazine slightly, like a practiced bidder with the auction catalogue, a gesture that whispered, did not shout, its message. He put his banner down beside his place. His desire to keep up, I noticed, did not stop him from breaking off in the middle of an article.

With a mouthful of coffee in me and no more than the usual grievances against the world, I said, without even a trace of irony, "That's admirable."

"Yes, I was a chemist, you know." I did not know, but I hardly felt like quibbling. "Still—as I always say to Harvey —someone has to do our job."

"I shouldn't wonder." My mind was really on my coffee, or I would have caught the name Harvey. Coincidence had worked well enough for me this far; there was no reason why it should break down now.

"Not that he blames me."

"For what?"

"For shifting into the publicity end. Oh, I didn't mention. I'm John Karome. I'm in publicity out at Galaxy Motors."

"You write all that stuff about the new automobiles? Dyna-magi-miraflow, with knee-action exhaust and knee-room second gears. Big-car prices with small-car comforts. That sort of thing?"

"Oh, no. I'm in the chemical end. Galaxy does everything, you know." This I did know; I read *Fortune*. "I do publicity for the chemical stuff. In this day and age—as I always say to Harvey—it isn't enough to discover, you have to sell. I sell."

"You're in sales, too?"

"Not that kind of *sell*. I mean spread the word around. I could have stayed in the laboratory, like Harvey, but somebody has to let the world know what's going on there. That's where I come in."

"What does Harvey say?"

"He says, it's your life, John. That's what Harvey says."

"Sounds a little nasty to me."

"Oh, no, not Harvey."

"Who is this Harvey? Is he your brother or something?"

"Well, almost, I guess. I've known Harvey for years. We went to high school together and then we went to college together. I was best man at his wedding and he was best man at my wedding. That was my first marriage. When we were still at Ann Arbor. We're both chemists. I was one, I mean, and we went to work for Galaxy and so we're almost like brothers you see. Except I don't see him much any more. Melinda says it's just too much trouble to get into town to see Harvey and his wife. We live out, you know. Toward Bloomfield Hills."

"In Bloomfield Hills?"

"Toward. Not in. Melinda thought we ought to move in that direction." There was nothing for me to say, but he went on without my priming him. "I was never as good a chemist as Harvey, you know. That's why I got out. That and the money. And Melinda. Not that Harvey blames me."

"Why should he blame you?"

"Well, Harvey and I kind of thought being chemists was being something important." He laughed suddenly, without amusement. "Only you know what he's working on now —has been for years?" I shook my head. "A fertilizer. That's funny. All our talk about cures for this and cures for that, and Harvey's working on a fertilizer. He doesn't see the joke of it."

"There's a serious side to fertilizer, too," I said. "Even to natural fertilizer."

"Maybe you're right. Anyway, there I sit out in that big place with Melinda and my expense account and all that, and there sits Harvey Williams"—I did hear clearly this time—"in a worn-out two-story house in a tacky neighborhood with his wife and three kids and his damned fertilizer. But he doesn't envy me very much." In silence, he signaled for the steward, settled the bill, picked up his journal, and scraped his chair away from the table. Standing, he paused and said, smiling limply, holding out the magazine, "I try to keep up."

The street I found when I went in search of Harvey Williams was lined with solid, middle-class houses, built probably in the twenties. It was as quiet and pleasant as the trees that lined it. The children, some white, some Negro, that played in front of the houses were involved in those games—cowboy, skiprope, catch—that could be carried on comfortably under the ever-watchful eyes of mothers who called now and then to keep out of the street, off the lawn, close to home. The block was caught at that moment of suspension, after the street has been safely open to Negroes, after the panicky whites have moved, when the remaining residents—white and Negro—suspect, hope even, that a balance has been achieved and that they can all live comfortably together, before the howling need for decent homes rises more strongly in Paradise Valley and the remaining whites are forced out to the edges of the city.

Harvey Williams' house stood in the center of the block; it was, as John Karome had said, two stories high. It was also closed, or seemed to be, except that two boys were pushing toy cars across the cement porch.

"Hi," I said, but they did not look up. Absorbed in their automobiles, or warned by their mother not to talk to strangers? "Hi," I repeated. "Does Harvey Williams live here?"

"Mickey lives here," said one of them. "And Tom. He's big."

"And Red," said the other one. "He's a dog."

"Are they home now?" One of the boys shook his head; the other one did not offer even a shake. "Do you know where they are now? Mickey and Tom and Red?" No answer.

"Are you looking for Mrs. Williams?" A woman's voice, from the porch next door. "They're on vacation. Won't be back for three weeks."

"Do you know where they went?"

"They go to one of the lakes, but I never remember the name. My husband knows, but he's not at home."

"Oh, well. It can wait."

As soon as I had said that it could wait, I knew that it could. No use tracing a vacationing chemist to his lakeside lair. Confrontations are always possible. Confrontations? Confrontations was right, by God. I holed up in an air-conditioned hotel room in Detroit, coming out only to eat or to visit Dearborn Village or something foolish like that; so I had time to ask myself where I got off dragging my ass all over the country, like some spook from a Shakespeare play, whispering, *swear, swear,* to men and women whom I did not know and who could never know me. I had decided to sell my interest in the ornamental box to oblivion, to burn the list and go somewhere—anywhere—when boredom pulled me out of the hotel to Belle Isle Park. I elbowed my way through the crowds at the zoo and, then, tiring of that, I walked down one of the paths that led away from the masses of people. I sat for a moment on the grass, resting, paying no attention to anything, when the song of a bird came to me from one of the trees. I did not know what kind of bird was singing, but I knew that whatever branch he sat on was really an ornamental box I had once held in my hand. And I knew that I could no more leave Detroit than I could fly up into the tree and join my voice to his.

On an evening, three weeks and two days after I first set foot on Harvey Williams' street, I was back again in front of his house.

So was Harvey Williams. At least I assumed that the man cutting the lawn was the master of the house. There is something in the way that a man handles a lawn mower—at least the old-fashioned hand-propelled variety—that stamps him as owner or stranger. The householder does not cut with the neat efficiency of the regular yard man or the indifference of the casual worker, but with an uneven mixture of love and vexation that allows some corners to be cut and recut carefully, fondled and cared for, and others —those that come last in the cutting—to be only poked at, a token touch of wheel and blade.

Nothing that John Karome had said prepared me for Harvey Williams' being a Negro. I was never to understand how Karome, who seemed like the kind of man whose every idea, every prejudice is prepacked and standard brand (except for that nagging sense of having deserted), could have stumbled into a friendship with Williams—a hero worship with reverse English—that had survived adolescence, college, and a first marriage, only to wither—not die, never die—under a second and success. Melinda was easy enough to figure. Her reluctance to visit her husband's oldest friend in town was not a matter of geography, as he had said, or of economics, as I had supposed.

Karome had seemed indefinitely middle-aged over the dining table. Williams seemed indefinitely young as he pushed the mower across the lawn. They were both, I suppose, in the hazy years on the near side—my side—of forty where the perennially young have not yet started to go at the seams and where the others already show their age. In his dress, his movement, his concern with his lawn, his backdrop—the house, the street, the family hidden somewhere inside—in everything but his color, Harvey Williams was the perfect middle-class father from the *Saturday Evening Post* advertisement. He was stabbing the mower under the edge of a rosebush, trying to top the tall grass along the flower bed's border—it could only be done on the knees with a clipper—when I interrupted him.

"Are you Harvey Williams?"

"Yes." He left the mower—gladly, I think, from the way he let go the handles—and walked to where I stood on the sidewalk.

"I'm E. D. Anodyne. I understand you're doing some interesting work in fertilizer."

He was immediately suspicious. Perhaps you cannot simply walk up to a man and start talking fertilizer. For all I know, there may be fertilizer spies. Perhaps—more likely —he had old and visceral reasons for distrusting strangers who used fertilizer or anything—even harmless or curative —as an opening gambit. He said only, "Where did you hear that I was working in fertilizer?"

"From John Karome."

"And what did you find out from Johnny?"

"That you were doing . . .

". . . some interesting work in fertilizer. Yeh, we got that far. But what?"

"I hoped to get the details from you."

"I'm not at work as you can see. You arrange with Johnny Karome to come to the lab one day and I'll explain what I'm up to." He walked back to the lawn mower. "Good evening, Mr. Anodyne."

"I didn't do that very well, did I?"

"Do what?"

"Get into a casual conversation with you so that I could gradually work my way around to the reason I came to see you."

He walked back to me. "I didn't think you were interested in fertilizer." His voice was harsh now. "All right, what is it you want? Are you from Oak Park? Have you heard that I was asking about a house out there?"

"No, I'm not from Oak Park. I was there once and I can testify that the trees are better and bigger here. But if you want to live under little trees in Oak Park and if someone sells you a house out there, that's your lookout."

"Then what neighborhood do you represent, Mr. Anodyne?"

"The neighborhood I represent, Mr. Williams, you already live in and will live in even if you move to Oak Park."

"No riddles. Please, no riddles."

"Your not wanting a riddle won't make it less a riddle. I came about the ornamental box."

"The box! What about it?" He was trying to speak calmly still, but excitement—fear maybe—quickened his words. "Don't tell me that list is restricted now?"

"Not that I know of."

Relief. A little relief. "What brings you to me then—to me—out of all the possibilities?"

"Don't be vain, Mr. Williams. What makes you think I haven't been to others on the list? For that matter, what makes you think I have so many people to choose from? Have you seen the list?"

"No, but I've seen the box. Everyone must want the box."

"I don't think so. Everyone hasn't seen the box. Every-

one cannot have felt what we felt when we held the box
. . ."

"You've held it, too?"

"Of course. You're a scientist, Mr. Williams. What is it about that box?"

"There are three possibilities, only one of which is a possibility. Either the box is alive, which is impossible, or has something alive in it, which, since there are no air holes, is also impossible. The real possibility is that what we hold is illusion, our own life transferred to the box."

"Or that all three are true. Isn't that a possibility? Hang onto that, Mr. Williams. That should please the scientist and the child in you."

"The scientist is the child in me."

"Then fertilizer wasn't irrelevant, after all. So few things are."

"It wasn't always going to be fertilizer. It was once going to be a cure for something."

"Even a fertilizer might be a cure for something."

"Only a temporary alleviate. Like Johnny Karome's friendship."

"Or a house in Oak Park?"

"Yes, or a house in Oak Park."

A voice from the front porch—"What are you doing out there on the steps, Harvey?"—reminded us that we had sunk, unthinkingly, to the front steps where we sat, talking, in the dusk that was turning to night.

"Come inside, stranger," said Harvey, "and talk about something innocuous like baseball or the movies."

"O.K., stranger," I agreed. As we started up the steps, he put his arm about my shoulders . . . tentatively.

CHAPTER TEN

THERE'LL BE PIE

THE NOVELTY of Harvey Williams, for me, was his family. All the other names to whom my travels had given flesh were loners—as I am—men and women who had discovered that you can accept no substitutes and who had gone on accepting them and transforming them, with limitations—oh, the hedge of the ornamental box—into the finally genuine. Candy Stick had her Angela, of course, and P. R. Eferred has his phalanx of secretaries, but these were finally decoration. Integral they were not.

The uniqueness of Harvey Williams did not strike me that first night when we—strangers both and still—went into his house and joined his wife in a summer drink. Perhaps it was because essential differences must always wait on apparent ones. More than likely, it was simply that the children were already in bed. Tom, the big one, according to my car-pushing informants of three weeks earlier, was a tall seven; Mickey was five; the daughter, whom the boys on the porch had failed to mention, probably because she was only a girl and barely three years old into the bargain, was called Nella, after her mother. All this I learned as we talked that first evening—not about movies or baseball, but also not about ornamental boxes, or fertilizer, or homes in Oak Park.

I was introduced as a stranger in town—accurate enough heaven knows, and in any town—and a friend of Johnny

Karome—stretching a train breakfast into a blood pact. If I remained something of a mystery to Nella during our brief
. . .

Oh, hell, use the word.

. . . friendship, she was difficult enough to understand on that first night. I could fit her into no neat category, not at least until the next day.

The label is godsend. If you can stamp "shrew" or "mother's boy" or "do-gooder" on the forehead of a person at a first meeting, you are saved the effort of discovery. The exploration into self is so hazardous a journey that you are likely to outrun your supply lines; how can you afford side trips into strangers? Post lands and post them quickly and if the sign is the wrong one no one knows unless he is looking out from the inside.

Nella was an extremely attractive woman, dressed in a summer cotton, but the simplicity seemed to be planned to pull your eye away from her to the room, the house as a whole. She gave every impression of intelligence and she had a quick sense of humor, a laugh ahead of the scientist, the husband, but these qualities too were muted. It was as though she were saying, *not me, not me,* watching to see that I got the message, as the three of us sat in the consciously correct living room, drinking gin and tonic, with the dog Red—a mongrel, picked up by Harvey at the pound —at our feet.

The next day confirmed what I only sensed that night. "Come back tomorrow for dinner," said Nella. "We're going to try a cook-out."

"She made me build a grill in the yard," said Harvey. "She got it from some magazine."

When I saw Nella in the back yard the next afternoon, I finally did get the message. The well-spread table, the three smiling children, the romping dog, the husband at the grill (in an apron)—the image of the American family, invented by spinsters and divorcees who live in expensive furnished apartments, childless and grill-less with blooded toy dogs instead of cheerful mutts. Nella played actively at that image. She *had* been saying *not me, not me,* which is another way of saying *us, us, us.*

Because an image is active does not mean that it is not also actual. I know a preacher who plays at being a preacher and is a preacher.

Harvey Williams' family *was* a family. I do not know what prompted Nella to ask me to come to their picnic on the lawn. I suspect that she asked the friend of John Karome—*go tell that second wife of his how we live!*—but I prefer to think that she asked the stranger in town. Whatever the motive, I was glad of the invitation. Within a short time I—well, E. D. Anodyne anyway—was a stranger no more.

I played catch with Tom. I was proficient enough, thank God, not to look too foolish against the skill of his seven years, and not so expert that I got bored with the endless back-and-forth, back-and-forth, back-and-forth. I was lured away by Mickey to crawl on my hands and knees around the roots of a big old maple, pushing tiny cars through underpasses built by nature, with an assist from his five-year-old hands and a sharp-pointed stick. I let the young Nella tell me a complicated story involving names that I did not know and would never know, and I let the older Nella draft me into carrying paper plates and pastel napkins to the card tables set up in the back yard. I turned the steaks for Harvey while he checked to see if the ice had finally cooled the beer. At last, having eaten well, I moved a little out of the charmed circle and sat to one side, my back against Mickey's maple, and felt a little sorry for myself as I watched the five of them, a unit, around the tables.

Deception in the summer's sun? Even if the quest for fertilizer were not enough, why shouldn't the fact of family —here, now, touchable, not Annette Despere's memories— be enough? Since all Adams are little boys who carry snakes around in their pockets, all Edens have their serpents. I had a vision under that maple tree: the ornamental box as snake trap.

I saw the Williamses a few times after the picnic in their backyard. I had to go on playing my own pretend, wearing the Anodyne label that I had slipped on at our first meeting. I can be almost anyone for a short time and I can be someone else for a longer time if another plays the game with me, as I was Will to Candy Stick's Sylvia, but I cannot lose Connie Firth forever. Connie returned which meant that I moved on. I would have had to go in any case. Even Connie Firth could not have been for long tangent to a family circle. There is in and there is out and that is all.

Besides there was a woman to see in Chicago—Patsy Werkman. Or a man? Well, maybe . . . Constance, after all.

Even after I said good-by to Harvey and his family— "Take any wooden boxes you can get," he said—I stayed around Detroit. Unconscious celebration, perhaps, because it was almost Labor Day. When that day came, however, I never made it to any of the formal celebrations where labor leaders and imported politicians joined their voices in bromidic chorus to a victory long since won. I had watched the newspapers for details of time and place, but when the time came I was not in any of the places. The heat that had forced the mobile young to beaches over on the Canadian side of the river had forced me into a bar in Hamtramck.

It was early afternoon and the place was almost deserted. A big man, in shirt sleeves, a touch of gray at his hair, stood at the bar, using the occasion of the day to tell again a story that he had told many times before . . . 1941 and the Ford strike, how he had fought and with whom, and how it had all been gravy in Detroit since then.

"Gravy my ass," said a young man. "How about '56? That's the year I lost my house. How about since '56? Who knows he's working?"

"I know I'm working," said the storyteller.

"Working and talking, sure. You're just like my old man. You guys sit around on your seniority and make speeches about how it was back in the depression." He flipped the collar of his summer shirt up at the neck and held it in front with both hands, as though it were a threadbare coat, his only defense against the winter of 1932, and, hunching his back, began to quaver, "You young smart alecks don't know what tough times is. Why back in '33 a family of four had to live for three weeks on a jar of peanut butter and a box of Kleenex." He stood up, smoothing his collar back down. "Shit on that old man. I wasn't even born in 1933."

The older man cocked his fist. Not a threat. Simply a gesture of dismissal, of disavowal, saying *no son of mine* . . . Aloud, pushed through clenched teeth, "I ought to break your back, you young poop."

"You couldn't break a cherry, you old poop."

"I can outfuck you any day in the week, sonny."

"Well, now. Well, now. Will you listen to this old man talk? Come on, pop, admit you couldn't get it up without an overhead hoist."

Next only to having his sexual prowess praised, a man likes to have it doubted. It looked as though the quarrel would dissolve in a bath of good feeling. And it would have, if the older man had not added, "I can outfight you, too. And what's more I can outwork you. None of you young punks can do a real day's work. Coffee break. Smoke break. Pee break. You'd take off every hour if they'd let you."

"And so would you, and you damn well know it. Don't tell me you work because you love the company. You work for the money they pay you and anything you can steal."

"What do you mean, steal?"

"This old man's got the only house that uses hub caps for ash trays."

"You just try getting a hub cap out the gates." That was the line that got the laugh, but it was not a laugh the speaker wanted. "This used to be a pretty good bar," he said to the bartender, "before these lazy-ass kids started filling it up. I'll leave them to you. I'm going home."

"Time for your nap?" asked the young man.

The older man did not answer. It was not that he was playing it for dignity, the silent exit that capped the young man's crack; it was simply that he could not think of an answer and did not want to risk a second wrong laugh. "See you tomorrow," the young man called after him as he got to the door.

"Tomorrow," he said, lifting his hand. He disappeared smiling.

"Jesus, that old man shoots the bull." The speaker was a man who had been sitting alone at a table, playing with an almost empty beer glass while he listened to the story and the argument. Now he joined us at the bar, holding out the empty for a refill.

The older man's opponent, turned suddenly ally, wheeled on the newcomer. "What do you mean, bull?"

"Bull means bull, doesn't it? The old crapola. All that stuff about 1941. Hell, that's almost twenty years ago."

"Look, trucker, that old man was in the Ford Strike and that was a rough one, let me clue you."

"So who cares?"

"So he cares. So I care. I'm a friend of his." He paused for a long drink of beer and when he spoke again his voice was soft with nostalgia for a time he could not have known. "In those days at least they could do something. Now we just stand around while the big boys talk."

"That's right," grinned the trucker. "You boys belong to the talking union."

"Better that than the stealing union."

"I been working steady and the pay's good. What have your honest Johns done for you?"

"For Christ's sake," the bartender broke in, "why don't you two knock it off. What's all this union chatter? You senators or something? Don't you know it's Labor Day? Talk about baseball. Tell a dirty joke."

"That's right, trucker," said the auto worker. "Tell us some lies about the women who spread for you between here and Chicago."

"Chicago?" I asked.

"That's right," said the trucker. "Red Bird Express. Detroit to Chicago every three days. I go tonight." He stopped to wonder why he was pouring out information at me as though I were a traffic cop. "If it's any business of yours."

"I have to go to Chicago," I said. "I was interested."

"Can't give you a ride. Company rule. Union rule, too."

"Well, ain't he a nice one," said the auto worker. "Mama's little boy here always obeys the rules." He began to mince up and down in front of the bar. "I'm sorry, dear, but I just can't go against the big old company and the big old union." He slipped back into his normal voice. "For God's sake, give the man a ride."

"I told you there's a rule . . . ."

The auto worker choked over his beer. Sputtering in mock hysteria, he pointed derisively, "Get him. Get the big, tough trucker."

"O.K., O.K., I'll give the man a ride." To me, "You be out in front of this bar at eight o'clock, buddy, and I'll take you to Chicago."

I should have refused, should have let him off the hook, but he stood there pointing and preening at once and I found myself saying, "Thanks. I'll be here."

"Though I must be nuts to do it. If they catch me with a passenger, it's my ass."

"That's what you were going to tell us about," said the auto worker.

"What? Oh, yeh . . . well, there was this dame in Niles . . ."

I felt like a fool for being there, but at eight o'clock I was standing, suitcase in hand, outside the Hamtramck bar. I did not really believe that the trucker would show at all and, what's more, I would have been happy if he had gone back on his word. There is one moment in every boy's life when he dreams of being a trucker himself, of shepherding one of those motored monsters across the night highways, making incredible turns on mythical dimes, saving families of eight from death beneath his wheels. That moment had passed for me twenty-five years earlier. I knew now that a trucker is a man who puts in miles as other men put in hours. The only break in the routine of road disappearing beneath his headlights is a stop where he can get a cup of coffee, take a shower, greet another driver, kid an unresponsive counter girl, and buy a T shirt for his seven-year-old with MY DADDY IS A TRUCKER written across the front. The romance had gone out of it. I had hitchhiked with enough rule-breaking drivers to know disenchantment. But there I stood, as Labor Day died in the dusk, and waited for my ride.

It came. It was nothing so ponderous as a trailer truck, but it moved hugely down Conant Avenue, promising me almost three hundred miles of discomfort. REDBIRD EXPRESS was painted in giant letters across its side, with *Detroit, Michigan* and an address printed in smaller letters in one corner. The redbird itself, as tall as a man, as formless as a sign painter's skill, sang in soundless joy from its perch on the truck's side, its huge beak open to the gas fumes and the dust of the road. I had visions of its coughing its way out of a contract.

"It'll be my ass," was my host's greeting. "Get in. Get in."

"Have a good trip," came a voice behind me. The auto worker stood, smiling, not at me, but at the driver. "I thought I'd stroll down to see you off, trucker."

"Up yours," said the driver.

Above the noise of the motor, I heard one last shout, "Have a good time in Niles."

The ride was a long and a dull one. Danny Ridjiesc— that was my trucker's name . . .

How did he suddenly get to be *my* trucker? We acquire. We acquire.

. . . had seemed garrulous enough that afternoon in the bar, but now he was clammed over the steering wheel, his eyes

on the road, his mouth shut. Forced by direct questions—
"how long you been driving?"—he pushed out monosylla-
bles resentfully—"five years"—as though I were someone
from the welfare office and he had asked for relief. On one
of our stops the man at the cash register asked, "What's
that you got with you, Danny?" He nodded at me. "You
don't have a relief man on your run."

Danny, whose only lies were sexual, stumbled into an
embarrassed stammer, from which I, a better liar, retrieved
him. "They may put me on this run," I said. "They figured
I ought to see it once with a good driver."

"If you do come this way, don't forget us."

"Well," I said, honestly, although he mistook my meaning, "I'll never forget your coffee."

Outside, Danny thanked me for pulling him out of a
tight spot. "That guy mouths to everyone who comes into
his place. Everybody on the road would know that I had a
passenger if you hadn't made up that story. You're O.K."

O.K., I may have been, but not enough to start him talking. So that was it. Ordinary fear, like that that a junior
executive feels when the man above him sees him lunching
in a place too cheap or too costly for his expense account.
Fear that runs to the first open arms for shelter, whether
sanctuary lies there or not. My lie, after all, was so flimsy
that if there was really danger of word getting back to a
company or a union that cared, his job was still not safe.

I found myself angry. At him. At me. At the world. *What
are these rules,* I wanted to shout into the night, *that make
so big a man walk tippy-toe across an eggshell landscape?
Who are you,* I wanted to shout at me, *that you should take
a ride you do not need, carrying panic like a Typhoid Mary?
What kind of man are you,* I wanted to shout at him, *that
you let yourself be shamed into an unnecessary act?*

What I did say was, "Do you have a son?"

"Yeh. Nine years old."

"Suppose some kid dared him to fight and he didn't want to because the kid was bigger or tougher or faster than him. Because he knew he would be beaten up. What would you tell him? Fight or not fight?"

"Fight. What else could I tell him?"

"That's what I thought."

So what was I, after all, but a black eye carried away from a corner fight.

It was just as well that by this time we were coming into Chicago, floating down from the roadways on stilts, passing distant foundries and clusters of cottages, bumping finally into deserted Stony Island, where he said, "Do you mind if I drop you here? I don't want to take you on downtown."

"I know," I said. "It would be your ass . . ." I thanked him and said good-by.

Don't misunderstand me. I was quite ready to leave the nervous Danny, but I do not think that I would have agreed so quickly to being left in Stony Island in the middle of the night if I had not seen an idle taxi parked along the curb. The driver was so deep in the *Sun-Times* that he did not even look up as I approached him.

"Are you free?" I asked.

"Sorry, Mac. I'm through for the night." His head still in the newspaper.

I had to argue. "I'm stuck here if you don't give me a ride. I just got out of a truck . . ."

"Out of a truck?" His interest pulled his eyes into my face. "Firth, my benefactor," he shouted.

"Johnny Bucks, the poet," I shouted back. It was like running into an American in a French cathedral town.

"Johnny Bucks, the taxi driver," he said. "Get in and I'll tell you the story of my life."

"You already told me that story."

"Not lately. Not the latest installment. You remember what happened to Saul on the way to Damascus. That light and a voice from heaven: *You don't have to be a poet at all.* Man . . . oop, sorry . . . it's hard to get it out of the blood . . . anyway, I went around for days with my head under my arm. Then, one day, I heard your words clear and fresh and sweet across the meadow . . ."

"A meadow in Chicago?"

"O.K., Grant Park. The words blew in from the Chicago Basin."

"I *had* gone east."

"That's the idea. I walked out of that night club I told you about . . . where, I might add, I was bombing . . . and got myself a job as a taxi driver."

"And?"

"And, dammit, I like it. I'm a good driver. I was a lousy poet. How about you? Are you still on your mysterious business?"

"Mysterious business? What mysterious business?"

"Don't kid me, Firth. I'm an old con man myself. I always knew you were up to something you couldn't talk about. No one who had anything he could talk about would have let me go on and on and on the way you did when we whipped across the northern plains."

I smiled a smile that was supposed to say *that's nonsense, but let's play it your way.* I actually said, "All right. I am on mysterious business, but I still can't talk about it. Do you suppose you could drive me to a hotel where I could find a pillow for my tiny head?"

"I could do better than that. I could take you to my place and give you a pillow of my own. Besides I want you to meet my wife."

"Wife? What wife?"

"My wife."

"When I left you on the Fourth of July you were a single man—a divorced one, at least. It is now Labor Day and you're married?"

"A working man needs a helpmate. Besides we're not completely married." I must have looked incredulous. "Consummated, yes. Legalized, no. We'll take care of that soon. You will come and stay with us."

"No, I'm afraid not. I will come and have dinner with you some day when you're not hacking. I'll let the two of you show me—God forbid—the sights of Chicago. I'll even offer myself as best man or ring bearer or flower girl if this wedding ever gets off the ground. But I will not move in on your honeymoon home. Do I make sense?"

"Sense of a sort," he admitted. "What kind of hotel you want? What can you afford?"

"I'm still solvent . . ."

I was not Solvent, nor had I ever been. People who knew us both might have noticed a human resemblance.

"Yes?" he said into my hesitancy.

"I can afford comfort. Downtown, I think. Something solid with the look of the twenties about it—the Stevens, maybe, or the Palmer House."

"Why the twenties?"

"I'm retrogressing. I had the thirties yesterday."

"I won't understand you if I live to be six."

Without waiting for understanding, he drove me to the Loop and let me out. I paid him in a promise to see him soon. By way of change, he forced the *Sun-Times* into my hands. "Here. Learn to know and love your adopted city."

□   □

Checking into a hotel in the middle of the night, I would not have thought of buying a paper. Still, there the *Sun-Times* was in my hand and there I was going up in an elevator. I had either to study the bellboy, who looked tired and cross, and the elevator man, who was no happier, or I had to occupy myself with the front page. I chose the newspaper, and looked, unseeing, at a full-page picture of a large man, smiling crookedly, ducking his way through the white anger of flashbulbs. Beneath the picture, in heavy type, were the words LOCAL LABOR LEADER LEAVES COMMITTEE. I was too tired for the small print that followed the caption. It was all I could do to wonder why the man on the copy desk had not found one more L to complete the alliteration and to mutter to myself about how the same guy seemed always to be coming from the same committee in the blare of the same flashbulbs. My eyes wandered to the back of the bellboy's head (he needed a haircut) and stayed there until the elevator gentled onto the correct floor and the shaggy-headed bag carrier led me down a hallway.

After I had made the bellboy disappear—by making the magic sign—passing a half buck into his hand—I climbed under a shower to let the ache and dust of the Redbird Express soak out of my body. I came out refreshed and—I had not planned this—completely sleepless. I walked back and forth across the room trying to decide to go out into the night streets of Chicago in search of food—or something —when my eye found the newspaper where I had thrown it on the bed. I stretched out on the bed, the paper in hand, to follow Johnny Bucks's admonition. A name screamed out of the small print that I had so pointedly ignored on the elevator: Patsy Werkman.

There she was, only of course she was not she, but he,

and the big man smiling and bobbing past the photographers.

Inside, under the headline PATSY CHARGES CORRUPTION was a by-lined story:

Washington, Sept. 7—Before a surprise Labor Day hearing, Patsy Werkman, vice-president of the International Bag and Burlap Workers, told a Senate subcommittee investigating corruption in industry and labor that Simon Oliff, international union president, had accepted five thousand dollars from Bayswater Bags, Inc. In exchange, Werkman charged, Oliff agreed to keep workers from striking in the Bayswater and Croydon plants.

Werkman, president of Chicago Local 409, said in a prepared statement, "Simon Oliff has hurt the reputation of every member of International Bag and Burlap. His usefulness to the union is at an end."

There was Patsy Werkman in the limelight in Washington and here was I in bed in Chicago. I did what I could. I went to sleep.

If this were an intimate diary, the day-by-day, moment-by-moment account of my life during the months in which I was entangled with the ornamental box, I would cheerfully give the details of the next week or so. I would tell what hours I spent in the John Crerar Library reading comparative physiology and how long I stood outside of Carson Pirie Scott wondering why they do not build department stores like that any longer, but you quickly get the point. I did not go to Washington. Wisely, as it turned out, for Patsy Werkman's play for power was to take him to several cities before he came home, decked with honors. If you do not count my attendance at Johnny Bucks's wedding, the only activity of mine that was in any way relevant to this story was my faithful trailing of Werkman through the daily papers. The headlines tell the story.

St. Louis, Sept. 8:   'IS THIS A JOKE, PATSY?': OLIFF
Bayswater, Sept. 9:   B. BAGS SAYS NO CHECK PASSED
Washington, Sept. 10:   PATSY PRODUCES EVIDENCE
St. Louis, Sept. 11:   OLIFF COUNTERCHARGES CORRUPTION
Washington, Sept. 12:   'OLIFF RUNNING SCARED': WERKMAN
Washington, Sept. 13:   OLIFF ARRIVES WASHINGTON
Miami, Sept. 14:   AFL-CIO MAY DROP BAG & BURLAP
Washington, Sept. 15:   OLIFF HINTS PATSY IN DEAL
Washington, Sept. 16:   BELOIT FIRM INVOLVED
Beloit, Sept. 17:   BELOIT SAYS NO DEAL
Miami, Sept. 18:   PATSY ARRIVES MIAMI
Miami, Sept. 19:   PATSY IN SECRET SESSION
Miami, Sept. 20:   'PATSY CLEAN': AFL-CIO
Washington, Sept. 21:   OLIFF CHARGES POLITICS
Miami, Sept. 22:   AFL-CIO DEMAND OLIFF GO
Cleveland, Sept. 23:   BAG AND BURLAP CONVENTION
Cleveland, Sept. 24:   OLIFF ARRIVES CLEVELAND
Cleveland, Sept. 25:   PATSY RECEIVES OVATION
Cleveland, Sept. 26:   OUST OLIFF MOVEMENT
Cleveland, Sept. 27:   PATSY HOLDING BAG

Patsy Werkman had replaced Simon Oliff as president of the International Bag and Burlap Workers. He arrived in Chicago on September 28 and made statements at the airport about the ethics of the labor movement and the need for constant vigilance within the unions.

The day after the new president came home, I turned up at union headquarters. The place was manic. Old union men and new public relations men trampled each other in the press to see or to be seen. Busy secretaries scuttled in and out scattering publicity releases like Johnny's appleseeds. I had no hope of getting through to Patsy Werkman, but I had come that far with something other than bag and burlap on my mind and I was going to make a try for it. I watched the newspapermen mill around in the anteroom, waiting for a scheduled press conference. The chance of a private interview dimmed before my eyes until Charles Seeker, the old journalist in me, broke through and saved the day.

A phone booth stood against the wall farthest from the door that led to the lion's den. Why there should have been a phone there I do not know unless it had been put in in less happy days to discourage passing union members from making calls on official lines. There was no phone book in sight and I could hardly ask one of the secretaries, but with the help of information I found the number I wanted, dialed, and heard a girl's voice: "International Bag and Burlap."

"*Look* magazine," I said. "Put me through to Patsy Werkman."

"One moment please," I could not see the girl who had taken the call. She must have been somewhere on my side of the room. My booth, though, gave me a perfect view of the man who sat at the desk outside of Werkman's office. He craned his head toward one corner of the room, as though trying to hear something above the noise around him. He gestured impatiently and a girl came to the desk, leaned down and whispered to him. He nodded toward the corner and picked up the phone. A click and then, "Yes?"

"Charles Seeker. *Look* magazine. Is this Mr. Werkman?"

"This is Mr. Werkman's assistant."

"I want to see Werkman."

"There's a press conference in forty-five minutes."

"I don't want to go to a press conference. I want to see

Werkman. I'm in the neighborhood. I only need ten minutes."

"How about tomorrow or later?"

"Tomorrow there may be some one else on the front page."

"Just a minute, please."

I watched him as he put the phone down on the desk and disappeared through the door that he was guarding. By the time I pushed an imaginary hat to the back of my head—like in *The Front Page*—he was again at his post. "Did you say that you were quite near, Mr. Seeker?"

"Quite."

"Mr. Werkman would like to see you. Can you come right now?"

"I'll be there almost before you hang up."

I was not quite that fast. I watched him hang up and go back to the door of Werkman's office, apparently to nod that I was on my way, and, when his back was toward the phone booth, I stepped out of the booth, out of the room, even out of the building. I turned around on the sidewalk, smiled helplessly at a passer-by's amiable, "Did you forget something?" and went back up the steps.

My entrance, my introduction—"I'm Charles Seeker"—my reception were as matter of fact as the workaday world. The assistant showed me into Werkman's office and closed the door behind me.

When Werkman stood up to shake my hand, I realized that he was not nearly so big as he had looked, framed with flashbulb light, on the front of the *Sun-Times*. He was a good half head shorter than I am and no one could call me tall. Although I had the height on him, he had the reach on me, and the poundage too. He had broad shoulders, draped now in an expensive suit coat, and the face of an old fighter—once-broken nose, crinkled ear. Even now I see Werkman as a boxer. Perhaps because in the first few minutes we sparred so obviously.

"How do you feel about your victory over Si Oliff?"

"It was not my victory. It was the victory of honest unionism. What kind of article did you have in mind doing?"

We circled each other, warily, tentatively jabbing, never coming in to land blows that hurt. It came to me in the middle of our handkerchief dance that I was not really Charles Seeker from *Look* magazine and that I had got so involved in the game I was playing that I had practically forgotten what brought me to Patsy Werkman in the first place. I began to laugh. I laughed so spontaneously, with such sudden force that I could hardly get my breath. Werkman stood in front of me, the edges of his mouth waving as though they wanted to laugh with me. "What is it? What is it?" he kept saying.

"It's us," I gasped. "It's us. We're both phonies. We're . . ." But I was off again. "You keep . . . you keep," I sputtered, "spouting speeches . . . speeches someone wrote for you . . . to me . . . me . . . because . . . because . . . and I'm not . . . I'm not a reporter at all."

Patsy began to laugh. Explosive shouts pounded up, out of his wide-open mouth, hacking great pieces out of the air. At the first shout, the door flew open and the assistant hovered helplessly on the perimeter of our helplessness. Patsy waved him away, weakly but surely, and continued to laugh with me.

When at last we trickled into titters and chuckles, pain behind our eyes from the exertion, our stomachs, minds, spirits pumped of infection, we began finally to talk to one another. He seemed not surprised, not annoyed, not worried that I had come about the box. He was as calm, almost, as Annette Despere. But he was no help. He knew no more than any of the others. Not where the box was nor what it contained nor why it was necessary.

"All that I know," he said, "is that when I had my hands on the box I kicked the power monkey off my back. Just for a moment."

"Power monkey?"

"Sure, power monkey. That's why I rang up TILT on Si Oliff's pinball machine."

"To replace him?"

"That's right. Hey, wait a minute. Don't get me wrong. I'm not that simple a bastard. Si was a crook and crooks are a drag on the union. I've been around unions years enough to care. But, between you and me, I mainly wanted his job. I wanted to run Bag and Burlap."

"And after Bag and Burlap?"

"Something must be after that."

"And after the something?"

"Something . . . and something . . . and something more."

"Is there a last something?"

"Are you crazy? You're the one who started talking about the ornamental box."

YOURS FOR THE MASKING

I DO NOT ALWAYS understand why old union men who have slugged their way up to power and position, suites in Miami or San Juan, good clothes, good cars, the ear of Washington, should surround themselves with innocuous young men, interchangeably alike in their gray neatness and their horn-rimmed anonymity. Sometimes I wonder why their muscled old friends of the picket line should be buried safely in locals. Special entree to headquarters, of course, but not regularly on the premises. This day, sitting in Patsy Werkman's office, while his assistant hopped nervously at the door, invisible behind my back, almost invisible even when I turned, I thought I knew what his pale presence meant to Patsy. When we had stilled his pleading hops by breaking off our conversation —"If you find out, let me know" was all that Patsy Werkman said by way of farewell—and moving out into the large room where every eye turned toward the labor leader, I was certain I knew.

I remember a girl named Minnie Fairbanks who went to high school with me. She was a tall, well-built redhead with a full mouth, large brown eyes and a skin as free of adolescent blemish as a cosmetics ad. She held herself straight, indifferently proud, and walked softly, glided even, despite the scudding saddle shoes. The male eyes turned away from the lockers as she passed, away from the pinned-up Oomph girl or the more daring nude, and watched the barely perceptible pump of her behind as she disappeared along the corridor; with itching hands, the watchers slammed the locker doors shut and twisted the combination locks, savagely or comically, to show need or resignation—actually to make sure that the door was locked.

Inevitably Minnie's best friend—a frog-faced girl named Lulie something or other (the name of Minnie Fairbanks I have not forgotten)—clomped clumsily, fatly, heavy-footedly alongside the floating beauty.

Although I had transacted my business—the same old business: no sale—with Patsy Werkman, I lingered at the back of the crowd of reporters to see him perform. The assistant stood to the left and one pace to the rear, like a lieutenant trailing a colonel at inspection, occasionally whispering a fact, more often hovering silently, like the prop that he so obviously was. Patsy did well what had to be done. Having just taken over International Bag and Burlap, he had to give off an air of command, of assurance, of ability, but, having deposed Si Oliff to get control, he had to suggest the simple honesty of the average card-bearing burlapmaker.

I will bet my album of labor songs against a lifetime subscription to *U. S. News and World Report* that half the kids' rooms in half the burlapmakers' homes have burlap bedspreads, cunningly dyed by clever wives, run up from material carried—almost by accident—home in voluminous lunch pails.

Patsy turned from one questioner to another, looking into the eyes of each asker, speaking confidently, but hedging a little by letting a touch of *it's only me* creep into his voice.

"What about Si Oliff?"

"I'd rather not talk about that," said Patsy, rising above it all. "That's in the past. It's the future of I. B. & B. that concerns us all now." His hand made an encompassing, an including gesture that said that the pale assistant, the pretty secretaries, the jostling hangers-on were all shoulder to shoulder in a newer, purer cause.

"Beloit. Will you comment on Beloit?"

Patsy shrugged. He became the beleaguered father who knows that his boy is troublesome but loves him all the same. *Son,* I expected him to begin. "Beloit?" he actually began, saying the word as though it were a new one he was trying to learn. "Beloit. I thought that little misunderstanding had been cleared up." The reporters waited; the answer seemed incomplete. "Poor Si. Poor Si was reaching for straws when he tried to put the dirty label on me."

"Poor Si? You sound sorry for him."

"Si Oliff did a lot for this union in the old days. I don't want to remember only what's happened in the last few years. And I don't want to talk about Si at all. Let's talk about I. B. & B."

It was not quite as simple as Patsy wanted it to be. But it was simple enough. True, there were a few more questions about Si Oliff and there were questions about the Miami meetings and about the Cleveland convention, questions that could not be answered comfortably by generalizations, but Patsy turned them into launching pads for familiar clichés about unionism and social responsibility and the future of America. Any labor reporter worth his Guild card could have written the interview without ever leaving the city room. Still Patsy had charm, rough at the edges like unfinished brick, and it was plain that he would get as good a press as the publishers' politics would allow.

One fencing match is like another and you have to be a

genuine enthusiast to hang around watching parry and thrust, waiting for the referee to cry up a touch. Patsy was good, but not good enough to hold me for many minutes.

I had moved toward the door, out of the circle of reporters of which . . .

And of any circle.

. . . I was not a part. I was half-sitting, half-leaning on the edge of a desk at which a dark-haired girl, plainly pretty in her alertness, sat, staring fondly at Patsy as he talked to the newspapermen.

"He's good," I said.

"In the Aristotelian sense, yes," she said. "I don't know about the other."

My God, I thought, in this town even the secretaries have picked up the university patter. I answered, "Who does know about the other? The certain ones, of course, but they're always wrong."

"Always?"

"As always as possible. Aristotelian goodness a man can judge. Or," I nodded, flirting a little, for no man can keep from flirting with a girl behind a desk, "a lady."

There seemed nothing more to say. I looked up in time to catch Patsy's eyes as he pivoted from a question at one end of the circle in search of the next asker. A private smile, not the public-relations one that he used to back up his answers, climbed into the corners of his mouth, whispering *I've got a secret,* and I sent back a conspiratorial grin of *Cross my heart and hope to die.* His head turned on around the arc; the personal smile gave way to the public one.

A shout broke the calm of the press conference, smashed my half-formed resolve to complete my quiet exit. "Patsy,"

boomed a voice, "Patsy, you old son-of-a-bitch, you did it."
The boomer was a big man, six inches over six feet, heavy
shoulders stuffed into expensive suiting. He stood at the
door, beaming, arms outstretched, ham hands pleading for
a brother's embrace. Repeating Patsy's name as though it
were an *open sesame*—which it may have been—he marched
across the room, his giant strides cutting its expanse down
to closet size. The line of reporters opened as he surged
past them. They grinned as he clutched Patsy, still muttering his name and that he was a son-of-a-bitch and that he
had certainly done it.

"Who in God's name is that?" I asked.

"Marty Clinton," said my neo-Aristotelian acquaintance.
"The lawyer. You know, handles lots of labor stuff."

All I could think of to say and it was silly enough was,
"He doesn't look like a lawyer to me."

"That's what he's counting on. He's running for sheriff."

Sheriff. To me a sheriff is either a fat illiterate in a high-
powered car, victimizing honest folk—like in the movies—
or a fat illiterate in a tobacco-juice-stained office, feeding
his family on public trust because he has not been able to
do so by the sweat of his brow—like in most rural counties.
With that vitality and his connections why, I wondered,
should he want to be sheriff. In fact I said it out loud, "Why
should he want to be sheriff?"

"In Cook County, so goes the legend, the sheriff's office
is a steppingstone."

I stood and watched the tall rugged man who wanted to
be sheriff and the short rugged man who wanted to be . . .
who knows what exactly, but with my . . .

The possessive will creep in.

. . . ornamental box under his arm . . . slap each other's
shoulder, shake each other's hand, smile each other's smile.

They maneuvered for position like actors at a benefit, as the cameras went *flash,* and I went, slower than *flash,* out the door of International Bag and Burlap.

It had got to be like one of those board games we used to play when I was a child. You line the men up at the start, you remember, and then shoot dice to move them past obstacles—*go back three spaces*—and over hazards—*skip two turns*—toward the eternal city, the rainbow's end, home. When finally the end of the game is in sight, your man only a few jumps from his final goal, the need to get him there rises like a scream in the throat. And yet, even in the urgency, you know that it is nothing . . . nothing special, at least . . . and that even if your man does beat everyone else home, he and all the others will be swept off the board and put into a box. Someone else will come along and take over the board and when the new game begins it will be a new game for certain and an old victory will not make any man run faster or surer. Still the need to run, the need to operate as efficiently as possible within the allowable margin of the rolling dice remains. Play it cool or play it intense, the game has to be played even if the goal is ephemeral and the only reward a glass of grape Kool-Aid on childhood's hot summer afternoon.

I sat in my hotel room and looked at the now-worn, now-dirty page that I had torn so many months ago from Solvent Derritch's diary. Was I throwing the dice or was I being moved around the board? I still do not know. I did know that I had moved past obstacles and over hazards, that I had only one roll of the dice—the name of B. Wright Prommiss and the address in Indianapolis—between me and home, if this game had a home. My difficulty was that at no time had I had a full view of the board.

"There's no promise in Prommiss," I said to myself and I meant it. Which did not mean that I would not seek him out. If I had been able to quit after Rodney Salvay or Professor Pick, I might have walked away from the game with only the barest tug of doubt, wondering vaguely who if anyone would win. I was too few jumps from the finish now to bow out. There was eagerness, expectation in my packing, but when I left for the station I carried not only my bag but the suspicion that I was reaching the end of the yellow brick road and would, alas, find no Emerald City. I might find simply the end of the road.

The train that I caught was named for James Whitcomb Riley. I sat in the comfortable club car and watched my fellow passengers—heavily built expense-account men in double-breasted blue suits and neat, dumpy, wool-suited women, married not to these men but to others like them. Everyone has a line or two of Riley buried somewhere in the back of his mind, sunk in the old swimming hole of his consciousness. As I listened to the babble of estimates and sales rising above the Bourbon-and-branch-water and the rustle of hem-lines and kitchens hovering over the Bourbon-and-ginger-ale, I dredged up my half-remembered line, the one about the boy who knew what he wanted to do when he grew up: *I'm ist go' to be a nice Raggedy Man! Raggedy! Raggedy! Raggedy Man!*

"Old Riley," I said to the man next to me, a fat, graying man with tiny eyes and the full mouth of a pouter, "Old Riley would have dug all this."

"Old Riley who?"

"James Whitcomb Riley. The gent they named this train after. You know, the poet with the pince-nez."

"I'm not much for poets, son, but I do know my Riley.

When I was a boy in school—that's fifty years now—I shook James Whitcomb Riley's hand. I recited 'Little Orphant Annie' in front of the entire school and then I shook James Whitcomb Riley's hand."

"That must have been a grand moment," I said. I kept my voice straight. No snottiness crept in, but pure as the line was I felt a twinge of guilt as soon as the words were out of my mouth. After all, damn it, it may have been a grand moment. Which recognition did not keep me from saying, "I'd like to shake the hand of the man who shook James Whitcomb Riley's hand."

That was too much . . . well, almost too much. The man turned his little eyes on me suspiciously, pouted his fat lips doubtfully, but I stared at him from open, honest eyes. I extended my hand and he took it gingerly. "If you really mean it," he said. Then, "What do you mean that Riley would have . . . *dug* . . . all this?"

"I mean all these comfortable well-off people. This car. *This.*" I lifted my glass. "He would have plunked himself down in one of these seats and ordered up a double and ripped off a poem about walking barefoot through the fields. Back to nature with no chigger bites. Besides," I said, raising my drink toward my neighbor, "the old boy was on the sauce."

"Are you trying to say that James Whitcomb Riley was a drinking man? Because if you are trying to say that James Whitcomb Riley was a drinking man, I am going to protest. I shook his hand in 1908 and I can testify that he was certainly not a drinking man and the man who wrote 'Little Orphant Annie' could not be a drinking man." Exhausted by his defense of the Hoosier poet, he signaled for another drink.

Not anger exactly, but annoyance at least hung around

my neighbor's head, as though, in coupling Riley and drink, I had done him a personal wrong, such as naming his mother in a curse or noticing his halitosis. "I bow to your superior knowledge," I said graciously and I insisted on buying his drink. We were friends again.

"What do you think of the election?" was his way of saying that all was forgiven.

My kind of traveling—the roundabout road from the Bridgeport kitchen of The King to the club car of the *Riley* —is not designed to keep me up on the political news. I had to think quickly to remember that it was an election year at all. I tried to imagine what election my companion had an emotional stake in. Failing that, I searched the conversational corners of my mind for the conventional comment. I need not have bothered.

"Old B. W. is going to the Senate. That's my bet."

"Do you think his chances are really that good?" I asked, wondering who old B. W. was.

"I've been an active Democrat in this state for forty years, son, and I cannot honestly say that I have ever seen a candidate with as good a chance to win as old B. W. has this year. And a better man for the job I do not know."

"And you, sir?" I asked. "Are you a candidate, too?"

"I am always a candidate. But I am never elected." He laughed. "Always a bridesmaid, never a bride." As though defeat had become so customary that it had become precious, he began to tell me of his failures—beginning with an unsuccessful councilmanic contest in 1922, ending with his present, almost certain defeat in the race for county sheriff. I found myself thinking that he had the build for the job. "My county is stanchly Republican, you know. But even when the Democrats do win, I somehow don't make it. I get beat by a widow or a veteran or something that has more claim on people than the party."

He went suddenly silent over his drink. And I over mine. I could think of nothing to say. Then a phrase came into my mind, one that I had heard spoken by an army captain, an ex-football hero, in a training center where I was learning to handle a bayonet to defend myself from the Germans and the Japanese: "It isn't whether you win or lose; it's how you play the game."

I said the phrase aloud. The fat man smiled manfully above his built-in pout.

Make a note: when in doubt use a cliché.

My neighbor brightened visibly. "But old B. W. is going to carry most of the state. You can bet on that." The brightness stayed all the way to Indianapolis. As the train felt its way past warehouses and factories in search of the station, a billboard rose up shouting its message. "There's one of old B. W.'s signs."

Old B. W. was not old at all. The face on the board was professionally young, a typical American boy in his mid-forties. As straight as a die, as clean as a pin, as slick as a whistle. Like an insurance advertisement or a *Fortune* young executive.

But, for me, the words were more important than the face.

BE RIGHT WITH B. WRIGHT

B. WRIGHT PROMISS

YOUR

DEMOCRATIC CANDIDATE

FOR SENATOR

I never got to the address that I had torn from Solly Derritch's book. I did not need to chase out to the periphery of Indianapolis in search of the Promiss land. I knew what it would be like. An expanse of lawn dotted with nursery evergreens—instead of the maples turning yellow and red in less affluent parts of town. A house of stone and glass, elegantly comfortable, like a cover picture of *Better Homes and Gardens*. A large dog and two small children, suitable sizes for newspaper photographs.

I did not need to go because B. Wright Promiss's face and name assailed me when I stepped off the train and followed me past the cheap restaurants and army-navy stores that surrounded the station. I was on foot, my bag safely stored in a locker. The signs not only shouted that I must, we all must BE RIGHT WITH B. WRIGHT, they also played a variation on the exclamation that had dropped from me back in my Chicago hotel room: A PROMMISS PROMISE IS A PROMISE KEPT.

I walked along Madison Avenue, into the circle where the Soldiers and Sailors Monument shot its shaft toward the sky and the wartime governors crouched at the four corners like respectable bulldogs on guard duty. I sat on the steps—an October day like a gift from heaven—breathing the exhaust fumes from the endless ring of cars, biting its own tail, revolving around and around the circle. A new car entered to take the place of any link that broke away, turned down one of the exit streets to tend to its own business or to find romance. A car, plastered with streamers and signs, a loudspeaker fastened to its roof, turned in from Washington Street and added its seasonal noise—BE RIGHT WITH B. WRIGHT, BE RIGHT WITH B. WRIGHT, BE RIGHT WITH B. WRIGHT—to the perennial scream of brakes and the peremptory hoot of horns.

The offending loudspeaker faded out of my consciousness. Not that the car left the circle, so fertile a ground for dropping its seed, but my mind began to busy itself with B. Wright and the hum of its own activity pushed the roaring political message (or was it a moral dictum?) to the back of my consciousness, a whisper. B. Wright. B. Wright. What was that *B.* hiding? Bertram? Bonaventure? Boniface? Beulah?

Well, Beulahland Wright Promiss, I said to myself, I might as well get on with it.

I had been sitting long enough to attract the surprised, the amused, the disapproving looks of shopping, of idling citizens who moved, like the limbo crowd in Dante's book, around the circle of sidewalk that lay beyond the revolving chain of cars. I made my way to a crosswalk where the cars parted like the Red Sea on a red light, and I passed to the other side without even wetting my feet. In limbo now myself, I sought a policeman to find out where Betram Wright Prommiss might have his headquarters. One policeman, two policemen, three policemen—none of them seemed to know, although the third man did direct me to a store-front operation, which the forces of Prommiss had taken over from a failed haberdasher and set up as a button-and-sticker outlet.

The window was almost covered with a blow-up of Boniface Wright Prommiss's face, clear-cut and outsize, and a smattering of smaller signs, some even for lesser candidates, patched over the few remaining expanses of window as though the volunteers preferred to operate in the dark. Inside I found no handful of conspirators crouched around a rough deal table, a candle stub stuck in the neck of a wine bottle. I found a single volunteer worker sitting at a scarred, rented desk under an unshaded bulb that gave its substitute light for that shut out by Promiss's picture. The worker was an attractive woman in her thirties, plump enough to insist on cottage cheese at lunch, a suburban matron in an expensive jersey dress, a single string of pearls at her neck, a fur coat thrown back over the chair on which she sat.

"Can I help you?" she beamed.

"I'm looking for Mr. Prommiss."

"Oh." That was a new request. "Oh, he's not here. He's never here. Do you want a button?" She held up a Be-Right-with B. Wright button, which, being a gentleman, I accepted.

"Actually it was the man I wanted, not a button."

"Maybe he's at headquarters, although I don't suppose so. He's always talking somewhere. But maybe."

"Maybe you could give me the address." This she could do and did, searching the unfamiliar desk for a pencil, finally rummaging up a small gold one from her purse, and writing an address across the front of a Prommiss pamphlet: *The Man and the Record.*

"This way you get a message, too."

I thanked her and turned toward the door when her voice stopped me, "Are you terribly busy just now?"

"Not terribly."

"I shouldn't ask, I suppose, but I wonder if you would sit here for a few minutes while I run to the drugstore on the corner."

"Could I bring you something?"

"Well, you could, of course. But the fact is I'd rather go myself." I tried to look as though I was not thinking that she was probably going to buy something intimately female, but I apparently failed. "It's only coffee I want, but I would like to get into the sun for just a second. It's so murky in here."

"Go," I said gallantly. "I will make the time." She went, *are-you-sure*-ing me until she disappeared through the door.

I settled myself in the absent matron's chair. I surveyed the desk where she had neatly stacked the Prommiss pamphlets, where she had pushed the Prommiss buttons into a ragged but respectable pile. If I were playing politician, I thought to myself, I would scatter this stuff all the hell and gone across the desk; I would make myself believe that the room was alive with activity, with controversy. The telephone, carefully squared on the corner of the desk, glared at me balefully, refusing to ring, refusing to give me a chance to play the executive. I was tempted to put through a few calls of my own. How, I wondered, was my old friend Annette Despere in Atlanta? Or P. R. Eferred in San Francisco? My fingers played along the back of the receiver when suddenly the bell went and I drew my hand back as though it had been burned. I picked up the receiver and, on the assumption that *Hello* was not a suitable greeting, I said, "Be Right with B. Wright."

"What?" said an incredulous voice. "Maryanne?" continued the questioner. "Is that Maryanne Bright?"

"Is Maryanne Bright a good-looking woman who can afford a real fur coat?"

There was a choked *yes* at the other end of the line.

"And is she giving her all for Bonaventure Wright Prommiss?"

"What? Who? What are you talking about?"

"Because, if that is Maryanne Bright, she is not here. She has gone out for a bromo, and I am swamped with business and can talk no longer." I lifted my voice, commandingly. "All right, ladies and gentlemen, line up for your Prommiss buttons." I made a noise like a crowd and then put the receiver down, wondering whether the gasping woman at the other end was a Prommiss volunteer checking from headquarters or a member of Maryanne's bridge club in search of a luncheon date.

My only customer came in just as I hung up the phone. A short, thin man in a neat, inexpensive black suit. Rimless glasses, a prim mouth. He looked like a cartoon clerk.

"Will you . . ." I started to say, holding out a Prommiss button.

"I certainly will not," he interrupted. "I would not pin one of those badges of corruption on my collar to save my immortal soul, if I had such a thing. Your B. Wright Prommiss is no better and no worse, no different certainly than his Republican adversary. Two sides of the same coin. What difference does it make which party wins? The same forces are always in power. This country is run by the banks and the generals and the big businessmen. If you want to save the country, vote this ticket."

He handed me a throwaway from one of the splinter parties—Socialist Labor or Labor Socialist or Socialist Socialist or Labor Labor—a list of names—his perhaps—who were standing for the state offices. He turned on his heel and tried to make a dignified exit. He would have succeeded if Maryanne Bright had not been coming through the door, her fur coat hanging precariously on her shoulders, a paper cup of coffee in her hand. "See," he said to me. "See what I mean."

In a way I did see.

"A little business," the lady said, bustling back to her job, draping the fur coat, opening the coffee.

"He brought us this," I handed her the throwaway.

"Oh, dear," she said, crumbling it up and throwing it in the wastebasket. "Why does everyone want to run for office?" I shrugged that I did not know. "Is there anything else you should tell me?"

"Yes, Mrs. Bright," I said, "you really should quit taking cream in your coffee." I pointed to the paper cup on her desk. Her eyes followed my finger and played around the rim of the container. Her head bobbed, smiling uncertainly, puzzled—by my use of her name? by my suggestion? "It really isn't done, you know." I waved and went.

The Promiss headquarters—a hotel suite—were as busy as Mrs. Bright's station had been quiet. Teenage politicians raced around, carrying messages, looking as though it was all they could do to hold the country together. Harried girls licked envelopes. Men shouted into telephones. A desk, marked information, sat unmanned, uninformative at the door of the suite. I stepped around it and began prowling for myself. No one stopped me; no one asked if he might help me or told me to get the hell out. I wandered from room to room, listening to snatches of conversation—"I thought that son-of-a-bitch said he could swing Montgomery County"; "They want a race statement in Gary"; "He can't—he just can't speak in every one-horse town in the goddamned state"—looking for someone who had come to rest, even momentarily, and who might tell me where B. Wright Prommiss was. No one stilled, not even for a moment.

Thumbtacked to the wall of one room was a large chart, marked off in squares for days and hours. Someone—a humorist with a talent for lettering and none for spelling—had printed "The new SENATOR's speech itinerery" across the top of the chart. I studied it carefully. Prommiss was booked in solid, sometimes six or seven speeches in a single large city; often three speeches in three different small towns in one day. My best bet for catching up with the flying young hopeful was a town called Calebsville, where he was scheduled to speak on the evening of October 10 and with no further booking until late the next afternoon. If he had any sense at all, it seemed to me, he would bed down in whatever comfort Calebsville had to offer and get one real night's sleep out of thirty.

"What do you want?" The question startled me. I turned, fingering my Prommiss button, and looked into the hard eyes of the woman who had asked the question. I had seen the type before. A brighter Mrs. Bright who had grown tired of being a volunteer and had signed on as a professional. As tough as Democratic votes in a Republican county, but—I suspected—as falsely sweet as early returns if the occasion demanded.

I played my suspicion. "I was hoping to get Mr. Prommiss to speak."

"Whom do you represent? What kind of audience can you muster?"

"The ministerial association in Paris. . . ." Every state has a Paris.

"New Paris?"

I nodded. ". . . and there are seven of us."

She had me by the arm immediately, sweet talking me not to insult the clergy, but I was headed, as fast as possible, toward the exit, loaded with her regret that Senator Prommiss—wasn't she jumping the gun a little?—was too tied up—alas, alas—to be able to speak to my group. If the door had been a meat grinder, I would have been a hamburger pattie in ten seconds. Good-by, and God bless you.

It was night when my bus came into Calebsville. I had been through Indiana towns before. I could imagine the clapboard houses on tree-lined streets; I could guess the new homes—brick or Bedford stone—exposed to the sun of the new development on the edge of town. I knew the look of the drugstores, the liquor store, the lunchroom with its cry EAT, the musty movie house doing its bad business, the small groceries dying of progress and supermarkets. I could have predicted the hotel. Big, old, cheap and with practically no service, rubbing its surprised eyes in wonder that it should lose the drummers to the shiny motel out on the main road. I checked in, slept late, woke up to find that all I had imagined was really there.

What I could not know until I had worked my way through conversations in the hotel lobby, behind the EAT sign, on a corner, in a bar was that Calebsville was deceptively prosperous, that one of its two factories was on half time and the other had begun to lay men off. One hundred years before, such a situation would have assured a rousing reception for B. Wright Prommiss or his political ancestor, but judging from the men I talked to no one was interested in the election.

At Caleb Municipal Park—a few acres of grass and trees, a tennis court, a clutch of picnic tables—a platform had been erected to receive our Prommiss. When I made my way to the spot on the morning of the ninth, I found men hanging a great banner above the outdoor stage. Too early, I thought, a day too early; suppose it rains. But the banner was right on time, for it was not a Prommiss that it advertised, but his opponent who was scheduled to speak that night.

Once the banner was up—proclaiming Ray S. Publica, or whatever his name was—the men began to set up folding chairs, rented from or donated by the local undertaker. When I returned that evening to claim one of the chairs for myself, I did not have to fight for a seat. A handful of people waited for the candidate—ward workers, hangers-on, confirmed Republicans, one or two of the unconvinced and the curious. By the time the candidate arrived, the handful had become a small group, but why he was willing to come so far to speak to such a meager and so convinced an audience I did not know. But speak he did, after the town candidates, the county candidates, the district candidates had been introduced, had taken their bows.

Ray S. was good-looking, young-looking, alert-looking, intelligent-looking, in all ways a replica of B. Wright Prommiss, at least the Prommiss that I had come to know from his election posters. He exuded confidence. He spoke passionately as though his words had meaning.

Good men and women of Calebsville, it is an honor to appear before you. I have come to ask your support in the coming election that means so much to the American people, so much to you good people of Calebsville. Never has this nation been so prosperous. A murmur went up from the crowd—a murmur of protest even among the faithful. *I say again that never has this nation been so prosperous. And yet, and yet—oh how well I know—there are troubles enough for you in Calebsville. Where is the heart of your troubles? Not in the brave Republican administration which fights the good fight for a stronger, richer America, which fights the Communists abroad and the grasping labor unions at home. And with what help! The Democrats in Congress, in the Senate—my worthy opponent—would sell you out to the crooked labor leaders, would be soft on Communism, would rob you by pouring more and more dollars down the rat hole of Europe. . . .*

And so it went. When the candidate pulled up, sweating, at the end of his message, the applause was perfunctory, heartfelt. The people stood up, stretched, moved slowly toward the platform where Ray S. shook each hand, assuring each of them, by the touch of flesh on flesh, that he was a man among other men.

I put off the handshaking until the next day.

☐   ☐

B. Wright Prommiss was his election posters made flesh. Expensive orthodontia in his childhood had helped him retain his boyish smile, as warm and moving as a barefoot kid with a homemade fishing pole, a creature who still lives on a few barbershop calendars. Otherwise—even in his lateness—he was like his Republican opposite number. The waiting crowd was larger, Calebsville being a factory town, and an edge more informal in dress, but it was really the same meeting with a few words changed.

Good men and women of Calebsville, it is an honor to appear before you. I have come to ask your support in the coming election, that means so much to the American people, so much to you good people of Calebsville. Never has this nation been so prosperous. Last night's murmur became a shout of protest. *At least, that's what they tell you in Washington.* The laugh came. *Yes, that's what the Republicans tell you, and yet, and yet—oh how well I know —there are troubles enough for you in Calebsville. Where is the heart of your troubles? Not in the brave Democratic Congress which fights the good fight for a stronger, richer America, which fights the Communists abroad and grasping Wall Street at home. And with what help! The Republican administration—my worthy opponent—would sell you out to the big businessmen, would be soft on Communism, would rob you by pouring more and more dollars down the rat hole of Europe. . . .*

And so it went. When the candidate pulled up, sweating, at the end of his message, the applause was perfunctory, heartfelt. The people stood up, stretched, moved slowly toward the platform where B. Wright shook each hand, assuring each of them, by the touch of flesh on flesh, that he was a man among other men.

I took my place in the line of handshakers. If I was going to hack a minute out of Golden Boy's tight schedule this was the moment for me to bare my ax. He took my hand, a gentle but manly grip, and glazed his face in a smile of greeting, his eyes sparkling, friendly, unseeing. Across his muttered platitude of pleasure, I said softly, but clearly, "Can I see you for a moment? It's about the ornamental box."

"What?"

"Can I see you for a moment? It's about the ornamental box."

He turned to the man standing at his side—a secretary or a campaign manager or something—and whispered that he should take me to his car. The aide protested briefly and vainly. "I said take him to the car. I want to speak to him in private."

If our walk to the car had been in the best movie tradition, we would have moved silently through the shadowy darkness of the park, tight-lipped but apparently casual, toward the black closed car that was our destination. The secretary, or whatever he was, with no cinematic sense, filled our path with a running, whining monologue about how beat, bushed, bedraggled poor B. Wright was, how inconsiderate were the ordinary run of men (meaning me), how never, not even in the dead of night or the first bright crack of dawn, did the man, the poor man—and he doing it all for the people—get a breath to breathe alone. "What in the world do you want anyway?" he concluded.

"A little touch of Harry in the night."

Something—perhaps my answer, perhaps exhaustion—stilled his whine. He left me sitting in the back of Promiss' car waiting for the last hand to be clasped.

"Is it time?" The question was Promiss' greeting as he slid into the seat beside me.

"Time for what?"

"The box. The opening of the box. Soon, Doc's message said. He said he would tell us where and when, but I can guess where."

"I'm not the messenger."

"Then what do you want?"

"What you want. To be in on the opening of the box."

"You're not on the list." A simple statement. Prommiss thought more quickly, more clearly than his speech had suggested.

I decided to play it straight. "No, I'm not on the list. I've held the box in my hands, but I'm not on the list."

"I feel expansive, stranger. I'm about to be elected senator and I feel friendly. But that box means more to me than a seat in the Senate. I could cheerfully see you dead if I thought you stood a chance of doing me out of my place on the list. But I don't. I don't think so. So I'll give you a tip. Stick around."

"Around?"

"Around Calebsville. I have a hunch." He held out his hand for me to shake. Again. "I have to get on the road. Good-by, stranger."

I climbed out of the car, shut the door behind me, and then leaned in the open window. "Good-by, Mr. Prommiss. Tell me, Mr. Prommiss, what does the B. stand for?"

"Bethel," he said. "I couldn't risk being nicknamed Betty."

"Bethel," I echoed. "A hallowed spot."

"Exactly." He flashed me the expensive boy's grin. The car started. The grin still hung at the window as the automobile pulled away and left me to find my way out of the park.

CHAPTER TWELVE

WHEN THE BOX WAS OPEN

 I WAS LEFT in the dark in more ways than one.

Something had happened since I had laughed with **Patsy Werkman**. A message, and from Doc. An English detective would have known what to do with those random bits of information. He would have deduced an intricate plot, solved the mystery of the cryptic words in time to save the Queen, the country, the day, and all without removing his dressing gown. I am not a detective and am no Englishman and do not even own a dressing gown.

If Prommiss had chosen to get his one good night's sleep in Calebsville, I might have invented an unassuming alias, as transparently ad-honest as the face he was selling the voters, and used it as a wedge to pry my way into his secret. But his expanse of taillight had disappeared around the stone gate of the park. The ice-faced, smiley woman in his Indianapolis headquarters may have penciled in one more speaking engagement for him, perhaps he simply wanted the night's rest on some bosom that Calebsville did not own. Whoever or whatever, he was gone. At the end of my list (my rope), I was left to find some new hobby or else, as he suggested, to stick around. You know me by now. I stuck.

For a month after my whispered meeting with Prommiss —a month that saw him get that seat in the Senate—Calebsville was my home. I, a stranger, an outsider, became the stranger, the outsider, and finally their stranger, their outsider.

What, metaphysics aside, *did I do for a month in Calebsville?* Well, I walked. At first, through the downtown streets, poking into stores and bars and ice cream fountains. Then out into the rest of the town where the neat homes and the pattern of yard and tree repeated themselves like variations on a familiar theme. Finally, out to the limping factories, brick-solemn for all that the hive hum of meaning that should have come from them was turned down low, and past the graying, dirty houses that had long since lost their battle with factory smoke—poor relations across the tracks.

When I had come to know the town well, when no walk offered any surprise, I began to vary the search for the unexpected. Sometimes, I stood in the lobby of the hotel and watched the bus unload its passengers—sometimes as many as three for Calebsville—praying that at least one of those who stepped down would not be a Calebsville housewife back from a day's shopping in Indianapolis. Sometimes, I hired one of the four local taxis and had the driver take me past the edge of town, down one of the country roads that led to look-alike crossroads villages.

I managed to fill my time. I also managed to attract attention. My presence was enough to start the talk. Who was this man who had washed up in the wake of the two political meetings? My walks—*what's wrong with him anyhow?*— swelled the volume. It was my trips by taxi that really set the tongues a-flying. Speculation followed me like a dog on a leash. I was, by unanimous vote, the local enigma. I found myself stepping around discreet inquiries. Some questioners were more blunt. The waitress in the lunchroom demanded, "What is your line of work anyway?"

"I'm a developer," I said, and I let it go at that.

The word passed around. I was a developer and, although no one knew what I developed or how I developed it, the assumption was that it was profitable to me and might be good for the town. A few people approached me cautiously, bankbooks in hand, hoping to get in on a good thing. I almost wished at those moments that I was a swindler because I could have made a good thing out of these touching evidences of human faith through greed. More people approached me to show me good land, choice home sites, the best place for a launderette or a cocktail lounge.

I was C. M. Firth on the hotel register and C. M. Firth Associates in most of the minds in Calebsville. It was fun in an old-fashioned way, like a fancy-dress ball, and I became so involved in playing at being that I almost forgot why I was hanging around the town at all.

If a man thought only of the ornamental box, I suppose, he would paralyze himself and, waiting, never move again.

Still, the box played at the edge of my consciousness. It broke through on one of my taxi rides outside the rim of the town. Just past the city limits, out a road that I had been over before, lay a large field where tall grass grew. Weed grass, wire grass, hip high on the edges of the field, trampled by feet or wheels over much of the space. I knew it was there, if an indifferent glance implies knowledge, but on this trip—*kick went the box*—I really looked. A large wooden trailer sat in the field. Like an antique huckster's wagon, it had a door that opened down from the top to form a counter or a platform, only this door was as big as the whole side of the trailer.

"What's that?" I asked.

"Michaelson's field," said the driver. "It's where circuses and revivals—things like that—put up their tents."

"I don't mean the field. I mean that trailer."

"Oh, that belongs to Doc Holiman. He sets up on Michaelson's field most winters."

"Who is this Doc Holiman?"

"A medicine man. He travels around to the fairs and carnivals in the summer. Sells something called Holiman's Tonic. Some folks say it really works."

"Works on what?"

"On what ails you. Kind of a cure-all, you know."

I knew. Oh, I knew.

My walk the next morning was longer than usual. Fortified with an extra cup of coffee, strengthened by curiosity, I walked all the way to Michaelson's field. The trailer turned out to be the variation on the huckster's wagon that it had seemed at a distance. No horse grazed near by, eating badly on the worthless stand of wire grass, for Doc Holiman's wagon was a once conventional trailer truck converted now to the functional glitter of show business.

The blank, blind, shut-door side of the trailer still faced the road. Hoping to find more than its eyelessness could tell me, I walked all the way around. On the end two messages called out to whatever cars followed Doc down whatever highways: one, commercial, in large red letters, HOLIMAN'S TONIC; the other, admonitional, in smaller black letters, PLEASE PASS ON LEFT. The far side wore the face of a house trailer, a door, windows with curtains, the suggestion of a home on wheels.

I knocked. There was no answer. I knocked again. Still, no answer. The windows, what with the height of the trailer and of the wheel base on which it sat, were too far out of reach for relaxed peeping. Still, I did my best. I was on tiptoe against the side of the trailer, trying, with no luck, to get a look at Doc Holiman's home and castle, when a voice behind me said, "Can I help you?"

If I did not blush, I should have. I turned, embarrassed, and began to stutter an excuse, "I was just . . . well . . . kind of . . ." I heard my own voice stumbling through the ruin of my words and pulled myself up short. "I was trying to see inside," I said simply.

"I could see that," he answered.

"But your windows are too high."

"I'll have them lowered."

"Then, they are your windows?"

He nodded.

If I had not been chewing nervously at the edge of my guilt—it's hard to break in as a Peeping Tom at my age— the splendor of the man would have hit me at once. He was stout and heavy-headed, with a thick mustache spread all across his lip. He wore a brown derby and a matching brown frock coat, striped trousers and a paisley waistcoat that would have been as old-fashioned as the rest of him if the college men's shops had not rediscovered it a few years ago. A massive gold chain hung across the front of the vest and he wore an egg-sized onyx ring on his right—his gesturing—hand. Dressed in period, like the road side of his wagon, he too had his touch of the contemporary. His feet were encased in space shoes.

"You're Doc Holiman?" I asked, knowing the answer. He nodded. "I came out to see you."

"You're C. M. Firth?" he asked, knowing the answer. I nodded. "I heard about you in town. What do you want with me? I haven't anything to develop."

"I wonder."

"What does that mean?"

What it really meant—if it meant anything—could as well be left unspoken. I made a gesture toward the back end of the trailer. "Oh, Holiman's Tonic, I guess."

"You guess."

"Holiman's Tonic, I know."

"And is that why you came to see me? My tonic?"

"No," I said almost truthfully. "I came because I wanted to see a medicine man. I didn't know there were any left."

"I'm left," he said. "Would you like to come in?"

The invitation was direct, easy, uncomplicated. My reaction was not so simple. I did want to go inside, and I did not. If this was B. Wright Prommiss' Doc, then maybe inside his trailer the ornamental box sat on an end table—are there end tables in trailers?—like an ordinary decoration. I needed to see, and yet I was afraid that the box might not be sitting there or that it might be and that I would not, could not touch it. In the end, what could I say to such an invitation? "Yes, thank you. I would like to come in."

If the box is in the trailer, I told myself, as I followed my host inside, I will know it, I will feel the pull of it. That was surely my longing talking, my yearning to hold it again in my hand, to feel again the rustle of life—life?— that had frightened me when I lay stretched out on my Providence bed and held it for the first, the only time.

Doc Holiman closed the door behind us. I knew nothing. I felt no pull. There was no sight of the ornamental box. No hint, no whisper, no indication at all.

The medicine man's trailer differed from the run of the breed only in that its space had not been broken up into a handful of matchbox rooms. Otherwise it was just a home.

The only unusual piece of furniture was a floor-to-ceiling cupboard at one end of the room.

"Holiman's Tonic," said my host, nodding toward the cupboard.

There were no decorations on the walls, no bric-a-brac on the table to say that this man had traveled fairs and carnivals for years. The only picture was a bird print—Audubon perhaps—which by its singleness commanded my eye.

"The *Sialis sialis*," said Doc Holiman. "The Eastern bluebird. Handsome, I think."

I nodded my willingness that the bluebird should flourish.

Doc Holiman gave me a drink, ignoring my complaint that it was too early, that it was still morning, and began to talk. For almost three hours I sat in the trailer and trouped through the years, the states, the towns of carnival America. His speech, once his stories began, lost the directness of our exchange outside the trailer. I began to hear the classical beat of the barker. From his boyhood days as an errand runner and bottle carrier, through his years as an entertainer, to his transformation into the world-famous Dr. Holiman, I followed the life of the medicine man.

"So you see," he concluded, "so you see, Mr. Firth, the traveling medicine man is almost as dead as you deem him. That soothing syrup, his voice, that soft-soaped and sold so many generations of the American people is stilled, killed by the dancing television puppets who prove that new cure-alls cure all more surely than ever the classic colored water could. He has lost his jugglers and his fire-eaters for such artists are artists no longer unless a camera tracks them beneath klieg lights. He exists if he exists at all—I exist *if I exist at all*—not as an anchor riding out the sea of change, but as an anomaly in a world in which his clothes and his speech, both once correct, have become quaint and funny. A world in which his customers come not to save their bodies and their souls, but as a joke, a lark, a fifty-cent diversion between the Ferris wheel and the caramel corn. They need him still. They need *me* still. Sophisticated our nation may be, knowing and clever our people may have become, but in some form or other there must always be a bottle of colored water held high above a head held just as high, while a rich voice assures that this is the elixir, the cure-all, the panacea, the fountain of youth, the pot at the end of the rainbow. I am still in the business, Mr. Firth. I am still in the business."

When at last the flow of words stopped, I thanked my way out of the trailer and walked back to town. Doc Holiman seemed to me to be only a tired old medicine man, clinging to his own bottle of cure-all, his vocation, in a world which had declared it obsolete. If that was all there was to him, then he was not the Doc that Prommiss had promised, he was not sitting at the end of my rainbow. Every doctor, every dentist, every druggist, every man who has had even a nodding relationship to disease or drugs or learning of any kind is likely to be called Doc in an Indiana town. There was no shortage of Docs and yet the coincidence of Holiman's presence and Prommiss' suggestion that I stick around was still too much to pass off. Besides, the medicine man's eloquence, the skill with which he built the story of his life, like a careful novelist with an eye for detail, the final moment in which determination mixed with sadness—all these suggested contrivance. That might mean art or artifice. The good old charlatan in the brown derby may have sold me a smoke screen. Under which shell was the ornamental box?

By the time I got back to town my speculations were academic. As I approached the hotel, I caught a glimpse of a blimp in a blanket, topped with a straw skimmer. My gun-bearing friend from the Hotel Chevron was wedging his unlikely way into a taxi. When the cab passed me, the fat man was staring straight ahead, as though there were something he needed to see past the driver, beyond the windshield. His lips moved soundlessly, framing, I am willing to bet, the words to "Bye, Bye Blackbird."

The parade had begun.

I took up the fat man's song. Whistling, I pushed through the hotel door, but the whistle died on my lips before I had gone two steps across the lobby. A pair of long legs, encased in rough black cloth, jackknifed out of a chair in the corner. The head that belonged to them was bent over a book with a title that I could not have read even if I had been sitting on the absorbed man's shoulders. It was in Greek.

I wanted to go up to Professor Pick, to shake hands, to say hello, but I stopped myself. It was not the memory of his hanging on the fence, kicking out at me, that kept me from approaching him. It was not memory at all, but its failure. I did not know who I was. Who I had been, at least. I was not Connie Firth in Ravenna, I was sure of that. Eddie Anodyne? Charles Seeker? C. M. Rosmer? Which one and why was no longer clear. I had been so many different people in the presence of so many names on the list that I knew suddenly that I had now to be no one to all of them.

□

A rose by any other name is likely to change shape, color, smell.

I told myself, climbing the stairs to my room, that I could not approach any of the people who had been stations of the cross-country quest of mine. *Be sensible,* I said to myself, Doc's call will bring them all together and, chameleon though you may be, you can not be five men at once. I did not know until I came back down just how much pain there would be in my separateness. Annette Despere was sitting there, as delicate and as enduring as she had seemed that day in Oakland Cemetery. I wanted to lean down and kiss her on the cheek, as I had before over her cup of tea. Instead, I turned away from her. I sidled out of the hotel, my face toward Professor Pick, who was oblivious to everything except his book.

Outside, I heard a soft voice saying, "Stay in the car, Angela, I'll see what the hotel has to offer." Out of the anonymity of a rented car came first one remembered leg, then a second, finally the whole girl—tweed-coated now like a coed. Candy Stick—the ghost of Sylvia—disappeared through the door of the hotel.

I stepped into the doorway of the drygoods store on the corner to let a king and his retinue roll by. A heavily built young man was pushing a wheel chair in which a crumpled figure sat wrapped in a cocoon of blankets; two girls—handmaidens or secretaries—followed, one step to the rear. Before any face had registered on my mind, I knew that the potentate had to be P. R. Eferred. He did not look to the right or the left; he stared down at his gloved hands.

A Homburg and a dark blue overcoat hung on one of the wall hooks in the lunchroom. A Homburg in Calebsville? The sight of it kept me from going in, kept me from

running into Rodney Salvay, who sat alone at one of the
tables, his pale face bent over a bowl of soup. At a neighboring table, also alone, sat Patsy Werkman, digging into
a meal of ham and navy beans with the reminiscent pleasure of a man who has not always known the Pump Room.
The two men seemed not to know each other, even to see
each other. The names from Solly's diary were still a list.
They were not yet a group.

With the gathering of the box-hunters, my journey—one
way or another—was almost at an end. By all the laws of
sentimental drama I should have been too excited to eat,
but those laws had apparently been repealed. Anticipation
rode me like a jockey, which may explain why I was hungry
as a horse. There sat Salvay and Werkman, filling themselves and filling seats which I, with my month of squatter's
rights, considered my own. Barred from my usual restaurant, I had to choose between a drive-in sandwich stand out
on the edge—and not Doc Holiman's edge—of town and a
chili joint over where the two factories stood. I chose the
chili. It was nearer and quicker; it would keep me away
from downtown for the shortest time and there I thought
I needed to be, to busy myself with seeing and not being
seen.

With a bowl of chili rumbling in my belly I started back
toward the center of town. Ahead of me, on the other side
of the street, a big man half sat, half leaned against the
fender of a car. His massive head was bent over a notebook
in which he seemed to be writing. From time to time, he
glanced over the edge of the notebook at the yard of the
house in front of him—just dirt enclosed by a broken fence;
the rusty skeleton of a motorcycle, three discarded tires, a
scattering of boxes and pans were all the lawn decorations
that the house could boast. I was tempted to cross over for

a better look at his preoccupation. A step this side of intrusion, I realized that it was Arthur Krafft, who was transferring the huddle of junk, a still life, into his sketch pad. I kept to my own side of the street.

Downtown Senator Prommiss stood outside the hotel surrounded by a group of admirers. The editor of the local paper was trying to get a statement. "No," said the senator. "Not at all. My visit to Calebsville has no political significance whatever. I am here to visit a few friends." Over the mumbled questions of the editor, "No. No, I would prefer not to say. Let me put it this way. If . . . if at any time I have an announcement of importance to Calebsville I promise that the *Times and Continuer* will have it first. For the time being, for the moment, kind friends, if I might be permitted . . . ." His boy's smile cajoled an opening in the charmed circle. He passed through it and into the hotel leaving an aura of good feeling that must have seemed to the deserted circle a little like an ache.

If the senator had not gone into the hotel, I might have looked to him for answers, because to him I was simply *stranger*. There was no counterfeit identity that I had to live up to. But I could see him standing in the lobby, talking with Patsy Werkman (a political or an ornamental-box connection?); Annette Despere and Professor Pick sat where I had seen them earlier. I went on past and up the street, down the other side. Up and down, up and down, I wandered in and out of stores, talking to owners and clerks to whom I was almost a local fixture. "A lot of strangers in town," was the universal greeting. "Is something going on?"

"Coincidence," was my inevitable answer.

As I walked and talked, I looked. I glanced at passing license plates. I slowed down so that footsteps behind me might reach and pass me. I was not at first aware that I was looking for Harvey Williams, the only one from the list who had not turned up. Finally, sitting in the drugstore over a lime coke, I knew that it was Harvey that I had been waiting for and I knew why I had not seen him.

A Negro boy, perhaps fifteen years old, came into the store and ordered a milk shake. "To go," said the girl at the fountain.

"I'll drink it here," said the boy, sitting uneasily on the stool.

"To go," said the druggist, firing from his redoubt behind the cash register.

"To go," said the boy. He took his milk shake in a paper cup, the straw sticking straight up in the thick mixture, and stepped out into the November afternoon. Not uncongenial weather, but not milk-shake-on-the-street weather either.

"A visitor, I guess," said the druggist.

A Southern Indiana town. Harvey Williams had not turned up at the hotel because he would not have been admitted. I had not seen him in the lunchroom because he would not have been served. Even if he had finally got that house he did not need in Oak Park, he would still have been a strange colored man to Calebsville. For Harvey, in memory of our cook-out on his lawn, I should have said something, registered a protest. I did nothing, except push my lime coke away and follow the boy into the afternoon.

Whatever happens, I told myself, is not going to happen in town. I needed the walk to blow the Negro boy and his November milk shake out of mind . . .

Ostriches do not hide their heads in the sand, I learned from Trader Horn; they simply lower their heads into bushes in the hopes that their long necks will not be seen and cut off.

□
. . . so I headed for Doc Holiman's trailer. The meeting would have to be there and it would have to be this day, at the latest this night. Some of the names made flesh—Miss Despere, for instance—might not be in a hurry, but men like Patsy Werkman, Senator Prommiss, P. R. Eferred, would not have come days early even for this meeting. They, after all, had a world to win.

Before ever I reached Doc Holiman's trailer, I saw an expanse of blanket standing on the edge of the road talking to two small boys. I edged off the road into a grove of trees that stood to one side of Michaelson's Field and moved in as close as possible without stepping into the open. The side of Holiman's trailer was down, a stage in readiness, but the medicine man was nowhere in sight. The voice of the blanket carried to where I stood. "You kids get on out of here now."

"We want to see the show," said the biggest of the boys.

"No loiterers," said the fat man with the implacable tonelessness that had once been aimed at me. "Move along. No loiterers."

The boys took a step or two away and stopped. "This is a public road, mister."

"No loiterers," repeated the fat man as though the words had some magic power.

At this moment, Doc Holiman came around the corner of his trailer. "What's the trouble, what is the trouble here?"

"I say *no loiterers* and I say *no loiterers* and they don't move," lamented the fat man.

"We just want to see the show, Doc," said the oldest boy.

"There's not going to be a show, son," the old man answered. "In November, son, you can't expect to see medicine shows. They're summer shows." The boy pointed toward the opened side of the trailer. "Oh, that," Doc went on. "I'm cleaning her out, getting ready for the winter. You want to look around?"

He held out both hands and a boy caught onto each one. They moved away from the fat man who stood—pouting, I'll bet—on the edge of the road, refusing to join them in their inspection of Doc's home. The kids stood for a moment on the platform, gesturing at an imagined audience, and then they followed Doc inside. When they came out, each one carried a licorice whip. Doc walked them back to the edge of the road. "That's show business," he said. "So now you know how medicine men live." The boys, nibbling at the whips, stood watching Doc, as though they expected something more. "You boys better get along now," he said. "What would a goodhearted old man like me do if someone came along and asked if I had seen a couple of boys who had skipped school?" The boys got along. Doc waved after them. "See you in the summer."

"Do you think," he said to the fat man, "do you think that you can pass the word along that this is a private party without making it sound so attractive that every farmer-in-the-dell around here will want to stay and clap hands?"

Doc, I was tempted to say, if you want to look inconspicuous do not use a fat man in a blanket overcoat and a straw hat to wave the crowds away. Still, the watchman did his job. A few passing cars slowed, stopped and, after a word from the fat man, moved on.

At dusk the nine began to gather. Harvey Williams came first from wherever he had been waiting in town. He got there just as Doc Holiman and his blanketed assistant began to set up folding chairs in front of the platform. Harvey and Doc shook hands, muttered a greeting, and then Harvey helped the two of them open the last few chairs. The others followed quickly. It was no surprise to see Senator Prommiss and Patsy Werkman arrive together, but I had not expected Rodney Salvay to be with them. I was prepared to see Candy Stick drive up in the hired car, having dumped Angela somewhere for the night—where in Calebsville?—but not to see Annette Despere sitting beside her. P. R. Eferred arrived without his nurse and his secretaries; it was Arthur Krafft and Professor Pick who climbed out of his limousine and helped him out and into his wheel chair.

Sometime during the afternoon, while I stood in the grove and felt the deceptively warm November go chill through my overcoat, the strangers in town had ceased to be strange to one another. Perhaps, although I cannot see how, Doc sent some kind of message that brought them together. More likely, they recognized one another. Expectation and suspicion, lightly masked in most men's faces, had risen to the surface on these nine, drawn up by the promise of the box, and their eyes must have told one another that they were the elect.

Now, here they were, huddled on folding chairs, waiting for the medicine man to begin his show. There were two lanterns, one on each side of the platform. From where I stood the nine figures—ten counting the fat man who came from the back of the wagon and stood behind the seated audience—were a common black cluster against the light of the lamps. A movement, a lift of the arm, a turn of the head and an individual silhouette stood for a moment outside the solid mass, but faded again, quickly, into the community of waiting.

Doc Holiman stepped to the center of the platform. In his hand was the ornamental box. A gasp went up from the folding chairs; at the sight of the box everyone present—

and I was present—caught his breath in anticipation. I moved out of the edge of the trees, confident now that I would be protected by the dimness of the light and by the fact that every eye was on the platform.

Doc wore his regular costume, even to the derby, and I expected somehow that he might lift the box above his head and begin a spiel about its curative powers. He did not. When he spoke, he spoke softly. "My business is panacea. When this box is open, you will know what to do."

I could not see what Doc did to the box. I would have sworn that that day back in Providence I had pushed, pulled, and punched every pushable, pullable, punchable rosebud on its carved exterior. Still, a simple movement with his fingers and the box lid lifted. He held it toward the figures, who strained forward on the chairs in front of him. A cry went up . . . a lament. They rose from their chairs; even Eferred tried to struggle to his feet, to lift himself out of his wheel chair. Their heads lifted toward the sky; their arms reached upward, grasping nothing.

The first clear voice in the babble of disappointment and anger was Patsy Werkman's. "Well, I'll be goddamned . . . ."

There was confusion in front of the platform. The voices crossed one another, the words shapeless sounds that carried no meaning. Except for Eferred, slumped now in his wheel chair, only Miss Despere still sat down. The others were on their feet. A step this way, a step that, every movement was amorphous. The activity of loss, unmeaning busy work in the glare of the lamps. Not by plan, not by organization, but as though by accident, an unexpected eddy, the disjointed movements joined into a forward surge. The group moved toward the edge of the platform.

"WAIT!" Doc Holiman's voice broke above their heads. He stood now, taller than himself, taller than life, his right hand stretched forward, the incongruity of his dress lost in his transmutation from charlatan to prophet. "When the box is open, you will know what to do."

The pushing figures stopped, held as though frozen, waiting for the words that had to follow Doc Holiman's single oracular sentence. They came, but not from the medicine man. It was Annette Despere who spoke. Through all the confusion she had sat as quietly as she had that first day when the uncontrollable Emma had boiled all over the memorial services. She seemed not to be speaking to anyone in particular, certainly not to the huddle of disappointed people in front of Doc Holiman's platform, their backs a wall in front of her. "Before I left Atlanta, I got word from a collector in London who had come across some missing Despere papers—seventeenth century." Her voice was calm, clear, confident. "If someone can give me a ride into Calebsville, I will see if I can get an early bus out. I have work to do on my family history."

It doesn't fill my time! it is my time. The ornamental box had become simply an ornamental box. It might have become a miniature coffin. I wanted to hug Miss Despere.

The silence that followed her simple statement was so heavy that only strong men could lift it. When the voices began to break into the stillness, they came singly. It was as though each person had been touched into testimony. An orderly revival meeting. No shouting. No singing. And, thank God, no one on the mourner's bench.

"Something odd has been going on in machine tools," croaked P. R. Eferred, out of the depths of his chair, from under his blankets. "I should have checked on my holdings weeks ago."

"I promised a manuscript by March," said Edward Pick, "and I still have a dozen poems to go. I must get back to Avis."

"I should have been in Beloit a week ago," said Patsy Werkman. "With a contract ending on January 3 and no new one signed, how can anyone have a merry Christmas?"

"If I don't get to New York immediately," said Arthur Krafft, "that imbecile at my gallery will make a mess of hanging my new show."

"If I don't get to Washington soon and do some friendly talking," said B. Wright Prommiss, "I'm going to find myself with the ass-end of committee appointments when the new year comes."

"There hasn't been a service at Pacific Hall for three weeks," said Rodney Salvay. "I wonder what those poor bastards are doing with my doors closed."

"If I don't get back to the laboratory and stay there," said Harvey Williams, "that fertilizer will never get off the ground . . . or on the ground."

"I must look awful," said Candy Stick. She laughed. "Good God, I haven't thought of my looks for days."

They had been holding themselves stiff, like children in an Easter pageant, and now, their pieces spoken, they broke into natural activity. They moved away from Doc Holiman's trailer, talking among themselves. Within seconds the four cars were loaded and had disappeared toward town.

Doc continued to stand in the center of the platform. The fat man took first one, then the other lamp and blew them out. Doc was now almost invisible in the pale light of the stars. I still stood there. At last the medicine man's voice

came to me, "You there. You in the dark. Isn't there something you should do?" I turned and walked back to town.

Early the next morning I was standing on the road, my
suitcase at my side, my thumb in the air. A string of cars
passed me because I looked too prosperous or too disreputa-
ble or too sure of myself to touch the drivers' hearts. In the
end, of course, I got a ride. My benefactor was a salesman
in plastics, an amiably inquisitive man, with miles to go
and me to fill the miles.

"Going far?" he asked, as he unlocked the door for me to
get in.

"Yes, I'm going quite a distance."

"May I ask where? Or is it a secret?"

"It's no secret. Bridgeport. Bridgeport, Connecticut."

"Business in Bridgeport, eh?"

"Not business, pleasure. I'm going to spend Christmas
with my brother and his wife."

And so I was. Christmas with The King and Queenie.

I sat beside the plastics seller, aware that his mouth was
moving, that words were piling up on the seat between us,
but I heard nothing. I was daydreaming about what might
lie beyond Bridgeport and Christmas. The heater in the
car was on. As I dreamed and as he talked, I slipped out of
my overcoat and tossed it into the back seat. I pulled my
suitcoat straight and with a gesture of tidiness stuck my
hands into the pockets. My right hand found and brought
out the page from Solvent Derritch's diary. I looked at it
for a moment and then tore it across the middle and then
again and again until it was only a handful of wastepaper.
As I began to roll down the window, I was aware that the
driver's voice had stopped. I sat for a moment, my hand

on the handle, but there was only the whisper of the motor. He had asked me a question, of course. "I beg your pardon," I said. "My mind was somewhere else."

"All I asked was your name. If you don't mind my knowing. It makes the ride more friendly."

"C. M. Firth," I said. I held my hand out the half-open window and let the scraps of paper blow away. As the wind whipped them off my hand, I added, "Constance Firth. My name is Constance Firth."

That much, Doc Holiman, I could do.